"For years I've dreamed of having a family, but no man wanted me."

Now Tristan knew Caroline's motives. They were pure and painfully simple. She wanted to be a mother.

She paced up to him with her eyes blazing. "I'd do anything—even marry you—for the sake of two beautiful children. Does that confession satisfy you, Major Smith?"

A wry smile lifted his lips. "You're a brave woman, Caroline."

"I'm not brave at all," she murmured.

"I think you are," he answered. "I'd be pleased to marry you…for the sake of the children, of course."

The moment called for a handshake. They were sealing a business deal. But Tristan couldn't bring himself to offer merely his hand. Neither could he kiss her, not even as a token of friendship. Moving slowly, he touched her cheek. "You should call me Tristan."

D0483252

Books by Victoria Bylin

Love Inspired Historical

The Bounty Hunter's Bride
The Maverick Preacher
Kansas Courtship
Wyoming Lawman
The Outlaw's Return
Marrying the Major

VICTORIA BYLIN

fell in love with God and her husband at the same time. It started with a ride on a big red motorcycle and a date to see a *Star Trek* movie. A recent graduate of UC Berkeley, Victoria had been seeking that elusive "something more" when Michael rode into her life. Neither knew it, but they were both reading the Bible.

Five months later they got married and the blessings began. They have two sons and have lived in California and Virginia. Michael's career allowed Victoria to be both a stay-at-home mom and a writer. She's living a dream that started when she read her first book and thought, "I want to tell stories." For that gift, she will be forever grateful.

Feel free to drop Victoria an email at VictoriaBylin@aol.com or visit her website at www.victoriabylin.com.

VICTORIA BYLIN

Marrying
the Major

Love Inspired

Recycling programs
for this product may
not exist in your area.

™ LOVE INSPIRED BOOKS

ISBN-13: 978-0-373-82887-6

MARRYING THE MAJOR

www.LoveInspiredBooks.com

Printed in U.S.A.

Which of you, if your son asks for bread,
will give him a stone? Or if he asks for a fish, will
give him a snake? If you, then, though you are evil,
know how to give good gifts to your children,
how much more will your Father in heaven
give good gifts to those who ask him!
—*Matthew* 7:9–11

This book is dedicated to my sons,
Joseph Scheibel and David Scheibel.
One's traveled the world and the other is a soldier.
They both influenced this story. Love to you both!

Chapter One

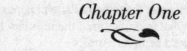

Tristan Willoughby Smith didn't like to be kept waiting, and he'd been waiting for three days for the arrival of the quinine he needed to treat his malaria. He'd also been waiting for the arrival of the Bradley sisters. He'd hired the youngest, Miss Caroline Bradley, to be the governess to his children. He'd hired the elder sister, Miss Elizabeth Bradley, to serve as a nurse and advisor for the treatment of the disease he'd contracted in the West Indies.

Tristan had a high tolerance for the fevers that came with malaria, but he had no patience at all with tardiness. A former major in the British army, he expected people to do what he told them.

He expected such obedience from his children.

He expected it from the men who worked his cattle ranch.

Mostly he expected such discipline from himself.

He also expected discipline from the stage line scheduled to deliver the quinine he needed to control his fevers. With his hands on his hips, he stared down the windblown street that made up the heart of Wheeler Springs. The

stage was three days late. He'd contracted the disease four
months ago. The year before it had taken his wife, Molly,
leaving him alone to care for their two children. To protect them from the disease, Tristan had come to Wyoming
with Jonathan Tate, his best friend and former second in
command. Wyoming was as far from malaria—and his
home in England—as Tristan could get. It was also eigh-
teen hundred miles away from the Philadelphia pharma-
ceutical company that manufactured the quinine. If the
quinine was lost, he'd be in dire straits.

As much as Tristan needed the medicine, he needed
Caroline Bradley even more. The new governess didn't
know it, but he had plans for her that went beyond tutor-
ing his children. He had plans for Jon, too. If malaria put
Tristan in an early grave, his best friend would be the ex-
ecutor of his will and guardian of his children. Under no
circumstance did Tristan want his children returned to his
family in England. As the third son of a nobleman, Tristan
had no importance. That fact had been drilled into him by
his father, Harold Smythe, the Duke of Willoughby, and he
didn't want Freddie and Dora growing up under the same
cloud.

He also wanted them to have a mother, especially if the
malaria took his life. Whether Tristan lived or died was up
to God, a being he viewed as a Supreme Commander who
gave orders without discussion. Tristan would submit to
God's decree, but he couldn't bear the thought of leaving
Freddie and Dora without a family. That's where the new
governess came in. It was high time Jon settled down. If
Tristan died, he expected Jon to marry her and give the
children a mother. He'd ruled out the oldest sister for this
particular job. The Bradley sister, named Elizabeth, was
twelve years older than the younger one, and in her letters

she'd stated her dedication to nursing. The governess, however, had written eloquently about her love of children.

The wind kicked a tumbleweed across the street. For the first day of October, the air held a surprising chill. Or had the chill come from within, the first sign of yet another attack of illness? Tristan glanced up at the sky. The fevers usually started late in the day, and the sun had yet to reach its peak. Still, the chill was enough to show him that he couldn't wait any longer to find out what had happened to the stage. A military man, he sized up the obstacles between the railhead in Cheyenne and Wheeler Springs.

The Carver gang could have held up the stage.

Indians could have attacked.

An afternoon storm could have washed out the road and taken the stagecoach with it.

Tristan had a fertile imagination—a blessing to a poet but a curse for an army officer and a bigger curse for a man with malaria.

The door to the stage office swung open and Jon strode forward. He was forty-two, seven years older than Tristan, but he hadn't lost an ounce of the muscle that made him a formidable captain in the West India Regiment. Neither had he lost the dour expression he wore around everyone except Tristan's children. Five-year-old Dora had Uncle Jon wrapped around her little finger, and Freddie, almost ten, lived in the man's shadow.

Jon had gone to speak with Heinrich Meyer, the owner of the inn that served as the stagecoach stop. Looking at his friend, Tristan felt a familiar dread. "It's bad news, isn't it?"

"Yes, sir."

In private, Jon had stopped calling Tristan "sir" five years ago. The formality signaled trouble. In a habit from his days in uniform, Tristan laced his hands behind his back. "Go on."

"The bridge over the gorge is out."

Tristan blanked his expression, but his belly clenched. Two days ago a storm had ripped through Wheeler Springs. Runoff from the hills would turn the Frazier River into a torrent. The first time he'd ridden over the bridge that spanned the gorge, he'd called it a rickety abomination. Without the bridge, the stagecoach would have to take a longer route from Cheyenne or return to the city to await repairs. Even more worrisome, the coach could have been washed into the gorge. He imagined it lying on its side in the river, the quinine crystals saturated and useless. He thought of the governess and her sister injured or dead.

"We need to find the coach," he said to Jon.

"And quickly." His friend lowered his voice. "The Carver gang is in the area."

The Carvers had advanced from rustling cattle to robbing banks and stagecoaches. They were tough, crass and mean. The thought of the governess and her sister being trapped between Wheeler Springs and Cheyenne and at the gang's mercy made Tristan's neck hairs prickle.

"Get the horses, will you?" He'd have preferred to take a wagon to carry the women and their belongings, but the downed bridge made it necessary to go on horseback.

Jon gave him a quelling look. "You're not well. I'll go with Heinrich and his son."

"I'm fine."

"No, you're not."

"I am," Tristan said evenly. "I have to be. I'm almost out of quinine and you know it."

"And if you get feverish?" Jon knew how to be honest

but respectful. "You'll be more of a burden than a help. Stay here, Tristan."

"Absolutely not."

"But—"

"Don't argue with me." Tristan hadn't lived his life sitting on the sidelines, and he didn't intend to start now. He'd felt worse and done more. "Not only do I need the quinine, but the new governess and her sister are possibly stranded between here and Cheyenne. They're my responsibility. I'm going and that's final."

"If you say so, *sir*."

Jon emphasized *sir* not as a sign of respect but as a way of telling Tristan he was being a fool. If Tristan became ill, Jon would be stuck with him. An obvious solution loomed. He'd simply refuse to fall ill. He glanced at the sky. If they rode hard, they'd reach the river before dusk. "Get supplies. We'll leave immediately."

"I figured you'd be stubborn." Jon looked peeved. "Heinrich sent his son to ready the horses."

Shoulder to shoulder, the men paced to the mercantile. While Jon ordered supplies from the storekeeper's wife, Tristan weighed the facts. The ride to Cheyenne took two full days, three if the weather muddied the roads. A stagecoach station sat between the city and the town. He and Jon could be gone a week, maybe longer.

He had to get word to Bert Howe, the ranch foreman, and Evaline, his housekeeper and the woman tending to Freddie and Dora. Tristan had no worries about the ranch, but he worried greatly about his children. They tended to be nervous about his whereabouts. He had to get word to them that he'd be gone longer than expected. He kept a house in Wheeler Springs, and he knew just the man to deliver the message. Noah Taylor was Tristan's houseman,

Evaline's husband and a former sergeant in the West India Regiment.

"I need to speak with Noah," Tristan said to Jon. "Someone has to let Bert and Evaline know what's happened."

Jon nodded and went back to purchasing supplies. Tristan crossed the street at a rapid pace, glancing up at the sun and wondering again about the sheen of sweat on his brow. He hated being ill. It turned him into the skinny boy who'd grown up on his father's massive estate.

England had stopped being home the day he'd walked out of his father's study. As a third son, he'd known early that he had limited prospects. He just hadn't expected his father to be so blunt about it…or so cruel.

You have no place here, Tristan. Join the army. Become a clergyman. I don't care what you do.

That parting had been fifteen years ago. Tristan had never been interested in religion. In boarding school he'd been taught to believe in God as a father. If the Almighty was anything like the duke, Tristan wanted nothing to do with him. He accepted God's power, submitted to His authority, but felt no love for Him. Instead of joining the church, he'd used a portion of a large inheritance from an uncle to purchase a commission in the British Army. To make the break from his father complete, he'd changed the spelling of his name from the aristocratic "Smythe" to the more egalitarian "Smith." Tristan missed England, but he'd never go back to his father's estate. If the malaria claimed him as he feared, he wanted to buried at the ranch he called "The Barracks."

Of course he didn't want to be buried at all. He wanted to see Freddie become a man and Dora a wife and mother. Given a choice, he'd die an old man with a soft belly and a head full of gray hair.

But he didn't have a choice. God controlled his fate the way a commander waged a war. Tristan could only lead the battles in his control, which meant ensuring his children wouldn't be returned to England. It wasn't likely the duke would have an interest in Freddie, and it was certain he'd consider Dora a worthless girl, but Tristan had still made legal arrangements to name Jon as guardian. Silently he gave thanks he hadn't been born first. His oldest brother, Andrew, was heir apparent. He'd married Louisa Hudgins, the woman Tristan himself had hoped to wed. She and Andrew had probably produced a dozen children by now. Tristan's second brother, Oscar, would have married as well, though he'd been legendary for his romantic capering.

Putting his thoughts aside, Tristan strode to his town house. Stepping through the front door, he called to Noah. The man stepped immediately into the foyer. Tall and black, he carried himself with the military bearing he'd earned in the West India Regiment. The WIR was composed of free blacks and led by white officers from England. Most of the officers considered the post undesirable, at best a stepping-stone to another assignment. Tristan had felt otherwise. In his own way, he knew how it felt to be judged inferior. He'd led his men with pride and they'd fought with courage. When Tristan made the decision to settle in Wyoming, he'd invited Noah to work for him.

"Good morning, sir." Noah spoke with the singsong tones of the Caribbean. "Any word on the stagecoach?"

"The bridge is out. Jon and I are going to look for the passengers." He didn't mention the quinine. Needing medicine stung his pride, and Noah already knew the importance of it.

The former sergeant gave him the same look he'd

gotten from Jon. "If you'll excuse me, sir. Is that wise? You're not well, and—"

"I'm well enough." Tristan hated being questioned, a fact Noah knew better than most men. That he'd dared to bring up Tristan's health showed both respect and caring.

Tristan took the command out of his voice. "I need you to get word to The Barracks. The children will be worried."

"I'll see to it."

"Thank you, Noah." Tristan turned back to the door.

"Sir?"

"Yes?"

"Mrs. Harvey just delivered a letter." She was the postmistress and very conscientious. "It arrived with last week's stage. She apologized for misplacing it. I put it in the study."

"Who is it from?"

"Pennwright, sir."

Pennwright was his father's long-time secretary, a man who joked that his name had doomed him to his occupation. When Tristan had been sent to boarding school, Pennwright had written regularly. The correspondence had started at the duke's direction, but it had continued for years out of affection.

"I'll look forward to it when I return," he said to Noah.

"Yes, sir."

Satisfied, Tristan walked to the livery where he found Jon waiting with their mounts and two packhorses. If they found the women, the females would have to ride to Wheeler Springs. As for their possessions, they'd take what the horses could carry. When the bridge was repaired, he'd send a wagon for the rest. He welcomed the thought of having such a problem. The alternative—that they'd find the coach destroyed and the driver and women dead—couldn't be tolerated.

Looking grave, Jon handed him the reins to his favorite horse. Tristan preferred a spirited mount and the stallion he'd named Cairo had speed and intelligence. A sleek Arabian, Cairo was black with a matching mane and tail. The stallion obeyed Tristan, but he did it with an air of superiority.

Jon rode up next to him on the gray mare he favored. She wasn't old, but Tristan had named her Grandma because she rode like a rocking chair.

As he turned Cairo down the street, the sun hit him in the face. He swiped at beads of perspiration with his sleeve, then nudged Cairo into an easy canter. With the fever lurking in his body and the Bradley sisters in places unknown, there was no time to waste. Jon rode next to him, letting Tristan set the pace.

Three hours passed with no sign of the stage. The sun peaked and was halfway to the horizon when they arrived at the downed bridge. Tristan slid wearily off Cairo, shielded his eyes from the sun and scanned the gorge for the downed stagecoach. He saw only boards from the bridge wedged between rocks and the sparkling water racing past them.

Relief washed over him. "They didn't get this far."

"So it seems."

"We need to push on." Tristan inspected the sides of the gorge. A trail led to the river and stopped at a sandy bank. The men climbed back on their horses and headed for the crossing with Tristan in the lead. The storm had turned the path into slick mud, but they arrived at the river's edge without mishap. Cairo didn't hesitate to wade into the current, but Grandma needed coaxing. When Tristan reached the far bank, he turned and saw his friend urging the skittish horse to take one step at a time. He hoped the river would recede before they had to cross it again, hopefully with the stage driver and the two women. When Grandma found firm footing, she bolted out of the water.

Jon grinned at Tristan. "The old girl did it."

"Barely," Tristan acknowledged. "For a minute, I thought you'd have to carry her."

Jon smiled at the joke, then looked down the road. Tristan followed his gaze with the same questions in mind. Had the stage come this far and turned back? Had it gone off the road before reaching the bridge? He also had to consider the Carver gang. Fighting fever, Tristan acknowledged the cold facts. Anything could have happened. The quinine could already be lost, and the women could be hurt or trapped or worse.

With no time to waste, he barked an order at Jon. "We still have daylight. Let's go."

He nudged Cairo into a comfortable trot. Jon stayed with him, but at dusk Tristan admitted defeat. They hadn't seen a single sign of the coach. With the fever nipping at him, he gave in to Jon's suggestion that they strike camp for the night. They'd start looking again in the morning.

Caroline Bradley awoke on the hard ground with a jolt. Dawn had broken with startling splendor, but it wasn't the golden light that roused her from a troubled sleep. It was the snap of a twig, then the frustrated muttering of a male voice. She clutched the shotgun she'd found in the boot of the stagecoach. She'd slept with it for two nights, and she knew how to pull the trigger. If the Carver gang had come back, she'd use it.

Three days ago she and Bessie had left Cheyenne for Wheeler Springs. They'd had the coach to themselves, so they'd passed the hours speculating about Tristan Willoughby Smith, his children and what life would be like on a cattle ranch. Not once had they imagined the stagecoach being robbed by the Carver gang. Thanks to the sacrifice of the driver, they'd escaped while he'd challenged the outlaws with his pistol. She and Bessie had run for their lives and hidden in a ravine, listening as the Carvers killed the driver and ransacked their trunks and other shipments. When the outlaws finished, they'd stolen the horses and pushed the yellow coach into the ravine.

Cracked and lying on its side, the old Concord had offered adequate shelter from the sun, very little from the rain and none from the frightful howling of wolves.

In the scramble down the hill, Bessie had sprained her ankle. By herself, Caroline had piled rocks on the dead driver, then she'd salvaged what she could of their possessions. In the course of her efforts, she'd found a crate addressed to Major Smith from the Farr, Powers and Weightman Chemical Laboratory in Philadelphia. It had been opened and the contents had been dumped without care. In the pile of broken bottles, she'd seen a label marked "Sulphate of Quinine." Knowing the value of the medicine, she'd salvaged seven of the twelve bottles. They were wrapped in an old nightgown and hidden in the stagecoach for safekeeping.

She knew the major was ill, and she'd assumed he had a chronic illness or a war injury. Now she wondered if he was suffering from malaria. It had been a scourge during the war that had destroyed the South. Bessie had served as a nurse during the conflict, and she'd complained often that illness killed more men than mini balls. Major Smith, it seemed, was a very ill man. Seeing the medicine, Caroline had thought of his motherless children. Who would love them if they lost their father? Malaria was a fickle disease. It could take a man's life in a day or linger in his blood for years.

Outlaws had the same penchant for randomness. Aware of the slow, measured steps coming toward her, Caroline weighed her options. Bessie's ankle meant they couldn't run. Neither could they hide. Huddling against the undercarriage of the coach, she whispered into her sister's ear. "Bessie, wake up but don't move."

Her sister's eyelids fluttered open.

The footsteps were closer now. A bird took flight from a cottonwood. Caroline wanted to fly away, too. Instead she clutched the shotgun. The steps came closer. She heard the slide of dirt and rock as he reached the bottom of the hill, then the thump of leather on dirt as he paced toward the coach. A squirrel leapt from one branch to another, springing high and then landing with a bounce. Leaves fell like dry rain. With each step the stranger came closer to the coach until all noise stopped. Caroline took a breath and held it. Nothing stirred. Not a bird. Not a breeze. Bessie lay still, watching with wide eyes and signaling her with a nod to be brave.

Leaping to her feet, Caroline aimed the shotgun at the man's chest. "Who are you?"

He looked at her as if she were no more dangerous than a gnat. Refusing to blink, she stared down the barrel at a man who looked more like a scarecrow than an outlaw. Tall and gaunt, he had hair the color of straw and eyes so red-rimmed they seemed more gray than blue. His clothes hung on his broad shoulders, but there was no mistaking the fine tailoring. She took in the creases around his mouth, his stubbled jaw and finally the boots that reached to his knees. Black and spit-shined, they didn't belong to a shiftless outlaw.

She couldn't say the same for the pistol in his hand. It

was loose and pointed downward, but she felt the threat. She dug the shotgun into her shoulder. "Throw down your gun!"

He raised one eyebrow. "I'd prefer to holster it, if you don't mind."

That voice…it reminded her of a fog bell coming out of a mist, a warning she remembered from the Carolina shore, the place of her birth and the reason for her name. She heard the trace of an accent she couldn't identify, not the boisterous timbre of an Englishman or a German, but the muted tones of a man who'd worked to leave the past behind.

When she didn't speak, he holstered the gun then looked at her with his hands slightly away from his body, taking in her appearance with a flick of his eyes. Caroline knew what he'd see… A woman with an average face and an average figure, past her prime but young enough to want a husband. For a few months she'd once been secretly married, but he'd see a spinster. A woman desperate enough for a family that she'd decided to become a governess. If she couldn't have children of her own, she'd borrow them.

First, though, she had to get rid of this unknown man studying her with both fascination and fury.

"Get your hands up!" she ordered.

He kept them loose at his sides. "Perhaps—"

"Raise them!"

He let out a sigh worthy of a frustrated king. "If you insist."

Slowly he raised his arms, holding her gaze with a force that nearly made her cower. When his hands were shoulder-high, palm out so she that she could see the aristocratic length of his fingers, he lowered his chin. "Perhaps, Miss Bradley, you'd allow me to introduce myself?"

The accent was no longer muffled. Thick and English, it held a command that made her lower the shotgun. She didn't need to hear Tristan Willoughby Smith say his name to know she'd just met her future employer, and that she'd impressed him...in all the wrong ways.

Chapter Two

"Major Smith!"

Tristan arched one brow at the stunned brunette. "May I lower my hands now?"

"Of course." Most people groveled when they realized they'd stepped on his toes. Caroline Bradley snapped to attention but not in the way of an underling. She looked him square in the eye. "I'm sure you understand my reaction. As you can see, the stagecoach was robbed."

"Yes."

He wished now they hadn't stopped at dusk. As luck would have it, they'd camped less than a mile away. By the morning light he'd spotted in the debris a woman's shoe and a nightgown that had been mauled by dirty hands. Certain the two Miss Bradleys had been on the coach, he'd left Jon to search through the crates and had maneuvered down the ravine. He'd spotted the yellow coach lying on its side but hadn't seen the women. Until Miss Bradley had gotten the jump on him, he'd believed the sisters had been abducted by the Carvers or left for dead inside the coach.

Looking at her now, the one he assumed to be the governess, he decided the timing of his arrival had been fortuitous. If he'd arrived in the dark, she'd have shot him.

The elder Miss Bradley—the nurse—was struggling to stand.

Tristan stepped around the overturned coach and offered his hand. "Allow me."

"Thank you," she replied.

When the elder Miss Bradley reached her feet, the younger Miss Bradley put her arm around her waist to steady to her. Tristan couldn't address both women as "Miss Bradley." In his mind he'd think of them as Caroline and Elizabeth. If only one sister was present, he'd address her as Miss Bradley. When they were together, etiquette required him to address the eldest as Miss Bradley and the younger as Miss Caroline. Looking at the women, he easily discerned the difference in their ages and spoke to the nurse. "I presume you're Miss Elizabeth Bradley?"

"That's correct, sir."

He looked at the governess and wished the rules of etiquette weren't quite so clear. Calling this pretty woman by her given name struck him as too personal, even when he prefaced her name with "Miss." He studied her with a stern eye. "I'll address you as Miss Caroline. Is that acceptable?"

A populist gleam twinkled in her wide eyes. "Simply Caroline would do."

"Hardly."

"Then whichever you'd prefer, Mr. Smith."

"It's Major Smith."

He'd been out of the army for months, but he hadn't adjusted to being Mr. Smith. In England he'd have been Lord Tristan, a title that gave him indigestion but sounded normal to his ears. As much as he wanted to deny it, titles and ranks were in his blood.

Maybe that's why Caroline's tone struck him as insubordinate. Even more annoying, she reminded him of

Louisa. Not only did she have a lively glint in her eyes, but she also had Louisa's ivory skin and brunette hair. It was an utter mess at the moment, a tumbling pile of curls that had once been meant to impress him. He knew from her letters that she had a suitable education, but he hadn't expected the keen intelligence he saw in her brown eyes. Or were they green? Hazel, he decided. She had eyes that mirrored her surroundings, and today they'd been muted by the grayish sky. He couldn't help but wonder if her eyes had once been brighter or if they had faded with life's trials.

He'd taken a chance hiring a stranger to raise his children, but he had little choice. He hoped Jon would see Caroline's attributes as plainly as he did. His friend would certainly notice her female curves. Any man would— including Tristan, though the awareness had to remain fleeting.

She stood with her chin slightly raised, silent but somehow conveying her irritation with him. Tristan didn't like being challenged even with silence, so he paused to examine the overturned coach. He didn't expect to see the crate of quinine, though he held to a sliver of hope.

The new governess cleared her throat. "Sir?"

"One moment," he ordered. "Jon will be here shortly. There's no point in repeating yourself."

"Who's Jon?" she asked.

He glared at her. "He's second in command at The Barracks."

"A barracks? I thought you owned a ranch."

"I do," he said with aplomb. "*The Barracks* is a nickname. I assure you, Miss Caroline. You'll live in a perfectly proper house."

She gave him a doubtful look but said nothing.

Tristan cupped his hand to his mouth and called for Jon. "I've found the women. Get down here."

When he looked back at the two Miss Bradleys, the eldest was giving him a look he could only describe as scolding. Tristan's own mother had died when he was five, but he'd seen his wife give that look to Freddie. Tristan didn't like receiving it from an employee.

The new governess reflected the same disapproval. "Major, you should know—"

"Not now."

"But I have something to tell you!"

"I know enough," he snapped at her.

He must have established his authority because she sealed her lips. He looked up the hill, saw Jon navigating the incline and waited in stony silence for his friend to arrive. Tristan couldn't stop himself from wondering about the quinine. If the Carvers knew the value, they would have stolen it. Judging by the mayhem on the road, at the very least they'd smashed the crate. Without sufficient quinine, his next bout of fever would be a brute.

As Jon came down the hill, Tristan saw the look his friend wore after a battle when bodies lay askew and the price of victory was its most obvious. He hadn't found the quinine.

The man strode to Tristan's side, acknowledged the women with a nod, then spoke in a quiet tone. "I found the crate. It's been smashed. The bottles are broken or missing."

"I see."

"I'm sorry," Jon murmured. "There's nothing to salvage."

The younger woman cleared her throat. "Major Smith—"

"Miss Caroline!" He bellowed to make a point. "Do you *always* interrupt with such enthusiasm?"

"Only when it's important."

She said no more, leaving it up to him to humble himself and ask. "If you don't mind, it will have to wait. I'm expecting an important shipment. Jon is looking for—"

"Quinine," she said quietly.

Instead of scolding her again, Tristan stared into her shimmering eyes. "Go on."

"Part of the shipment was destroyed, but I salvaged seven bottles. They're hidden in the stagecoach."

He said nothing because being in her debt was humbling and he didn't know how to be anything but a man in command. Malaria had turned the tables on him. The disease was in charge, and it had been since he'd left the West Indies. Now Caroline Bradley was in charge. He didn't like being beholden to anyone, especially not a woman with brunette hair and intelligent eyes. Molly had been gone for more than a year. He missed her terribly, but his own illness had forced him to cope with the loss quickly. He had only one focus—to provide a family for Freddie and Dora in case of his death.

Jon offered Caroline his hand. "You must be one of the Bradley sisters. I'm Jonathan Tate. I keep Major Smith in line."

Tristan watched the woman's eyes for a flicker of interest. Jon was twelve years older than she was, but women found him appealing. More than once Tristan's second in command had been called a pussycat, while Tristan had been called "sir" by everyone including his wife and children.

Caroline Bradley shook Jon's hand, then introduced her sister. Apparently, the elder Miss Bradley went by Bessie. Tristan should have been doing the honors, but he disliked social pleasantries. They reminded him too much of the stilted formality of his childhood.

"It was terrible," the eldest Miss Bradley said about the robbery. "One minute we were riding along at a reasonable clip, and the next we were flying around the curves. The driver made it around a turn and stopped the coach. He told us to run for our lives."

"What happened to him?" Tristan asked.

"They shot him," Caroline said quietly. "I did my best to bury him, but his family might want to do better. His name was Calvin."

Tristan knew Calvin. He'd worked briefly at The Barracks. He had no family, but Tristan wouldn't leave him in an unmarked grave. He turned to Jon. "When we get to the ranch, send someone to take care of the body."

"Yes, sir."

Tristan turned back to the women. "Was there someone riding shotgun?"

Caroline shook her head. "There was supposed to be a second driver, but he didn't show up. Calvin made the decision to go alone." She gave him a deliberate look. "He was anxious to deliver the quinine."

Calvin would have known the importance of the medicine. Yet again, Tristan was beholden to someone. The debt couldn't be repaid except to live in a manner worthy of the sacrifice. That meant showing kindness to Caroline and her sister. Looking at her now, he saw a courageous woman who'd survived a robbery, buried one man and saved another by salvaging the medicine. Needing to focus on something other than her attributes, he changed the subject. "Do you know who robbed the stage?"

Bessie answered. "Calvin mentioned the Carvers before we left Cheyenne."

"That's the assumption," he acknowledged.

Caroline had the haunted look of a soldier reliving a battle. "The robbers ransacked the stagecoach. We heard them making threats, so we hid. We couldn't run because Bessie twisted her ankle."

Tristan couldn't stand the thought of the Carvers harming either of the women.

Bessie squeezed her sister's hand. "The good Lord had an eye on us."

Tristan doubted it. In his experience, God ignored the needs of human beings as surely as the duke had ignored his third son. Where was God when Molly lay shaking with fever? Neither did God care about little Dora, who still cried for her mother, or for Freddie, who didn't cry at all. Tristan had seen too much death to deny the hope of an afterlife, but he didn't see God in the here and now. He especially didn't see a loving Father when fever made him delusional and his bones caught fire.

Bessie indicated the area around the coach. "As you can see, we've been camping. Caroline saw to everything."

He studied the patch of ground sheltered by the coach. Caroline had done a commendable job of salvaging essentials from the wreckage. She'd built a fire, used a pot to fetch water from a stream and neatly organized food they'd brought from Cheyenne. The campsite was a testament to ingenuity, neatness and order, all traits Tristan admired. Nonetheless, he imagined the women would prefer his house in Wheeler Springs to another night in the open. They'd have to move quickly to arrive by nightfall, especially with packhorses laden with their possessions. He did a quick calculation and decided the women could ride together on Grandma. Jon could manage a packhorse, while the other carried what it could.

"We should be on our way." He turned to Bessie. "Miss Bradley, how severely is your ankle injured?"

"It's just a sprain." She looked at Jon. "I can walk up the hill if someone will give me a strong arm."

Jon turned on the smile that made him a pussycat. "I'd be delighted—"

"No," Tristan interrupted. "I'll escort Miss Bradley up the hill. You help Miss Caroline break down camp. Make sure you're careful with the quinine." Tristan would have preferred to carry it himself, but he felt wobbly.

Jon focused on the pretty brunette. "I'm at your service, Miss Caroline."

"Thank you, Mr. Tate."

"Call me Jon." He shot Tristan a sly glance. "Only the major insists on formalities."

The woman smiled. "Jon it is. For the sake of simplicity, Bessie and I go by our first names. You're welcome to call me Caroline."

Jon nodded graciously and Caroline smiled.

Though pleased by their budding friendship, Tristan felt envious. What would it be like to seek a woman's attention? To woo her the way he'd wooed Molly? They'd had a stellar courtship, even if he said so himself. He hoped Jon would show the same ambition for Caroline. If Tristan's plan worked, they'd fall in love and get married. If the malaria bested Tristan, they'd raise Freddie and Dora, and his children would have a family.

At Caroline's direction, Jon went to work gathering their meager possessions while she retrieved a bundled nightgown that presumably held the bottles of quinine. Tristan stepped to Bessie's side and offered his arm. "Shall we?"

"Thank you, Major."

As he helped the injured woman up the hill, he admitted to a sad fact. He didn't have to slow his pace to match hers. In fact, she'd slowed down for him. He glanced over his shoulder and saw Jon laughing with the pretty brunette. In other circumstances, he'd have given his friend a run for his money for the woman's attention…and he'd have won.

Caroline liked Jon, but Major Smith struck her as a pompous, arrogant, pigheaded fool. If he hadn't been so rude, she'd have told him about the quinine the instant she recognized him. She didn't expect her new employer to be overly friendly, but she'd hoped for common courtesy. She didn't like Major Smith at all.

Watching as he escorted Bessie up the hill, she saw the slowness of his movements and turned to Jon. "How long has Major Smith had malaria?"

"Four months." Jon stopped gathering blankets and looked up the hill. "He won't tell you anything, but you should know what he's been through. If you have questions, you should bring them to me. I know him as well as anyone. We served together in the West India Regiment. He's been to Africa, India, all over the world."

"And England," she added.

"Yes, but not for a long time." Jon's expression hardened. "That one is his story to tell. What you need to know is that he lost his wife a year ago. Molly was a peach. We all loved her."

"Was it malaria?"

"Yes. It struck hard and fast. She died within a week. Tristan wanted to leave the West Indies for the sake of the children, but his transfer request wasn't approved. He had no choice but to stay until he caught the disease himself."

Caroline ached for the entire family. "The children must be terribly frightened."

"They are," Jon replied. "Dora cries at the drop of a hat.

It'll break your heart. Freddie doesn't show his feelings, but they're deep. He's like his father in that way."

Caroline glanced at the arrogant man struggling to climb a hill. "How sick is he?"

He hesitated. "I've seen Tristan at his best and at his worst. He's a fighter. If anyone can beat the malaria, he can."

He hadn't answered her question. "Is today his best or his worst?"

"It's typical."

Later Caroline would ask Bessie about the course of the disease. "How did he come to be in Wyoming?"

"It's as far from swamps and England as he could get."

Caroline understood his aversion to swamps. His dislike of England baffled her, but she knew Jon wouldn't explain. She followed his gaze to the top of the ravine where the major had just crested the ridge. Caroline didn't know why God hadn't answered her prayers for a family of her own, but she saw a need here. Major Smith didn't like her, but his children needed someone who wouldn't leave them.

She wondered if he'd made arrangements for a guardian in case he succumbed to malaria. She couldn't bear the thought of growing to love these children and losing them to a distant aunt or uncle. She turned to ask Jon more questions, but he'd finished gathering their things and had tied them in a blanket. "Do you have the quinine?"

She indicated the bundled nightgown. "I'll carry it."

With the pack of clothing slung over his shoulder, he offered his elbow. "Shall we join them?"

"Yes, thank you."

Holding the quinine in one hand, she took his arm with the other. When the path narrowed, they broke apart and she climbed alone. It seemed a fitting way to end the ordeal in the canyon. Soon she'd be in Wheeler Springs.

She'd be able to take a bath and sleep in a bed. She'd meet Major Smith's children, and she'd have people who needed her. Feeling hopeful, she stepped from the ravine to level ground and saw Bessie and Major Smith at her trunk. In addition to clothing and a few personal treasures, it held her sister's medical bag. Bessie needed it to give the major a dose of quinine.

"I'll get it," Caroline called.

She didn't want Major Smith looking at her things. It struck her as too personal, plus she'd hidden the one photograph she had of her husband. Their marriage had been secret, and she had always used her maiden name. Charles had been a black man and a crusader, a gentle giant and a man of great faith. He'd died at the hands of a mob because he believed in educating all children regardless of color—and because he trusted people too easily.

Caroline had no idea what Major Smith would think of her choices, and she didn't care. She would always admire Charles and had no regrets, but it hurt to be an outcast. She didn't want to fight that battle again, so she hurried to the trunk before the major could look inside. She handed Bessie the quinine bottles, lifted the medical bag and unbuckled it. Jon walked up to them with a canteen in one hand and a tin cup in the other. Major Smith took the cup and looked at Bessie. "The quinine, please."

Bessie opened a bottle and poured a dose of crystals into the cup. "Quinine is most effective when mixed with alcohol. I have some in my bag."

Caroline opened a tightly corked flask and handed it to the major. He poured a swallow in the cup, returned the bottle to her, then swished the liquid to absorb the crystals. He downed it in one swallow and turned to Bessie. "You're experienced with malaria."

"I'm afraid so," she answered. "I nursed hundreds of soldiers during the war."

Caroline put away the bottle, set the medical bag in the trunk and glanced around for a wagon to take them to Wheeler Springs. Instead of a wagon, she saw four horses. Two were saddled. Two carried supplies.

"I don't see a wagon," she said.

"There isn't one," the major replied. "The bridge over the gorge is out. We'll use one of the packhorses for your things. Jon can ride the other one, and you and your sister can share the gray."

A shiver started at the nape of Caroline's neck and went to her fingertips. Horses terrified her. She and Bessie had grown up in Charleston where their father had been a doctor. They'd been city girls. What little riding she'd done as a child had been slow and ladylike. She hadn't enjoyed it, but she hadn't become terrified of horses until the night she'd seen her husband lynched. As long as she lived, she'd never forget the sudden bolt of a horse she'd believed to be gentle.

No way could she ride to Wheeler Springs. She had neither the skill nor the confidence to sit on a horse. Neither did she have the courage. How she'd make that clear to Major Smith, she didn't know, especially when he was looking at her as if he'd just had the best idea of his life. What that idea was, she didn't know. She only knew this man was accustomed to giving orders, and he expected them to be followed.

Chapter Three

Tristan saw a chance to bring Jon and Caroline together and took it. "On second thought, perhaps you'd prefer to ride with Jon? I'll take your sister, and we'll use both pack-horses to transport your belongings."

The eldest Miss Bradley nodded in agreement. "That's a fine idea, major. Our possessions are modest. Perhaps we can bring everything with us."

Caroline didn't seem to concur. She was gaping at him with wide-eyed horror. Surely she wasn't so modest she couldn't see the practicality of his suggestion? Tristan frowned. "Is there a problem?"

"Well…yes."

He waited five seconds for her to explain. Considering he didn't wait for anyone except Dora, five seconds was a considerable compromise. When the new governess failed to find her tongue, he lowered his chin. "Spit it out."

The elder Miss Bradley gave him a critical look. "My sister is afraid of horses."

"*Afraid* of horses!" Tristan couldn't help but sputter. "I own a cattle ranch. How does she expect to travel?"

Caroline glared at him. "You hired me to care for your

children, not round up cows. I expect to walk or ride in a carriage or wagon."

Tristan looked at Jon. "How far is it to Wheeler Springs?" He knew quite well, but he wanted her to hear the answer from Jon, who she seemed to like.

Jon's brow wrinkled in sympathy. "It's a good thirty miles."

She turned ashen. Tristan almost felt sorry for her. He'd been afraid many times in his life, ironically less often on the battlefield than in his own home. He'd been afraid of his father when he was boy, and he'd been afraid when Molly had fallen ill. Now he was afraid of the malaria. He tried to offer consolation. "You're obviously a resolute woman. You'll be fine with Jon. He's an excellent horseman."

"I'm sure he is. It's just that…" She shuddered. "There's no choice, is there?"

He shrugged. "You could walk."

Bessie touched her sister's shoulder. They exchanged a few quiet words, then the nurse turned to him. "I think it would be best if my sister and I shared the gray as you first suggested."

Tristan preferred his second idea, but he was tired of arguing. "Very well. Let's get moving."

When Caroline hesitated, Jon gave her the reassuring look he often gave Dora. "The horse's name is Grandma. She couldn't be gentler."

She managed a smile. It was tentative and sweet and so full of courage Tristan wanted to give her a medal. But they really didn't have time to dawdle if they wanted to get home before dark. "We need to go."

She glared at him. "I need to finish emptying the trunk."

Without waiting to be dismissed, she took her sister's

medical bag out of the trunk and set it close to her feet. Tristan had to admire her priorities. Except for Molly, the women he'd known would have reached for their jewelry before the medicine. Bessie reached into the trunk to help, but Caroline shooed her away. "Rest your ankle," she murmured. "We have a long ride."

So did Tristan and he already felt done in. He wanted to encourage the camaraderie between Jon and Caroline, so he offered Bessie his arm. "Come with me."

He escorted her to a flat boulder where they sat and watched the packing. Almost clandestinely, Caroline lifted a framed picture from the folds of her gowns. She put it with the precious quinine, then handed the bag to Jon. "This requires special attention."

"Of course," he answered.

Tristan called to his friend. "Bring it here. I'll carry it." He trusted Jon, but he didn't trust the packhorse to cross the river without balking. Tristan wanted the medicine in his care alone.

Caroline shot him a look. He figured the photograph was of her parents, though he wondered if it told other tales. Seated on the rock, he watched her expression as Jon set the bag at his feet and returned to help her. In a separate drawstring bag she stowed a black-bound volume he supposed was her Bible, a smaller book bound in cloth and what looked like a doll. She gave the bag to Jon and said something. Looking pleased, he tied the bundle to Grandma's saddle.

Just as Tristan hoped, the two of them quickly developed an easy rapport. Thirty minutes later, a packhorse was bearing all the women's possessions.

The time had come to mount up. Tristan leveraged to his feet and offered Bessie his hand. Together they ambled to the horses where Jon and Caroline were standing in front of Grandma. Jon was stroking the horse's nose, but it was the woman at his side who needed comforting. Looking tentative, she raised her hand to pet the horse.

Surprised, Grandma raised her head. Jon controlled her, but no one was there to control Caroline. She skittered away like a leaf in the wind.

The terror in her eyes reminded Tristan of Dora and how she came to him in tears after Molly's death. Dora expected people to help her. Caroline clearly had no such hope. She was staring at Grandma as if she were looking at a mountain. He felt sorry for her, but she had to get on the horse.

Jon motioned to Bessie. "Let me help you up first."

Leaning on Tristan's arm, Bessie limped to Jon's side, gripped the horn and put her good foot in the stirrup. With Jon's help, she landed gracefully in the saddle. Grandma didn't mind at all.

Jon looked at Caroline. "Are you ready?"

She looked close to tears, but she marched back to the horse like a soldier facing his second battle, the one where experience replaced ignorance and a man discovered his true mettle. Looking at her, Tristan wondered if she'd been thrown before. He could understand her reluctance to try again. He'd felt that way about love after Louisa rejected him.

Molly had mended that hole in his heart. It had threatened to open again with her passing, but she'd been adamant with him.

Don't you dare leave our children without a mother! I want you to marry again.

He'd made the promise, but he'd done it halfheartedly. He *would* give his children a mother, but she'd be Jon's bride, not his. Never his. The malaria had seen to that.

He studied Caroline as she listened to Jon, noting the

tilt of her chin and the way she held her shoulders. Her demeanor struck a chord of admiration. So did the way she swung up behind her sister in a flurry of petticoats and courage. When she rewarded Jon with a quiet thank-you, Tristan felt a surge of jealousy. Jon had his health. He had a future, and if the woman's smile was any indication, he'd have a wife as Tristan hoped and now envied.

Annoyed with himself, he lifted Cairo's reins from a tree and swung into the saddle as if he were a healthy man and not a feverish weakling. Frowning, he called to Jon. "Let's go."

He led the way, keeping the pace slow for the ladies but itching to nudge Cairo into a run. He wanted to leave his weakness behind—the illness, his worries—but he couldn't. All he could do was ride at a leisurely pace, listening to a pretty woman laugh at Jon's banter. The pleasantries should have given Tristan comfort. Instead he had to grit his teeth against the urge to one-up Jon with stories of his own.

For two hours he said nothing. When they arrived at the downed bridge, he turned to look at the women. Bessie had a steady way about her, but Caroline went chalk-white at the sight of the trail zigzagging down the canyon wall. Without a word, he led the way on Cairo with Grandma following and Jon at the rear with the second packhorse in tow. He could hear Caroline's unsteady breathing, but she didn't utter a word.

When they reached the water's edge, Tristan turned again to look at the women. Bessie had the stalwart expression of a veteran soldier. He suspected she'd experienced more difficult challenges than crossing a river. Caroline, however, could have been looking at a man-eating grizzly. Tristan followed her gaze to the rushing current. The knee-high water hadn't gone down since yesterday. Cairo could handle it, but Grandma would be skittish.

He slid out of the saddle. "I'll ferry the women across."

It was the first time he'd spoken in two hours. Caroline stared as if she'd forgotten him. "Are you sure it's safe?"

"Positive."

Jon dismounted, then lifted her off Grandma's back. She landed in front of him with her hands resting lightly on his shoulders. Envy poked at Tristan again. Next Jon assisted Bessie, and the four of them stood in a square of sorts. As if the women weren't present, Tristan addressed Jon. "I'll take Miss Bradley first. You'll wait here with Miss Caroline. When I take her across, follow on Grandma with the packhorses."

To Tristan's consternation, Caroline took a step back and turned away from them. He followed her gaze to the river and saw a tree branch floating by. Bessie put an arm around her sister's waist and murmured something. The younger woman murmured back loud enough for Tristan to hear. "I can't do this," she said. "It's just too much."

Bessie patted her back. "I know, but it's just a river. You can do it."

"But I don't *want* to!" Her voice rose in volume and pitch. "First we get robbed. Then you sprained your ankle and the wolves kept howling—" She shuddered. "When is it going to *stop?*"

Tristan ached for her because he felt the same way about his illness. It wasn't the river that had Miss Bradley in a knot. It was days, weeks, maybe years of frustration.

He stepped up behind her. Wondering if he'd lost his mind, he touched her shoulder. "Caroline?" He deliberately left off the "Miss."

She startled like a deer, then faced him. "I'm sorry, Major. It's just—"

"I understand."

He could have been speaking to Dora, but his daughter wouldn't have tried to be brave. She'd have reached to be picked up, fully expecting him to protect her. Caroline had no such expectation.

Her doubt challenged him. "The river isn't deep. I'm confident Cairo can handle it."

"Who's Cairo?"

"My horse."

She turned to look at the stallion. In the shadows of the canyon, his coat glistened black and his muscles were deeply defined. Poised and ready, the horse towered over Grandma.

"He's huge," Caroline murmured. "And he looks fast."

"He's practically a nag," Tristan said, joking. "The old boy can barely walk." He meant the horse, but she looked at *him*.

Anger flared in her eyes. "You're making fun of me."

"No," he said gently. "I wanted to make you smile. You can be assured that you'll be safe."

"I just don't know."

"I do," he said, deadpan. "No one disobeys me. Not even Cairo."

Jon laughed out loud. "Tell that to Dora."

"Well, yes," he acknowledged. "Dora has a mind of her own."

"So do I." Caroline squared her shoulders. "But there's no choice."

She'd spoken the same words earlier, and it bothered him. He wanted to tell her there was always a choice, but he hadn't chosen malaria. He hadn't chosen to lose Molly. Sometimes, there was no choice but to accept the inevitable. Today, though, he had a choice to make. He could be a sympathetic friend or an unfeeling tyrant. Before

Caroline could object, he took her hand and tugged her to Cairo. The horse stood with the expectation of royalty. Tristan took a peppermint from his pocket and offered it on his flat palm. Cairo took the treat, bobbing his head as he tasted the mint.

Caroline laughed. "Your horse eats candy."

"Yes." Tristan took another piece of peppermint from his pocket and handed it to her. "Hold it flat like I did."

"I couldn't—"

"Like this," he said, unfolding her fingers.

When she didn't argue, he put the peppermint in her palm and held her hand under Cairo's nose. The horse took the treat with the gentleness Tristan expected. More amazed than terrified, she turned to him. They were face-to-face, a breath apart. If he'd been a healthy man, he'd have wondered about kissing her. Not now, but later when he knew her better. But malaria had bent his life into a question mark. He could be gone in a week or a month…or he could live a long life. Looking at Caroline, he thought of his promise to Molly to remarry, and he imagined keeping it.

Blushing, Caroline looked away. "Let's go while I have the courage."

"Certainly."

Tristan pulled himself into the saddle, took the reins and guided Cairo to a flat boulder. Understanding his intention, she followed and climbed on the rock. He took his boot out of the stirrup and offered his hand. Nervous but determined, she placed her foot in the stirrup, grasped his fingers and looked into his eyes.

"On the count of three," he said. "One…two…three."

He pulled her up and over the horse. She landed with a plop and instinctively wrapped her arms around his waist, squeezing as if she'd never let go. For that moment, the malaria didn't matter. Tristan felt strong and capable. He might not live to see another Christmas, but he could get Caroline safely across the river.

"Are you ready?" he asked.

"Yes, Major."

He'd have preferred to be called Tristan, but a barrier had to be maintained. With Caroline clinging to his waist, he nudged Cairo into the current. The horse plowed into the river until the water rose above his knees. Ripples splashed against Tristan's thigh, and the hem of Caroline's skirt became sodden. She was trembling against his back, struggling to breathe evenly and holding him like she'd never him go.

"You're doing wonderfully," he said.

"We're halfway, aren't we?"

"Exactly."

They were dead center and in the deepest part of the river. Tristan looked up the canyon and saw a tree branch floating in their direction. He held Cairo back to let it pass, but the current aimed the branch straight at them. When Cairo sidestepped, Miss Bradley squeezed the breath out of him.

"We're fine," he said gently. "Just hang on."

He nudged Cairo to take another step. The horse refused to budge. Looking down, Tristan saw a submerged tangle of limbs and leaves. It was caught on the horse's hoof, and Cairo didn't like it.

Caroline trembled against his back. "Why aren't we moving?"

He thought of his boast that no one would dare disobey him. The stallion, it seemed, had decided to prove him wrong. Tristan would win this test of wills, but it would come at a cost. He put his hand over Caroline's stiff fingers. "Cairo needs a little encouragement. I'm going to dig in my heels. I want you to be ready because he's going to jump forward."

"Oh, no," she whimpered.

She held even tighter to his waist. Just before he nudged Cairo, the horse sidestepped again. The branch came with him and he started to rear. "Hang on," Tristan called to her.

He needed both hands to control the horse. Cairo whinnied in irritation, then reared up with the intention of stomping the branch. To Tristan's dismay, Caroline slid off the horse in a tangle of skirts and petticoats. With a splash, she landed in the river.

Chapter Four

The water went over Caroline's head with a whoosh. She couldn't see or breathe. She could only feel the sudden cold and the current grabbing at her skirt. The stallion was bucking and stomping. If she didn't get out of the river, she'd be pulled downstream or trampled. She tried to stand but stumbled because of the weight of her clothing.

"Get back!" the major shouted.

He had his hands full with the unruly horse. She didn't know why it had bucked, but the medical case was slapping against its side. She had a horrible vision of it coming loose. Major Smith would lose the quinine, and she'd lose her only picture of Charles. Bracing against the sandy bottom, she pushed to her feet. She wanted to run for the shore, but if the case tore loose she'd go after it.

Cairo reared back and whinnied. She half expected Major Smith to land in the river with her, but he moved gracefully with the horse, aligning his body with the stallion's neck and back. Behind her she heard Jon sloshing toward them on Grandma. Being caught between two horses terrified her more than drowning, so she hoisted her skirts and ran downriver.

She stumbled a dozen steps, tripped on her hem and

went down again. Rocks pressed into her knees and she cried out. She kept her head above water, but her skirt was tangled around her legs. Seemingly out of nowhere, male hands gripped her arms and lifted her from the current.

"Caroline." She heard the major's voice, the accent thick as he set her on her feet. "It's all right. I've got you."

She felt the strength of his arms and the sureness of his stance. As he steadied her, she wiped her eyes with her sleeve and became aware of his body shielding her from the current. She had no business noticing him in a personal way. She was merely an employee, a woman who was afraid of horses and had fallen in the river.

She pulled back from his grasp and staggered away. "I'm all right."

He splashed closer, reaching for her. "Let me walk you to the shore."

"No!" She didn't want to feel his arm around her waist. "Go take care of your horse."

"Jon has Cairo."

She looked past him to the shore where Jon and Grandma were leading Cairo up the sandy bank. The black horse had calmed, but he still looked on edge…much like the major. He stepped closer to her, his hand extended as if he were giving her a peppermint. "Come now," he said with authority. "There's nothing to be afraid of."

"Oh, yes there is!" She was afraid of *him*, afraid of her feelings because she couldn't help but appreciate the nobility of what he had done. With malaria symptoms, he had no business jumping into the river to help her. He should have taken his horse to shore and let Jon come to her rescue. Instead he'd risked getting a chill. Even more revealing was the compassion in his eyes. He looked both sincere and commanding, a man of courage who understood fear. She could imagine soldiers following him into battle, trusting him to lead them to victory.

She wanted to trust him, too. It had been so long since she'd had a man in her life that she could rely on. Charles had died seven years ago. After losing him, she'd become a pariah and no man had wanted her. It had been Bessie's idea to move to Denver. There they'd found Swan's Nest, a boardinghouse for women in need, and Caroline had found the faith to love again but not a man to love. She'd continually failed to measure up, though her friends had all found husbands.

Adie Clarke had married Joshua Blue, an unlikely but wonderfully happy match between a woman with a secret and a minister with regrets. Pearl Oliver had found a husband in Matt Wiley. A victim of violence, Pearl had married a lawman dedicated to justice and his little girl. And then there was Mary Larue. Two months ago she'd married outlaw J. T. Quinn, a man from her past whom she'd loved for years.

Caroline didn't begrudge her friends their happiness, but she very much wanted a family of her own. She wanted to belong somewhere, anywhere. That was what she'd hoped to find when she'd answered the major's advertisement. But now she wondered if she'd made a mistake. If she was *still* making a mistake, trusting too soon, believing she could rely on the major. In Denver she'd been safe. Since leaving Swan's Nest, she'd been robbed and nearly drowned. God had let her down, and so had Major Smith when his horse reared. She glared at him. "I thought no one disobeyed you, not even your horse!"

"Cairo startled—"

"He bucked me off!"

"Yes," the major said gently. "He became tangled in a branch and startled."

That voice… He could have gentled the wildest of creatures with that tone, the singsong of his accent. Suddenly she wanted to cry. She didn't blame the major for Cairo getting spooked, but neither would she forget that she'd fallen. She'd trusted him and suffered for it. Not only could she have drowned, but also he might have been harmed trying to save her.

"Accidents happen," she said bitterly. "I'm well aware of that."

"Yes," he said. "I apologize again. If you'll allow me to walk you to the shore, we'll rest for a bit while you dry off."

She didn't want to rest only to struggle through a long, tiring journey when the rest was over. She wanted to be safe and dry in a home of her own. She wanted an ordinary life in a place where she belonged. But she couldn't have any of that. She only had herself. Ignoring his offered hand, she met his gaze. "Thank you, Major. But I can manage."

She gathered her wet skirts and trudged to the shore, walking slightly upriver and feeling the tug of the current. He came up beside her but didn't speak. After she'd gone twenty paces, each more draining than the last, he looped his arm around her waist. She felt secure. She felt protected. And she was madder than a wet hen that she wanted to be more than a governess, more than an employee and a woman who'd fallen in the river.

As they slogged through the current, Major Smith acknowledged Jon with a reassuring wave. Mounted on Grandma, Jon recrossed the river to fetch Bessie and the packhorses, leaving Caroline and the major to make their way to the shore. When they reached the bank, he stepped away from her. Except for Cairo tied to a willow, they were alone. Caroline shivered with the chill. As soon as Jon brought the packhorses, she'd put on dry clothes.

With his back to her, Major Smith opened the medical bag to check the quinine. She thought of the picture of Charles. He'd see it. Good, she thought. If he had questions, he could ask. If he had prejudices, she wanted to know it.

"Is the quinine safe?" she asked.

"Yes." He looked deeper in the case. "Your photograph is unharmed, as well."

Would he ask who was in the picture? Did he expect her to give details that were none of his business? When he turned and looked into her eyes, she felt like a private in the presence of a general, but she refused either to cower or snap to attention.

Major Smith spoke first. "I was an officer in the West India Regiment. Have you heard of it?"

"No, sir."

"The West India Regiment is part of the regular British Army. It's led by men like myself, sons of England—" he said *England* as if it tasted bad "—but the soldiers are locals from the Caribbean Islands. They're free black men, Miss Bradley. I don't know who the gentlemen in your photograph is or what he means to you, but I presume he is—or was—someone important to you."

She'd been expecting rejection, prejudice. Instead she'd found another reason to like Major Smith. Wondering if the day could get any worse, she looked into his eyes and saw a loyalty that stole her breath, leading her to open her heart. "Charles was my husband. He died seven years ago."

"I'm very sorry."

"He was lynched," she said before she could stop herself. "It was ugly and violent, and I saw it happen. That's why I'm afraid of horses. The men who did it put him on a broken-down nag. Someone told me later they didn't intend to kill Charles. They just wanted to scare him." Her voice dropped to a hush. "They wanted to scare me, too. But the horse went wild. It bucked and Charles…died."

Major Smith held her gaze. "I've seen men die. It changes a person."

"Yes."

"And I've lost my wife," he added. "That changes a man, as well."

Caroline nodded because she truly understood. "I'm sorry for your loss, Major Smith."

"Likewise, Caroline."

He'd left off the "Miss," a fitting acknowledgment of the new accord between them. He also pronounced her name Caro-*line*. Most people called her Caro-*lyn*. It made her feel different from the woman she'd always been.

They looked at each other a long time, then both turned away to remember or think. Caroline was surprised at the sudden sense of kinship she felt with this man who had seemed at first to be so brusque and domineering. There was a kindness to him she hadn't expected. It was enough to make her hope that this journey hadn't been a mistake. Perhaps she truly had found a place where she could belong.

Still, she wouldn't get her hopes up yet. She knew too well how badly it would hurt if they were dashed once more.

To her relief, Jon arrived with Bessie and the packhorses. Her sister slid off the mare, ran to Caroline and hugged her. "You could have drowned."

"Or been trampled," she added.

"Let's get you in dry clothes," Bessie said firmly. "Then you can put the scare out of your mind."

Caroline agreed about needing dry clothes, but she

doubted today's ordeal would ever leave her thoughts. Somewhere between one side of the river and the other, she'd seen a new side of a man with whom she had believed she had nothing in common, a man from another class and another continent…a man who might finally be able to give her a home. It was a heady and frightening thought. Shivering, she went with Bessie to find a private spot to change. It was a long way to Wheeler Springs. She dreaded getting back on a horse, but she'd be fine with Bessie and Grandma. As for Major Smith and Cairo, the horse scared her and so did the man.

When the women were out of sight, Tristan thought of his own wet clothes. He was soaked to his thighs, but the sun and constant wind would dry the fabric. Feverish or not, he was more concerned about getting Caroline to Wheeler Springs without another incident. She'd most likely want to ride with her sister on Grandma, but Tristan had experience with both fear and horses. Fear had to be faced, and horses had to be controlled. Caroline had to get back on Cairo or her fear would fester. It had nothing to do with any wish on his part to keep the lady close, of course. No, he was convinced it was simply the logical response any employer might have toward a phobia on the part of a brave, stubborn, lovely employee. Turning to Jon, he saw his friend retying the bundle of clothing. "Caroline's badly shaken," he said. "But she needs to ride with me, at least for a time."

"I suppose so," Jon agreed.

"Of all the fool things," Tristan muttered. "Cairo's good in water. That branch came out of nowhere."

"We almost had two women in the river." Jon's brows lifted with admiration. "I had to stop her sister from going in after her."

"I hadn't noticed."

"I did." Jon's lips tipped into a smile. "You're a good judge of character, Tristan. The Bradleys are exceptional women. I expected the nurse to be a dour sort, but she's quite pleasant."

Tristan thought about his plan to match his friend with Caroline. Jon and Bessie were closer in age and possibly in temperament. The nurse would make a fine substitute mother, but he wanted his children to have someone young and spirited, someone more like Molly…someone with the courage to buck convention. Molly had done it when she'd defied her family and joined him in the West Indies. Caroline had done it when she'd married a black man.

Normally reticent, Tristan wouldn't have mentioned the photograph but he'd been surprised. He'd also been impressed by the defiant tilt of her chin. She was exactly the kind of mother he wanted for his children. If not for the malaria, he'd have been looking forward to riding with her on Cairo. Instead he found himself glaring at Jon.

His friend shot him a concerned glance. "You're looking rather dour, yourself. Are you feeling ill?"

"I'm fine."

"You're always *fine*," Jon said, mocking him. "If you're not up to ferrying a frightened woman, I'm sure the Bradleys would do well on Grandma."

Common sense told Tristan to agree. Male pride made him frown at Jon. "If the day comes that I can't handle a horse, I'll be ready for the grave."

"I didn't mean the horse," Jon said rather cheekily. "I meant the woman."

Tristan glared at him.

"You seem to be getting along quite well," Jon said too casually. "She's quite pretty, though of course you didn't notice."

Of course Tristan had noticed, but a man in poor health had no business courting a woman's affections. He was about to suggest Jon take Caroline on Grandma when the women approached from the bushes. Caroline had fashioned her hair into a braid and looped it around her head in a crown of sorts. The sun glinted off the dampness, giving it a sparkle. She'd put on an old calico, a gown he guessed to be comfortable and a favorite. She looked none the worse for wear. In fact, she looked lovely with flushed cheeks and a determined lift of her chin.

When the women reached the horses, she addressed him directly. "We're ready, Major."

"Yes, I see."

She turned to Grandma, where Jon was waiting to help Bessie into the saddle. His friend lifted a brow at Tristan, questioning him about the riding arrangements.

Tristan cleared his throat. "You'll be riding with me."

She faced him, her mouth slightly agape. "I don't think—"

"I do. We all know the adage about getting back up on a horse."

"And I will," she replied. "I'll ride Grandma with my sister."

Tristan put his hands behind his back, a pose he assumed to intimidate new privates. "May I be blunt?"

"Of course."

"Not only do I think it's wise for you to overcome your fear, I'm afraid I have a point to prove…to Cairo."

She wrinkled her brow. "Your horse's behavior isn't my concern. My safety is."

"Which leads to my second point." His tone stayed firm. "I'd like a chance to prove that Cairo isn't as dangerous as you've assumed. It's rather important, really. If you're to be living on a ranch, you need to be comfortable around animals."

"I don't mind animals," she replied. "But your horse—"

"He reacted to a fright," Tristan answered. "Surely you can understand. He'd like a chance to redeem himself." Tristan didn't want to admit it, but he had the same need. He glanced at Jon for help and saw a bemused look on his friend's face and then a twinkle in his eyes. Looking roguish, Jon addressed Caroline. "I can attest to the major's abilities as a horseman."

She glanced at her sister. Bessie gave a little shrug. "It's up to you."

Pale, Caroline turned back to him. "I don't think—"

"I do," he said gently. "The river is tricky for a horse. The road to town isn't."

She looked at him for several seconds. What she was gauging, he didn't know. Was it his ability, or her own courage? In the end, she walked in his direction. "I suppose you're right. I'll go with you on Cairo."

"Very good." Why he was so pleased, Tristan couldn't say. Neither did he know why he shot Jon a triumphant look, the kind they'd shared before he'd settled down with Molly, when they'd been young lieutenants and full of themselves.

As Caroline approached Cairo, Jon helped Bessie climb on Grandma, then mounted the packhorse. Tristan mounted Cairo, took his boot out of the stirrup and held out his hand. Without a rock to stand on, she had to leap and stretch, which is just what she did. She held his waist like before, but without the cinchlike grip. In silence he turned Cairo and headed down the road at a walk.

Clop. Clop. Clop.

She sighed.

Clop. Clop. Clop.

Tristan looked over his shoulder. "How are you doing?"

"Fine."

She sighed again. He said nothing. After a mile, she spoke over his shoulder. "Major Smith?"

"Yes?"

"How long will it take us to get to Wheeler Springs?"

"At this pace, about three days." When she laughed, he thought of lively piano music and the celebrations after battle. It felt good to know he'd restored her humor. Encouraged, he spoke over his shoulder. "Do you think you can handle going a little faster?"

She hesitated. "I suppose so. I'm eager to get to town."

"So am I," he replied. "I'm going to give Cairo a nudge. If you feel at all uncomfortable, just say so."

"Set the pace, Major."

When he urged Cairo into a slow jog, Caroline tightened her grip on his waist to keep from bouncing. He was tempted to ask if she wanted to go faster, but if she agreed then he knew she'd hold on tighter. He needed to keep her at arm's length the way an officer lived apart from enlisted men. That's how he'd think of Caroline Bradley...as a private in his personal army. Or maybe a sergeant because she'd be raising his children. With that thought in mind, Tristan rode with the pretty governess in resolute silence.

Chapter Five

Caroline couldn't fault the major's logic about having her ride with him on Cairo, but she felt like a sack of potatoes, one in danger of sliding to the ground and splitting open. With her arms belted around his waist, she heard every beat of Cairo's hooves. She distracted herself with questions about the man before her. Why had he come to America instead of returning to England? What had his wife been like? And the malaria… How did he cope with the fevers? And what provisions had he made for his children?

Unable to stand the silence, she decided the children were a safe subject and surrendered to curiosity. "Major Smith?"

"Yes?"

"I'd like to hear about Freddie and Dora."

He hesitated. "You already know their names and ages."

"Yes, but I'd like to know *about* them. What do they like to do?"

"They're children, Miss Bradley. They entertain themselves."

Miss Bradley made it clear his earlier kindness was to be forgotten. It annoyed her but not nearly as much as his refusal to talk about his children. He seemed cold again, even austere. Having lost their mother, Freddie and Dora needed their father's attention, and if his current behavior was any indication, he seemed unwilling to give it. If *she'd* been blessed with children, she'd have cherished every smile, every new adventure.

She rode with the major in silence, staring straight ahead until they reached the livery stable marking the beginning of Wheeler Springs. A row of buildings included a barber and bathhouse, a dress shop and a mercantile with its doors propped open. The shopkeeper stepped outside with a broom. Seeing their arrival, he waved a greeting.

Major Smith answered with a nod, a gesture that reminded Caroline of a returning soldier in a parade.

Across the street she saw a café with yellow curtains, and she thought of the wonderful food at the café run by Mary Larue, now Mary Quinn. At her wedding, Mary had placed her bouquet firmly in Caroline's arms, a gesture Caroline knew to be futile. For whatever reason, God had said no to her prayers for a family of her own. Instead He'd brought her to Wheeler Springs to love the Smith children, a cause she intended to embrace.

Halfway through town, the major turned Cairo down a road that led to a three-story house with paned glass windows, a wide porch and a cupola. Square and painted white with green trim, it reminded her of the houses in Charleston.

"Where are we?" she asked the major.

"My town house. We'll leave for The Barracks in the morning."

Once broken, the silence between them felt sharper than ever. Where was the man who'd helped her out of the river? The one who gave peppermint to his horse? The closer they rode to the house, the more rigid the major became until she felt as if she were holding on to a lamp-post. They were still several paces away when the front door burst open and a little girl came charging across the porch. Dark hair framed her face and accented her rosy cheeks.

"Daddy!" she cried.

The major heaved an impatient sigh. "I gave orders for the children to stay at The Barracks."

The thought of children being *ordered* to stay away from their father struck her as heinous. Why would he do such a thing? She wanted to take him to task, but she was in no position to initiate such a conversation...at least not yet. She settled for a calm observation. "Dora is lovely."

He said nothing.

"You must be very proud of her."

"I suppose."

Appalled by his apparent indifference and moved by Dora's obvious need, Caroline tried again. "Does she like to play with dolls?"

He said nothing, though he hadn't looked away from his little girl. Did he know what a gift he had in this precious child? Caroline wanted to lecture him, to warn him that such gifts could be snatched in a blink, but then she realized that he knew it. Major Smith was afraid to love his children because he was afraid of dying and leaving them to grieve.

Caroline watched over his shoulder as a boy with the major's blond hair and stiff posture joined his sister at the top of the two steps connecting the porch to the ground. "That must be Freddie," she said more to herself than the major. "He's a handsome lad, isn't he?"

Major Smith reined Cairo to a halt. "You should be aware, Miss Bradley, that I expect orders to be followed.

And I left specific instructions for the children to remain at the ranch."

She couldn't resist a bit of defiance. "Apparently not everyone obeys you, at least not when children miss their father."

Without turning or twitching, the major spoke in a tone just for her. "Courage becomes you, Miss Bradley. Rudeness does not. I suggest you mind your own affairs and leave me to mine."

He'd snubbed her, rightfully so, considering her position in his household. Stranded on his horse, she wanted to escape his nearness but feared sliding off and ending up in a heap. She settled for releasing her grip on the major's waist and looking for Jon. He rode up next to them, swung off the packhorse and helped her down with a gentleman's ease.

"There you go," he said in a friendly tone.

"Thank you."

Bessie halted Grandma next to the packhorse. After Jon helped her sister dismount, Caroline asked him to retrieve a small bundle from their possessions. It held gifts for the children and she wanted to present them now. Assuming Major Smith would introduce her, she waited while he tied the reins to the hitching post.

She turned her attention to the children. Dora's eyes were wide with curiosity. Freddie reminded her of his father, both in looks and in temperament. He had a stoic expression, a sign he'd learned sadness and loss too young. Dora needed a smile and a hug. Freddie needed to know she'd respect his quiet nature. Already Caroline felt challenged by the differences in the children.

Major Smith indicated she should step forward. For the first time since leaving the river, she had a clear view of his face. Creases fanned from his blue eyes, deeper and more numerous than she'd seen this morning. The line of his mouth pitched downward in a frown, or maybe it was a grimace against exhaustion. He wasn't a well man, and the trip to the stagecoach had cost him. Compassion tempered the frustration she'd felt toward him moments ago.

She came forward as he'd indicated, watching the children for their reactions. Freddie snapped to attention. Dora leaned against her brother and acted shy. Caroline was glad she'd brought the doll. Little Dora desperately needed something to hug.

The major spoke in a firm voice. "Good afternoon, children."

"Good afternoon, Father," Freddie answered.

Dora hid her face against her brother.

"Come forward, please," the major said. "I'd like you to meet Miss Caroline Bradley, your new governess."

Freddie took Dora's hand and guided her forward. The protective gesture touched Caroline to the core and reminded her of how the major had gently guided her out of the river. His cold attitude to the children hadn't always been a wall between them. She suspected that losing his wife and facing an illness had changed him.

When the children reached the ground, they stopped four feet in front of her. Freddie looked up at his father, a soldier ready to take orders. Dora looked at her toes, a little girl who didn't know what to do. Aching for her, Caroline stepped forward and dropped to a crouch so she could look into the child's eyes. They were blue like her father's and no less haunted. A harrumph told her she'd crossed the major, but she didn't care. *He* could be cold and distant if he wanted, but Caroline had no such inclination.

She smiled at the shy little girl. "You must be Dora."

Still looking down, the child nodded.

"That's a pretty name," Caroline said gently. "And you're wearing such a pretty dress. I bet you like to play with dolls."

Her head bobbed up and she nodded.

"Good," Caroline declared. "So do I."

The major spoke to her back. "Miss Caroline, I don't think—"

"I do." Ignoring him, she opened the drawstring bag and gave Dora the doll. "I made this for you."

The major's voice boomed behind her. *"Miss Bradley!"*

He sounded ready to court-martial her, but she had to give the book to Freddie the way she'd given the doll to Dora. She took the volume from the bag, stood tall and handed it to the boy. "This is for you, Freddie."

The major had said little about the boy's interests, so she'd taken advice from Mary Quinn's young brother and selected a science book with easy experiments. "We can use kitchen items to make a volcano. That should be fun."

Freddie's eyes lit up, but he looked to his father for direction.

Not wanting the boy to be a pawn, Caroline faced the major. She recalled how he'd ignored her when she'd wanted to tell him about the quinine. It went against her nature to be rude, so she gave him a wistful smile. "Forgive me, Major Smith. I was just so excited to meet your children. I'm sure you understand."

She'd meant to bridge the gap between the major and Freddie and Dora. Instead she felt as if she were in the middle of the river again, only this time Major Smith needed to be led to shore. He looked both stunned and bitter about his poor health. Caroline couldn't abide his attitude toward Freddie and Dora, but neither would she do him the dishonor of being blunt. His children were present, and Bessie and Jon were watching them with more than idle curiosity.

She softened the moment with a winsome smile. "I *do* apologize, Major Smith. With your permission, I'd like to speak to Dora and Freddie for a just another moment."

He made a sweeping motion with his arm. "By all means, Miss Bradley. Speak as long as you'd like. Take all afternoon…take all night."

Ignoring the sarcasm, she crouched next to Dora. "I thought we could name your new doll together."

Dora's bottom lip pushed into a pout, trembling until she finally spoke. "I want to name her Molly."

Freddie elbowed his sister. "You can't!"

"Why not?" Dora whined back.

"Because that was *Mama's* name."

The boy had the cold tone of an undertaker, but Caroline wasn't fooled. He'd built a wall to protect his bruised heart. Dora's innocent attempt to keep her mother's memory alive hit the wall like a battering ram. Behind her the major inhaled deeply, a sign he wasn't as indifferent to his children as he wanted to appear. Hoping to smooth the waters, she touched Dora's shoulder. "Molly's a fine name. It would honor your mother, but we need to consider your father and Freddie, too. We can give the doll two names, a special middle name and one for everyday."

"Do you have two names?" Dora asked.

"I do," Caroline answered. "I'm Caroline Margaret Bradley. Margaret is after my grandmother."

Dora looked at her father. "What's my other name?"

A five-year-old shouldn't have needed to ask that question. She should have been loved and schooled in family memories. When the major hesitated, she wondered if he knew the answer.

He finally cleared his throat. "Your full name is Theodora Constance Smith. Constance was your mother's sister."

Dora's eyes got wide. "I can't write all that!"

Caroline took the child's hand and squeezed. "I'll teach you."

Standing, she turned to Freddie. The boy's expression was strained, a mirror image of his father. She'd have to work to win him over, but she firmly believed God had brought her to this family for a purpose. Not only did the children need a mother, but they also needed a father who wasn't afraid to love them.

She motioned for Bessie to come forward. "This is my sister, Miss Elizabeth Bradley. You can call her Miss Bessie." Hoping to earn Freddie's interest, Caroline spoke to him directly. "She was a nurse in the war."

Freddie tried to seem bored, but his brows lifted with curiosity. Bessie greeted the boy, then said hello to Dora. Both children enjoyed the attention.

Caroline thought the first meeting went well. She turned to express her pleasure to Major Smith and saw a frown creasing the corners of his mouth. He dismissed the children with a terse order to go back inside, instructed Jon to report their arrival to the stage office, then motioned for Caroline and Bessie to enter the house. In the entry hall she saw a tall black man. When he broke into a smile, she thought of Charles.

"Good evening, Miss Bradley." He greeted her with a slight bow. "Welcome to Wheeler Springs."

Major Smith stood to the side. "Ladies, this is Sergeant Noah Taylor. Noah, I'd like you to meet the Bradley sisters, Miss Bessie and Miss Caroline."

She and this man were peers and equals, employees of the major. Caroline extended her hand. "Please call me Caroline."

"Yes, Caroline."

He greeted Bessie with equal aplomb. Behind him a black woman emerged from the kitchen. Tall and graceful, she looked at Major Smith with a mix of dignity and frustration. "Good afternoon, sir."

Major Smith answered with a nod. "Ladies, this is Evaline. She's Noah's wife and will show you to your rooms."

"Yes, sir," she said. "But first I must apologize."

He raised one eyebrow. "Does this have something to do with my children being here?"

The woman dipped her chin. "I know you left orders to keep them at The Barracks, but they were lonely for you."

Caroline loved Evaline on the spot. She'd risked a scolding to do right by the children. The major claimed no one disobeyed him, but his housekeeper had the freedom to follow her conscience. The major gave orders, but he wasn't unreasonable. Deep down, he cared about people. It showed, if one knew where to look.

Looking wry, he traded a look with Noah. "I seem to have lost all authority."

The man grinned. "No, sir. Just with Evaline."

The major harrumphed but made no effort to scold the woman. Instead he seemed to forget all about the transgression. "See to it the Bradley women have bathwater and whatever else they need." He turned back to Caroline. "Supper will be served at seven o'clock. The children will be present."

"Yes, sir," she answered.

Evaline indicated the stairs. "This way, ladies."

The housekeeper led the way with Bessie behind her and Caroline bringing up the rear. When she reached the landing, she looked down. At the same instant, the major looked up. Their gazes locked in a test of wills. She'd defied him when she'd spoken to the children, and he'd let her. Neither had he chastised Evaline. The major conducted himself with acerbic authority, but his final decisions showed respect, even a deep caring, for his friends and family. Why would he be so cold on the outside when he plainly loved Freddie and Dora?

They looked away from each other at the same time. Silent but determined to bring joy to this troubled household, she followed Evaline and Bessie up the stairs.

It was a sad day when a man's housekeeper disobeyed him and he let her. It was an even sadder day when he couldn't control the governess, or even his own children. Wondering why he bothered to issue orders at all, Tristan went to his study, shut the door and dropped down in the leather chair. It squeaked, yet another act of defiance against his desire for quiet.

He couldn't be angry with Evaline. He'd been happier to see Freddie and Dora than he could admit. But he'd held true to his resolve to keep his distance. With the malaria threatening his life, he had to stay strong for them. They had to learn they could live without him. The decision had seemed wise until Caroline skewered him by giving Dora the doll. He'd known how much his daughter missed her mother, but he hadn't realized how alone he'd left his children. It took discipline to stay strong for them, but that's what a father did…what an officer did. When everyone else succumbed to tears and flashes of temper, an officer kept his wits about him.

At the moment Tristan's wits were in tatters. He needed another dose of quinine, but he hadn't taken the bottles from Bessie's medicine bag because he'd been distracted by the children. Neither did he have easy access to the small supply he'd brought from The Barracks. It was upstairs in his bedroom, and he didn't want to pass his house-guests in the hall. He'd wait, but only for a bit.

To fortify himself, he picked up the letter that had been delivered before he'd left. Pennwright's neat script was badly smudged, but he expected the man's dry humor would be intact. He sliced the envelope with an opener, removed a single sheet and began to read.

Dear Tristan,
  I'm writing to you with a heavy heart. Both of your brothers are dead.

Tristan read the opening words again, then a second time. As the ramifications sunk in, his insides shook the way they did before weapons were drawn for battle. The shaking signaled danger and the loss of life…his life… the life in Wyoming he wanted for his children. With his brothers dead, he'd become his father's heir and the next duke of Willoughby. The clock in the entry gonged six times, a death knell to accent Pennwright's perfect script.

As if surveying a battle report, he took in the rest of the letter. Andrew had died of cholera, and he'd left no sons or daughters. Tristan immediately thought of his widow, Louisa, alone and grieving without even children to comfort her. She'd broken his heart when she'd married his brother, but he held no bitterness. He only wondered why she jilted him and if somehow he'd failed her. Oscar had died a week after Andrew. Pennwright's explanation chilled Tristan to the bone.

He died from a gunshot to the head. Your father is calling it a hunting accident.

Tristan knew his brother well enough to read between the lines. Oscar had called hunting the sport of fools. He didn't like horses, exercise or perspiration. With a heavy heart, Tristan acknowledged what hadn't been written. Oscar's "hunting" accident had likely been suicide. Tristan viewed the deed as cowardice, but he understood why Oscar had done it. A man of little discipline, he'd have become the duke's whipping boy.

Pennwright's next words carried no surprise, but they jarred him nonetheless.

You, Tristan, are now heir to your father's title and holdings. He wishes you to return to England immediately to assume your duties.

If Tristan had been healthy, he might have gloated at the irony. The son his father had dismissed as worthless now had value to him. But Tristan wasn't well... Chances were good his father would outlive him, and Freddie would fall under the man's influence. The thought chilled Tristan to the bone.

The duke could issue whatever orders he pleased, but Tristan wouldn't snap mindlessly to attention. He had to protect his son. The duke had turned Andrew into a pampered poodle and Oscar into an alley cat. Tristan refused to be paraded like a pet, nor would he allow Freddie to be turned into Andrew or Oscar.

In the same breath, he recognized the profound responsibility of being a duke. He'd been born a third son, but he'd become a leader of men. By blood and British law, he had a duty to the people of Willoughby and wanted to fulfill his obligation with honor.

But he was also a father and he had to protect his son. Tristan was the only defense between Freddie and the duke. He refused to allow his son to be used and manipulated. Dora would suffer, too. His daughter would be valued solely for her worth as a future wife, not for the charming little girl she was. As long as Tristan and his father were both alive, he had time to come up with a strategy. There was no need to rush back to England, at least not yet.

Weary to the bone, he left Pennwright's letter on the desk and headed to his room. After supper he'd speak to Jon about ways to protect Freddie. Tristan was a good strategist, but Jon had a more creative mind. First, though, he needed quinine.

He entered his suite and shut the door with a click. He took the dose of medicine, then washed his hands and changed into attire befitting a meal with the new governess and her sister. The women would talk throughout supper and so would his children. Jon would be charming, and Tristan would be stoic. With a bittersweet longing to be well again, he headed for the dining room, wearing the stiff upper lip he was so very tired of maintaining.

Chapter Six

Caroline had never had a better-tasting meal in her life…
or a more awkward one. She was sitting to the right of
Major Smith and across from Bessie. Jon was next to her
sister, and Freddie was next to Jon. Little Dora sat in a
child's chair to Caroline's right.

The instant she sat, Caroline had been determined to
bring an air of cheerfulness to the meal. Jon and Bessie
had been willing participants in the banter, but the major
ignored everything except the food on his plate. He could
have been eating in separate quarters, which she suspected
he'd have preferred to Jon's joking and the laughter of his
children. How could he not smile at Dora's face as she
tasted the raspberry tart Evaline had made for dessert? Did
he know Freddie imitated his every mannerism? Someone needed to open his eyes to the love he was denying
his children. She wouldn't do it tonight. His skin had the
pallor of exhaustion, and he'd eaten more lightly than she
would have expected. She couldn't help but worry about
him.

Unexpectedly Noah appeared in the doorway to the
dining room. "Sir?"

"Yes, Noah?"

"I apologize for interrupting, but a courier delivered this letter." He handed the envelope to the major. "He won't leave until you reply."

"That's odd," Jon said for them all.

Attempting to be nonchalant, the major opened the letter and began to read. His eyes flicked to the bottom of the page, then back to the top. As he read, his face turned into stone. Caroline glanced at Jon for a hint of understanding and saw his mouth tighten with apprehension.

Freddie broke the silence. "What does it say, Father?"

"It doesn't concern you." He stood abruptly and headed for the door, the letter dangling from his fingers.

Dora called after him. "Daddy! What's wrong?"

If he heard the child, he'd chosen to ignore her. And if he hadn't, he should have. These children had lost their mother and lived in a fragile world, one that could be easily shattered by their father's thoughtless behavior. Caroline put her napkin on the table and stood. She looked first at Dora. "I'm going to talk to your father, okay? I'll find out what's wrong."

Dora nodded too quickly.

Caroline looked at Freddie and saw criticism but spoke anyway. "I'll be back in a few minutes."

"You shouldn't go," the boy said coldly. "He won't like it."

Caroline ached for him. He was trying to earn his father's love through rigid obedience. It wouldn't work. The person who had to change wasn't Freddie. It was the major, and she intended to confront him. No matter what the letter said, he should have given his children more consideration.

After a glance at Bessie and a nod from Jon, she went to the entry hall. She saw Noah and the major speaking to a man she didn't recognize. No voices were raised, but she felt the tension as plainly as the sun on a hot day. Ducking into a room off the hall, she watched as the courier left. The major told Noah he needed air and went out the door. When Noah went back to the dining room, Caroline followed the major.

Tristan made a beeline for the carriage house. He needed to think about the contents of the letter still loose in his hand, and he wanted to be alone while he did it…or at least away from inquisitive women and little girls eating raspberry tarts, away from Jon who'd read his expression too easily and Freddie who'd forgotten how to laugh. Cairo was all the company he could stand in light of the news he'd just received. His father was in Cheyenne. He'd ordered Tristan to send two carriages—one for himself and his traveling companion and the other for his staff. He didn't name his companion, and Tristan hadn't quizzed the courier. It would be just like his father to travel with a mistress. Needing time to think, he had sent the courier back to the hotel with instructions to wait for a reply in the morning.

What Tristan would do he didn't know. But he'd learned to think before taking action, to make a battle plan before firing off a shot that would lead to a war he couldn't win. The war with his father was one he couldn't lose.

Stepping into the carriage house, he lit a lantern and read the man's demands a second time.

Perhaps you did not receive Pennwright's letter. I can think of no other reason for your lack of attention to your duties now that your brothers are dead. As the heir apparent, you are now the Marquess of Hayvenhurst, and I have come to escort you home

*to England. Send two carriages to the Dryer Hotel.
I expect them immediately.*

*I am traveling with a female companion, someone
who may surprise you.*

Harold Smythe, Duke of Willoughby

*P.S. I understand from Pennwright that I have a
grandson. I look forward to making his acquaintance.*

The mention of Freddie sent ripples of anxiety from
Tristan's spine to his fingertips. He'd written proudly to
Pennwright about his children. Not once had he imagined
his father would show an interest, but the duke had apparently
quizzed the secretary. Now Freddie had value. So did
Tristan, and he found the equation disgusting. He paced
down the row of stalls, pivoted and paced back to the door.

It opened a crack and he stopped. Female fingers curved
on the wood, pushing slightly so that the hinges creaked
and the opening let in a draft of air. Caroline slipped into
the circle of light by the door. He'd had enough of employees
ignoring his orders, enough of *her*. All through supper
she'd prodded him to engage his children in small talk, an
activity he found painful in Molly's absence. He'd hired
her to take care of his children, and he expected her to do
her job.

"*What* are you doing here?" he demanded.

Cairo added his support by snorting.

Miss Bradley startled but didn't retreat. Whatever she
wanted to say, she felt strongly enough to venture into a
barn populated by horses.

"We need to speak about the children," she said.

"Not now."

"Sir, they're frightened." She moistened her lips, a gesture
he found oddly distracting. "The way you left—"

"I had business."

"But they don't understand," she said patiently. "When a child loses a parent, the world becomes a dangerous place."

"Miss Bradley!" Her name exploded from his lips. "Do you think for *one moment* that I *don't care* about my children? Do you think you know them better than I do? Do you think you have the *right* to come out here and tell me that my children are upset because their mother is dead? Do you think I don't *know* that?"

She went pale.

"You have no such right!" Tristan waved the letter. "You have no idea what is about to befall this entire family!"

Her eyes glistened with genuine worry. "What happened?"

Tristan fought for a modicum of self-control. Not once in his years as an officer had he lost his temper. He considered the lack of decorum a weakness. Tonight he'd shamed himself. "It's none of your concern."

"I'd be glad to listen."

"No!"

She stood unmoving, staring with those hazel eyes that offered a comfort he couldn't accept.

"Tend to the children," he ordered. "It's their bedtime."

Instead of executing an about-face, she took a step closer. "I really am a good listener."

"I beg to disagree," he said in a superior tone. "If you were a good listener, you'd be walking back to the house instead of pestering me."

She stopped two feet away from him, a picture of womanhood in a russet-colored gown that matched the autumn hue of her irises. She'd put up her hair in a coif of loose curls, and her jaw had the strength of polished ivory. She looked determined and resolute but not cold or hard. Instead, she seemed to radiate sympathy and concern for him and his family. This woman had a heart for children. Judging by her first marriage, she cared about the downtrodden and needy. Tristan didn't like being on that list, but he knew she saw him in that light because of the malaria.

She looked calmly into his eyes. "I'll go, Major. But I'd be obliged if you'd do me one small favor."

He wanted to bark an order, but her gentleness held his temper captive. "What do you want?"

"Say goodnight to your children."

As simple as it was, the request tore at his gut. Molly had been the one to read to the children and listen to their prayers. She had also prayed for *him*... He'd prayed for her, but his words had been perfunctory until the end, when he'd begged God for mercies that hadn't been given. Tristan hadn't been surprised. God and the Duke of Willoughby had a lot in common. They both issued commands without feeling. Tristan had feelings, strong ones, but he didn't quite know what to do with them when it came to Freddie and Dora. With death breathing over him, he feared they'd suffer more if he loved them without drawing lines. Memories brought comfort, but they also caused pain. Even so, Molly would have been frustrated with how he'd been acting. She'd have been as concerned as Caroline, and she'd have been cheering for the governess.

"All right," he agreed. "I'll be in shortly."

The smile on her face couldn't have been more lovely. The light encircled her within a gentle glow, and he wondered what he might have done if he'd been a well man. Molly had been clear. *Don't grieve too long, darling. I want our children to have a new mother.* Now he lived on the brink of death himself and understood the clawing need to provide a family for Freddie and Dora. He also knew the depths of grief and the coldness of an empty bed. If he ever loved again, it would be in the distant future when the disease had been beaten and he could live a normal life.

He was staring at Caroline—admiringly, though he hoped he looked stern—when Jon walked into the carriage house. His eyes went first to the governess, then to Tristan. Surprise registered, then concern. "What's going on?"

Tristan strode to Jon, handed him the letter and aimed a look at Caroline, silently ordering her to leave. Good manners must have trumped her curiosity because she headed for the door.

"Wait," Jon said to her, indicating the letter. "You should know about this."

Didn't *anyone* follow his orders? Tristan glared at Jon. "It doesn't involve her."

"I beg to differ," he said mildly. "If your father's going to show up at The Barracks, it will be *everyone's* business. Whether you like it or not, Tristan, you're the next Duke of Willoughby. You're also ill, which makes Freddie the heir presumptive."

Caroline's eyes turned into saucers. "You're a *duke?*"

"No!" he shouted.

"Technically, he's a marquess, or maybe an earl." Jon looked at Caroline with understanding. "As an American, you're probably not familiar with the British nobility. As the heir apparent, Tristan will use one of his father's lesser titles, a courtesy title if you will. His father is Harold Smythe, the Duke of Willoughby."

Caroline stared at him in disbelief. "I had no idea you were a duke!"

"I'm not," Tristan retorted. "And when I advertised for

a governess, I wasn't heir apparent. My ties to England weren't important."

"They are now." Jon faced Caroline. "Tristan isn't fond of his father. It's his story to tell, but he left England to get away from his family. Because the duke had two elder sons remaining, he didn't interfere. But now that the major's brothers are dead, he is next in line. And after him, Freddie."

The poor woman looked torn between executing a curtsy and raising her chin in good old American defiance. She chose a middle road. "If you're a nobleman, should I still call you major?"

"Good grief!" Tristan erupted. "Of course, you should call me 'major.'" He glared at Jon. "Stay out of this. What's happened is no one's business but mine."

"If you believe that then you're a fool."

"Jon—"

"Be quiet, Tristan." He turned to Caroline. "The duke is a powerful man. He's also known to be pompous and prone to vices. He'll stop at nothing to get what he wants. If he learns Tristan is ill, he'll want Freddie."

Caroline turned to him with a quizzical look. "Is your father really that difficult?"

"Yes." He had no desire to elaborate.

She looked skeptical. "If I understand correctly, you haven't seen your father in years. Perhaps he has changed."

"He hasn't." Jon spoke for them both. "The duke belongs to a world you don't understand, and it has fixed his character in a way that makes him unfit to spend time with any child."

Tristan knew she'd push for answers. "I'm going to be blunt, Miss Bradley. My father has no time for anyone but himself. He turned my eldest brother into a weak man. My middle brother committed suicide rather than become his puppet. My father is critical and vain and a master of manipulation. As you know, my health is precarious. I do *not* want him influencing either of my children."

Jon broke in. "I have to agree with Tristan. The tone of the man's letter—plus Oscar's suicide—indicates he's as calculating as ever. In light of Tristan's illness, we have to protect the children."

Caroline gave Tristan a look of pity, then turned to Jon. "You both know better than I do. How can I help the major?"

When had Jon become the chief strategist? Tristan bristled. "I'm standing right here. I *do* have a say in all this."

"Of course," Jon acknowledged. "But you're too close to the problem. I can be objective. Does the duke know you're ill?"

Jon had a point. "Not to my knowledge."

"That's good," Jon said. "We have to keep him from suspecting you're in poor health."

The thought of his father discovering his weakness made Tristan sweat.

Caroline interrupted. "Bessie's a nurse. We'll have to explain her presence."

"That won't be hard," Jon explained. "She could have been hired for the children."

"What about people in town?" she asked. "Is it common knowledge Major Smith is ill?"

"I'm afraid it is," Tristan answered.

"Good point," Jon said to her, ignoring him yet again. "We need to get the duke to The Barracks immediately. The staff won't talk."

Tristan hoped not. The men and women he employed were loyal to him, but the duke would be bringing his own servants. They'd be watching him. "I don't see how to keep the illness a secret. If the malaria strikes, he'll know it." He gave Jon a hard look. "If I die, what happens then?"

Jon spoke in a hush. "We hide the children."

"Where?" Tristan couldn't imagine a place where Freddie and Dora would be safe.

"America's a big country," Jon answered. "The duke is a man of great influence, but even *he's* no match for an entire continent."

Tristan had his doubts. Did Jon plan to keep moving with the children? How would he make a home for them?

Caroline interrupted. "I could take them to Denver. I have friends who'd help us."

Stunned by the offer, Tristan looked into her eyes. He didn't doubt her sincerity. She'd braved her fear of horses to come to the carriage house to scold him for the children's sake. He knew she truly wanted to help them and he trusted her. He wished he could have trusted his father, but like God, the duke cared nothing for individuals, only for his own purposes.

"It would work," Jon said to him. "The Bradley sisters are Americans. They can live anywhere and not be noticed. Even better, Caroline's the perfect age to be considered the children's real mother."

Tristan thought of Molly. For years she'd urged him to make peace with his father, but she hadn't known the depth of his tyranny. If she had, she'd have been begging Caroline to hide Freddie and Dora. Jon's plan had merit, but it also had pitfalls. Tristan saw an obvious one. "She can't just run off with the children. If my father were to find them, he'd accuse her of kidnapping."

"I agree," Jon said with gleam in his eyes. "That's why you need to marry her."

"*Marry* her?"

"*Marry* me?" she echoed.

"Don't look so shocked," Jon said, sounding impatient. "A marriage in name only would give Caroline legal standing. It's perfect, really. Even taking your name is a benefit. What could be more common than Caroline Smith?"

Tristan shook his head. "That's a ridiculous idea."

"Is it?" Jon asked.

"Of course." Tristan had an uncomfortable awareness of the woman standing by the door, listening to the vehemence in his rejection. He didn't want her to take the rebuff personally, so he faced her. "I apologize for Jon. As you can see, he's lost his mind."

"I don't think so." She spoke gently, but her eyes were blazing as she turned to Jon. "I'd like to speak to Major Smith in private."

"Certainly." Jon headed for the door without giving Tristan a glance.

So much for being in charge… He'd been abandoned by his second in command. Tristan had waged war and tamed wild stallions. He'd fought fevers and delirious dreams. Looking at Caroline, her heart brimming with concern for his children and her eyes wide and bright, he prepared to do battle with the most dangerous enemy of all—a well-intentioned female.

As soon the door creaked shut, she faced him. "I'm considering Jon's suggestion."

"But why?"

"I can see how worried you are. You'd do anything to stop your father."

"I would."

"And I know you love your children." She gave him a forthright look. "If you didn't, you wouldn't be considering what Jon suggested."

He felt as if she were spinning him in circles. "Who says I'm considering it?"

"*Are* you?"

Yes, but he refused to admit it. "I can't possibly ask you to be my wife."

"You didn't ask," she reminded him. "Jon did, and I'm inclined to agree with him. As he said, it's a legal arrangement, one that's only slightly different than being a governess. The difficulty lies in the future." She gave him a meaningful look. "If you recover, we'd have to stay married or attain an annulment. With the children—"

"An annulment would be complicated," he replied. "They'd be hurt."

"Yes." She squared her shoulders. "If you survive the malaria—which I believe you will—would you return to England?"

"Eventually, but I have some flexibility as long as my father's alive."

"I see." She bit her lip. "Your obligations complicate the situation. I'm obviously not capable of being a duchess—"

"That's irrelevant," he said sharply. "I'm far more worried about dying than I am about living."

If he died, she'd be hiding his children and a marriage in name only would protect them all. If he lived, he could stay in America as long as his father remained healthy. Even so, he didn't want Caroline to be locked into a marriage she didn't want. He kept his voice even. "I realize going to England is above and beyond what you're prepared to offer. For that reason, among others, I'd insist on maintaining the possibility of an annulment."

"Of course," she murmured.

An annulment would give Caroline a way out of the marriage. The children had to be considered and their immediate needs outweighed a hypothetical problem in the future, but he still wanted to be sure that Caroline's chance for future happiness was protected. If he died, an annulment wouldn't be necessary. And if he lived, she could be rid of him soon enough. He brushed the depressing thought aside, but an equally disturbing one rose in its place. He didn't take marriage lightly. If they took vows, he'd keep them. Looking into her eyes, he saw the distinct possibility that he'd *want* to keep them. They'd been together less than a day, but they'd exchanged several letters beforehand and he'd been impressed by everything she'd done.

He didn't know what the future held and neither did she. He only knew he had to protect Freddie and Dora from his father, and he had to protect Caroline from being hurt. Her offer to marry him suggested she was vulnerable to the feelings that plagued every human being, and he worried she'd regret her kindness.

"It's a generous offer," he said to her. "But I can't take advantage of your goodwill."

"Why not?"

He didn't want to admit to his potential feelings, but the possibility of affection, or the lack of it, had to be addressed. "You've been married before. I presume you loved your husband just as I loved Molly. A marriage in name only strikes me as…inadequate."

She stood straighter. "Women marry for all sorts of reasons."

"Of course." In England men and women alike married for money and prestige. In America, women married for survival. He'd seen the advertisements for mail-order brides in cheaply bound catalogs. Those creatures struck him as pitiful. Caroline struck him as remarkable. He didn't intend to accept her offer to marry him, but he wanted to know why she'd made it. "If you'll forgive my boldness, why would you settle for an arrangement of this nature?"

Color stained her cheeks. "That should be obvious."

"It's not." At least not to him.

She held out her arms in a manner that put her life on display. "Look at me, major. I'm almost thirty years old. It's true I'm widowed, but my marriage was clandestine. In the eyes of society I'm on the shelf. I have no children, no family except for Bessie. My prospects for marriage are nil."

He couldn't believe she thought so little of herself. "That's simply not true."

"Forgive me," she said with a touch of sarcasm. "But you're either blind or an incurable optimist."

How this woman could believe she had no hope for a husband was beyond him. She was lovely, smart, brave and kind. She wasn't a naive girl anymore, but that hardly mattered to a mature man. Tristan preferred a woman whose character had been tested, someone who understood that life had ups and downs. He looked boldly into her eyes. "I assure you, Caroline. I'm not blind. As for being an optimist, I plead guilty. A man with malaria has little choice but to hope."

Her eyes misted. "You're carrying a terrible burden."

"Yes."

She lowered her arms like a bird that had decided not to take flight. "For the sake of the children, let me help you."

Never before had he admitted to the weight of his worries, but her kindness exposed his secrets. He didn't want to die. He loved his children and wanted to marry again. He and Caroline respected each other. What if their feelings ripened into love? What if he desired her and she desired him? As an ailing man, he'd vowed to never love again—or be loved—because he knew the pain of losing a spouse. If Caroline lost her heart to him and he died, she'd suffer.

Common sense told him to reject her kindness, but he was worried enough to consider her offer. Then a troubling thought occurred to him. Every angle had to be considered, even the ugly ones. He didn't think she was marrying him for his money, but he had to be sure. "There's another side to this. I'm a wealthy man. And after my father's death, I'll be even wealthier. If you think you'll inherit—"

"I don't," she said firmly. "If you think money can buy happiness, you're naive."

"I think no such thing, but perhaps you do."

"Absolutely not!"

"Then why do this?" he demanded. "What do you want?"

"A family!" she cried. "I want children and Christmas dinners and bedtime stories. For years I've dreamed of having a family, but no man wanted me."

Sadness gave her eyes a crystalline sheen. He felt like a louse for goading her into a humiliating confession, but he counted her discomfort as the cost of battle. Now he knew her motives. They were pure and painfully simple. Caroline Bradley wanted what most women wanted, what Molly had wanted and what his children needed. She wanted to be a mother.

Shamed but strong, she paced up to him with her eyes blazing. "As you can see, I'm a pathetic, childless spinster who'd do anything—even marry you—for the sake of two beautiful children. Does that confession satisfy you, Major Smith?"

They stood nose to nose, their breathing synchronous and close. Her chin was raised. His was pointed down. He could smell the soap she'd used to wash off the dust from the trip, and he saw the woman who'd bravely gotten on a horse after being bucked off. With a marriage in name only, he supposed she was getting on a horse of a different kind. She'd been hurt and rejected. He didn't want to be the man to trample her courage.

A wry smile lifted his lips. "You're a brave woman, Caroline. Perhaps the bravest I've ever known."

"I'm not brave at all," she murmured.

"I think you are," he answered. "If you're agreeable, I'd be pleased to marry you...for the sake of the children, of course."

"I'm agreeable," she replied.

The moment called for a handshake. They were sealing a business deal, not affirming a lifetime of love, but Tristan couldn't bring himself to offer merely his hand. Neither could he kiss her, not even on the cheek as a token of friendship. Moving slowly, as if she were a horse that needed a peppermint, he touched her cheek. He'd crossed a small but significant line, and he wanted to cross another. "You should call me Tristan."

"Tristan..." She said the name as if it tingled like the candy. "With your father in Cheyenne, we should move quickly, I think."

"Agreed." He'd need a license and someone to officiate. Wheeler Springs didn't have a church, only a monthly service when a minister visited from Laramie. Judge Abbott would have to do. "I'll make arrangements with the justice of the peace. Will that be acceptable?"

Sadness flitted in her eyes, a sign that this marriage in name only was indeed less than adequate. "A civil ceremony seems appropriate."

"Agreed." They were making a commitment to each other, one they'd both honor, but it would be based on respect instead of that mysterious kind of love that united a certain man and a certain woman.

"So tomorrow then?" he asked.

"The sooner, the better."

She smiled but it didn't reach her eyes. The moment called for a kiss…a caress. This time he offered his hand. They shook. A business deal had been struck, so why didn't he want to let go of her soft fingers, and why did she look like she wanted to cry?

Chapter Seven

In the morning Tristan penned a letter to his father explaining he'd send transport when the bridge over the Frazier River was repaired, possibly in three weeks' time. He said nothing of his new position as heir apparent, nor did he mention his pending marriage. He hoped the duke would wait in Cheyenne, but he fully expected him to leave immediately, taking the longer, more eastern route that avoided the river.

He took the letter to the hotel and gave it to his father's courier, a young man he'd never met. When the fellow addressed him as "Marquess," Tristan corrected him.

"In America I'm to be addressed as Major Smith."

"Yes, sir." The young man looked shocked, but Tristan remained as neutral as Switzerland.

Next he went to the courthouse where he obtained a marriage license and made arrangements with Judge Abbott to perform the ceremony at noon. He left the courthouse feeling both confident and ill at ease. In a few hours, he'd be a married man again. He'd be committed to a woman he barely knew but somehow trusted. He couldn't help but be impressed by her, and the feeling worried him. He liked her far more than was a wise for a man with malaria and a call to return to England.

He was tempted to renege on the entire arrangement, but the needs of his children pressed him to make one last preparation for the ceremony. He returned to the house in town and went into the attic, where he'd stored a particular trunk. He hadn't taken it to The Barracks because it was too painful to open. He'd seen it for the first time fifteen years ago on his wedding night with Molly, and now it held his dead wife's treasures—the quilt she'd made for their bed, her wedding dress, a few trinkets and her jewelry.

As he opened the lid, he felt as if Molly were in the room with him. He touched the quilt and recalled the promise he'd made to remarry. With his head bowed, he spoke to her in his mind. He shared his doubts and worries, then he said goodbye to her as his wife and hello as a cherished memory. Molly would have approved of the marriage and she'd have liked Caroline, but he also knew she'd want more for him than a marriage of convenience. She'd want him to love again.

He couldn't allow it, not with the malaria nipping at him, but he felt peaceful with Caroline. He'd do his best for her, and that meant honoring their marriage. Mixed in Molly's jewelry was a diamond ring that had belonged to Tristan's mother. Square-cut with tinges of pink, the stone was mounted on a platinum band. The day his mother died, he'd seen the ring unattended and he'd taken it. As a boy, he'd hidden it. As a man, he had kept it as a fond reminder of the woman he'd barely known.

Molly had never worn it, though he supposed she'd owned it in a legal sort of way. In the same legal sort of way Caroline was about to become his wife. It seemed fitting to give her the ring, so he put it in his pocket and went to his room to dress for the wedding. The ceremony was a legal affair, he reminded himself, a formality equivalent to hiring a governess. Even so, he selected a jacquard vest, a flashy ascot he arranged in a puff and his finest frock coat. His clothing didn't matter, but he wanted to honor Caroline. The ring mattered to him greatly, and he hoped she'd like it.

"Am I doing the right thing?" Caroline murmured to Bessie as they walked to the courthouse. Situated on the edge of town, the new building was a short walk from the major's house. He and Jon were five paces in front of them, just barely out of earshot.

"Only you can know," her sister replied. "But it's not too late to change your mind."

All night long, Caroline had been assailed with doubts. Her worries had nothing to do with the children. Tristan's determination to protect them had convinced her they were at risk. Dora had been instantly affectionate, and Freddie needed her, too. The boy had a chip on his shoulder, but the toughness merely showed his grief for his mother. The children filled her with confidence in her decision. What made her quake were the feelings inspired by their father.

A marriage in name only seemed logical, but then he'd touched her cheek and her heart had betrayed her. How could she not admire a man who'd do anything for his children? She would need all the discipline she could muster to keep from losing her heart to him. If the malaria didn't take him away from Wyoming, England would. Caroline was an ordinary American, a woman with average abilities and looks. She had no business being married to a man destined to be a duke.

If she'd needed proof, which she didn't, her clothing offered evidence. She'd come to Wyoming to be a nanny, not a bride and certainly not a duchess. Today she was wearing a gray moiré jacket, a navy skirt and a white blouse. There wasn't ruffle or frill in sight. She'd planned to wear the costume when she met the major for the first time. It was sleek and businesslike, which she supposed was as fitting today as it would have been for her position as a governess.

Except she wasn't going to be a governess. She was going to be a wife in name only and a mother to Tristan's children.

As the men stepped onto the boardwalk, Bessie gripped her elbow. "Are you *sure* you want to do this?"

It was the second time Bessie had asked her to reconsider a marriage. The first had been the night of her marriage to Charles. She'd been twenty-two years old and teaching the children of former slaves when he'd arrived in the war-ravaged town where she and Bessie had taken refuge. Born into freedom and schooled in Europe, he'd dedicated his life to the cause of education. She hadn't meant to fall in love with him, and he'd been even more reluctant. Love, though, had triumphed and she'd talked him into marriage.

I don't care about the risk. I love you, Charles.
You'll suffer, my dearest. We'll be judged.
I'll take that chance.

She'd been ready to pay the price for herself, but not once had she considered the cost to Charles. Bessie had tried to dissuade her, but Caroline had argued.

I don't care what people say.
But you'll have children—
We're saving money to move to Philadelphia. Life will be different there.

In the end, Bessie had stood with her in a church basement where she and Charles had spoken their vows in front of a young minister. Someone must have seen them, because gossip had erupted. Charles had been called uppity. A month later he'd been murdered and she'd become a pariah. She'd tried to continue his crusade for education, but the hate had been too much to bear on top of her grief. When Bessie suggested they travel West, Caroline had been glad to go. Privately she'd vowed to never again be an object of scorn.

Now here she was—an American woman about to marry an English nobleman—but it didn't matter. They had no future. If he survived the malaria and returned to England, they'd have to annul the marriage. Caroline was an excellent choice for a governess, and she made a decent wife under the circumstances, but a future duke would need a woman who was beautiful and accomplished. Caroline could only hope their effort to protect the children now wouldn't lead to worse heartbreak later. It was a risk Tristan had been willing to take, and she respected his opinion.

She took Bessie's hand and squeezed. "This is right. I'm sure of it."

Together they approached the courthouse. Tristan had gone ahead and was holding the door. Jon had hung back and now offered his hand to Bessie. Smiling her thanks, she took it. The two of them walked into the courthouse, leaving Caroline alone as if she really were a bride at the end of a processional. When she reached the door, Tristan offered his arm and together they went down the hall to an open door. Judge Abbott stood waiting for them in front of a judge's box.

A balding man with a beard, he cleared his throat. "Ladies and gentlemen!"

He'd shouted as if calling court to order. Startled,

Caroline drew back. Tristan consoled her with a pat on her arm.

The judge's voice boomed again. "I have business elsewhere, so take your places."

The couples fell into position, the women on one side and the men on the other. Judge Abbott cleared his throat. "Since this is a legal proceeding, let's not waste time. Do you Tristan Willoughby Smith take Caroline Margaret Bradley to be your lawfully wedded wife?"

Caroline's mouth gaped at the abruptness. She hadn't been expecting poetry or even a prayer, but she would have liked more than a deaf old man barking orders.

Next to her, Tristan frowned. "I do."

Judge Abbott looked down his nose at her. "And do you Caroline Margaret Bradley take this man to be your lawfully wedded husband?"

"I do."

Had Tristan asked for this cold, heartless ceremony? She'd offered herself to be a mother to his children. Surely the promise deserved some recognition. If this was how he intended to treat her, she had to question her decision to marry him. With her stomach in knots, she turned and saw the angry set of his jaw.

He lowered his chin, aiming his eyes at the judge the way he might have pointed a pistol. "Your honor?"

"What is it, Major?"

"I'd like to say a word to my bride."

His bride... Her stomach flipped. Did he have the same confused feelings she did?

Judge Abbott glared at him. "Make it quick."

Tristan gave him a stern look, then faced her. When he looked down at her hands, she recalled his touch in the stable and the way he'd lifted her from the river. Gripping her gloved fingers in his bare ones, he looked into her eyes. "My dear Caroline, I'm honored by your generosity of spirit, your kindness and your concern for my children. I will return that regard to the best of my ability…as long as I am able."

He'd made no mention of love, of course. Their marriage would be based on respect and honor. Friendship would have to suffice. But with the kindness of his words, she was once more convinced she was making the right decision. She raised her face to his. "I promise to love your children as my own, to protect them from harm and to give them a future. I am honored to become a part of your family."

With their gazes locked, his grip tightened on her hands. The gesture confused her, in part because she yearned to hold on more tightly than she had the right to do. She wanted more than honorable promises. She wanted to be loved and to love in return, but the commitment they'd made would have to be enough.

She broke Tristan's stare and focused on the judge. The man eyed Tristan with annoyance. "Do you have a ring?"

"Yes, sir." Jon put something sparkly in Tristan's palm.

She hadn't expected a ring, and she certainly hadn't expected something with a diamond. With her eyes wide, she took in the silvery band and the flash of light from a pink-hued stone. Looking up, she saw a twinkle in Tristan's eyes. He'd surprised her and was obviously pleased.

"Your glove?" he said.

"Oh!" She tugged it off a finger at a time, then offered her hand. Tristan took the weight of it, then looked at Judge Abbott expectantly.

"Repeat after me," the man said. "With this ring, I thee wed."

Tristan turned back to her. "With this ring, I thee wed."

Looking down, he slipped the cool band onto her finger. It slid like liquid and warmed against her skin, a reminder of what marriage was meant to be—a circle of unending love. Today the ring symbolized promises of a less romantic nature, but she appreciated having it on her finger.

Judge Abbott cleared his throat. "I now pronounce you man and wife. Major Smith, you may kiss the bride."

She wished the judge had skipped the gesture. A kiss had no place in a marriage of convenience. Even so, she turned to Tristan, lifting her chin for the token caress. He must have felt the same hypocrisy because he kissed her cheek as if she were a maiden aunt.

Suddenly stiff, he stepped back. Bessie pulled her into a hug. "Are you all right?"

"I'm fine," she whispered.

Behind her she heard Jon congratulating Tristan and wondered if he felt as off balance as she did. He turned to her. "We should leave for The Barracks."

"Of course," she replied.

Their gazes mingled long enough to make her wonder what he was thinking, then he offered his arm and escorted her to the house. Bessie and Jon stayed several paces away, giving them room for a private conversation. They hadn't discussed anything about the marriage, and the ring made the commitment more personal than she'd expected. She wanted to know about their sleeping arrangements and how they'd tell the news of their marriage to the children. She wanted to discuss everything, but she didn't know where to start.

When the house came into view, she saw a carriage waiting by the front door and realized they were leaving immediately for his ranch. Cairo stood next to the rig, saddled and ready to ride. Dora and Freddie were nowhere in sight.

"Where are the children?" she asked.

His brow furrowed. "I sent them ahead with Noah and Evaline."

"I assumed we'd tell them about the marriage—"

"We will." He spoke in a friendly but businesslike tone. "Come to my study at seven o'clock. I'll advise them of the change in your status, then we'll have supper as usual."

Caroline gaped at him. "We're becoming a family. There has to be a better way to tell them."

Judging by the look in his eyes, he didn't like the idea at all. The creases around his mouth deepened. "What did you have in mind?"

"I don't know exactly, but it seems right to tell them with smiles on our faces." They'd reached the carriage, so she stopped.

"They'll be informed. That's enough." He looked vaguely uncomfortable. "There's another matter to discuss. It's of a personal nature."

"Ah, yes." She'd been expecting this talk and welcomed getting it over with. "Our sleeping arrangements."

"Exactly." He looked like the stern officer he'd been. "There's a small room adjoining the master suite. The spaces are attached by a closet. You'll have total privacy, but we'll be able to speak alone whenever we wish. Will that be acceptable?"

"Of course."

"Very well," he said abruptly. "Let's be on our way."

He handed her into the carriage then mounted Cairo. Jon did the honors for Bessie, then climbed to the driver's seat. With Tristan in the lead, the four of them left town. She wondered about Grandma and figured Noah and Evaline had taken the horse with them.

Neither Caroline nor Bessie spoke until the buildings were a mile behind them. Surrounded by grass and cottonwoods, high sky and wisping clouds, Caroline marveled at the beauty of an ordinary day…only the day was no longer ordinary. For most married couples, the date would be marked on a calendar and celebrated. Caroline had no expectation of celebrating this landmark with Tristan, but the memories were engraved on her heart.

Bessie touched her hand. "How are you feeling?"

"Good."

"I'm glad," she said. "I thought you might feel a bit glum."

"I'm fine." Caroline inhaled the crisp air. "I came to Wyoming to borrow a family, and that's what I'm doing."

"You've done more than borrow the major's children. You just married him."

"I know."

"I'm worried, Caroline."

"Why?"

"Jon told me more about Tristan's father. He'll be a formidable enemy if Tristan succumbs to the malaria."

A breeze stirred through the trees, a reminder of changing seasons and the approach of winter. "He seems better today."

"The major and I discussed his health at breakfast. He's been ill for some time, and that's a good sign. Malaria kills quickly or it lingers for months, even years. I suspect he has the variety that lingers."

"That would be good," Caroline replied.

"Yes, but he needs to continue on the quinine. I suggested he increase the dosage."

"Will he have enough?"

Bessie looked confident. "A new shipment is already on the way."

Caroline stared across a meadow that seemed to stretch forever. "He has to live. That's all there is to it."

"That's up to God."

Caroline knew that fact too well. Not only had she grieved Charles, but she was also single and childless against her will. She'd had a few battles with her faith, but in the end she accepted her circumstances. She had learned to look for the good in all things, though she could see no good at all in malaria, and she saw even less in a child's loss of a mother. Nor did she understand the tensions between fathers and sons. For whatever reasons, Tristan had been terribly hurt by his father. Caroline intended to give the older man a chance, but Tristan's warnings had been dire and sincere.

She turned to Bessie. "Do you think the duke is as difficult as Tristan says?"

"I don't know, but he's likely to be critical of this marriage…and of you."

"I imagine so," Caroline murmured. If Tristan's opinion of his father proved accurate, the duke would treat her with disdain. She'd encountered such conduct because of her marriage to Charles. She didn't relish enduring the spite again, but she could do it for the children.

"The duke can say or do what he wants," she said to Bessie. "My only concern is for Freddie and Dora."

"When will you tell them about the marriage?"

"Tonight."

Bessie huffed. "I hope he's not planning on briefing them as if it's a war effort."

"That's exactly what he's planning."

"You can't allow it," Bessie said. "If he orders them to accept you, they'll resent you even more, especially Freddie. He'll think you're trying to replace his mother."

Caroline had no desire to replace Molly, but she very much wanted to be a family. She'd dreamed of having children her entire life. Her dream could come true, but only if Freddie and Dora shared it. She thought of being a child herself and saw a simple answer. She turned to Bessie. "Do you remember the game we played when we were little? The one where we dressed up in mama's things and pretended to be other people?"

"You called it the dream game."

"Tonight I'll play it with Tristan and the children."

The game would soften the news that the children had a new mother, and it would give Tristan a much needed glimpse into their hearts. More than anything Caroline wanted to unite him with his children. Judging from what she'd observed, he barely knew them.

She'd have to hurry once they reached The Barracks, but tonight's announcement wouldn't be made in the major's study, a room she felt certain would be dark, gloomy and lined with hunting trophies. Tonight they were going to celebrate with costumes, cake and laughter. This wouldn't be the wedding night she'd dreamed of, but it would be a new beginning just the same.

Chapter Eight

Tristan looked at the clock on the wall. It was two minutes after seven o'clock. He'd told Caroline to be in his study at seven sharp, and he'd given Evaline instructions to deliver the children five minutes later. Did *anyone* listen to him anymore?

Apparently not.

Intending to find Evaline, he stepped into the hall. As he turned, he saw the housekeeper coming in his direction. She wore an impish smile and a paper crown decorated with leaves and pine needles. Tristan gaped at her. "What in the world—"

"You're late, sir!"

How could he be late to a meeting *he'd* arranged? Noah came up behind Evaline. As he passed her, Tristan saw a dozen medals pinned to his chest. Some were medals the man had earned in the army. Others were made of tin and buttons and resembled playthings. To Tristan's consternation, Noah handed him a stick horse that had been painted black. "You better hurry, Major. You're late."

He took the horse without thinking. "Late to *what?*"

"Supper, of course." Noah assumed a formal pose, but his eyes were twinkling. "Mrs. Caroline requested the meal be served on the veranda. She and the children are waiting."

Tristan glanced again at the medals on Noah's chest. Maybe he was seeing things. Occasionally the fevers made him delirious. Maybe he was having an attack and didn't know it. Perhaps he'd imagined the crown on Evaline's head. As for the stick horse in his hand, it felt real enough to remind him of his boyhood dreams of being the finest horseman in England. He scowled at Noah. "What's going on?"

"You'll have to see for yourself, sir."

"I intend to do just that." He strode past Noah and Evaline, down the hall and through the children's playroom to the veranda. Through a window he saw lanterns on the railing, each one casting a circle of yellow light into the dusk. The glow reminded him of making camp with his men. He'd enjoyed the camaraderie around a campfire, but today he felt none of that ease.

Noah stepped ahead of him and opened the door to the veranda, indicating he should pass with a sweep of his arm. Tristan noticed the makeshift medals again and stopped. "*What* are you wearing?"

"You'll have to ask Mrs. Caroline."

"I certainly will." He raised the stick horse as if it were a king's scepter and instantly felt ridiculous. Annoyed, he marched out the door and saw Caroline and the children seated around a small table set with the china Molly had loved.

Caroline stood. "Good evening, Major."

They hadn't yet told the children of their marriage, so she'd addressed him formally.

"Miss Bradley," he acknowledged. "Children."

Before he could fully take in the gown Caroline had chosen, Dora ran to him. Instead of her usual pinafore, she was wearing a white dress with ruffles and pink ribbons. Molly had stitched it before she'd fallen ill. It had been for another child's birthday party, an event Dora had missed because her mother had died. Did the child remember? Tristan did... He'd found the dress with a needle still stuck in place, waiting for Molly to finish adding the trim. He didn't recall bringing it to The Barracks. Evaline must have packed it, though he felt certain Caroline had finished the ribbons and perhaps let out the side seams. The dress was a bit short, a sign that Dora had grown.

His daughter executed a curtsy. "Do you like my dress, Daddy?"

"It's lovely."

He hadn't seen Dora smile in a long time. To her the dress was a carnival of ribbons and lace, not a sad reminder of what she'd lost. Tristan looked at Caroline, wordless because he didn't know whether to thank her or scold her.

Dora tugged on his hand, the one not holding the stick horse. "We're having a party for us!"

"I see that." He disliked parties.

He glared at Caroline. When she answered with a smile, he felt like a curmudgeon. He had no idea what to say, so he turned his attention to Freddie. The boy was wearing his Sunday best but nothing outlandish. He looked as uncomfortable as Tristan.

Like father, like son.

The thought brought no comfort. Tristan wanted Freddie to enjoy life. Instead he was looking at Tristan the way Tristan had looked at the duke, stubbornly silent while yearning for approval. Whatever Tristan did, Freddie would copy him. If he disrespected Caroline, so would the boy. Aware his reaction would mark everyone at the table, he paused to give his wife of seven hours an opportunity to explain herself.

Her eyes brightened with the challenge and she stood, lacing her hands at the waist of a blue calico covered with a white apron. This morning her hair had been piled on her head in a mass of curls befitting a wedding. Now her brunette tresses were wrapped around her head in a braid. Compared to everyone else, she looked ordinary.

"What's going on?" he finally asked.

"We're playing a game." She spoke sweetly, but Tristan heard a dare in her voice. "Each one of us is dressed as the person we want to be someday. I thought we'd tell each other about our dreams for the future."

"I see."

"Sit down, Major." She indicated the chair across from hers. "We'll start with the children."

He wanted to get the silliness over with, but he had to admit her game had a certain charm. He'd been younger than Freddie when a groom in his father's stable had made him a stick horse like the one in his hand. He'd spent hours dreaming of being a cavalry officer. Looking at his children, he realized he had no idea what they dreamed of becoming. In his effort to protect them, somehow he'd stopped knowing them.

With his chest tight, he sat in the chair across from Caroline and propped the stick horse against the table. "Who goes first?"

"I do!" Dora jumped to her feet. "Guess what I am!"

"I have no idea," he said, teasing her a little.

"I'm a princess!"

"And a lovely one." He could hardly speak. Dora looked just like Molly, bright and eager and full of fun. She'd lost her mother, yet somehow she'd remained a hopeful child.

Caroline smiled at the girl. "Why do you want to be a princess?"

She thought a minute. "Princesses live in castles and they have ponies."

"I see." Caroline turned to him with a shine in her eyes. "Shall we ask Freddie to go next?"

In the most gracious of ways, she'd handed over the reins for the party and acknowledged him as head of the family. Looking carefully at her outfit, he realized the game had a deeper purpose than entertaining the children or getting to know them better. They'd each worn something to symbolize their deepest wishes. Caroline had worn a dress a mother would wear while baking bread or wiping a child's tears. Uncomfortable with the game but wanting to honor her, Tristan looked Freddie up and down. The boy was wearing a white shirt and a black tie, dark pants and a coat he'd soon outgrow. He looked formal and owlish, far more serious than the typical ten-year-old boy.

Tristan tried to sound cheerful. "You're dressed for business, I think."

"In a way," the boy replied.

"Are you a lawyer?"

"No."

"A banker?" The weight of not knowing his son hit Tristan hard. He should have known the answer without asking.

Freddie looked hurt, but he covered it up the way Tristan had covered hurt at the same age. He looked bored. "I'm a scientist. And I don't like games."

Caroline ignored the slight. "Science is a worthy pursuit."

"It is," Tristan agreed. So were silly games that revealed a child's dreams. "Why do you want to be a scientist?"

"Because they find answers."

"To what?" he asked.

"To everything," Freddie announced. "Even the cure for malaria."

Tristan felt his son's fear like a kick. It nearly broke him. "That's a worthy goal, Freddie."

The boy stared straight ahead, every bit as stalwart as Tristan had become in his fight against the malaria. He wanted to give Freddie hope, but his tongue refused to move. Even more powerful was the urge to pull the boy into a hug and never let go. Instinct told him to do it. Years of restraint kept him rigid in his chair.

Why, God?

Tristan stifled the angry cry. Whether he respected God or not, he had no choice but to take the Commander's orders. Caroline's gaze flicked from his face to Freddie's and then back to his. Just as she'd needed rescuing when she fell in the river, he needed someone to pull him out of his confusing flood of emotion.

She tipped her head. "It's your turn, Major. Knowing how you feel about horses, the children guessed you'd wanted a horse like Cairo since you were a boy."

"I did," he said, feeling more tense than ever.

Dora smiled at him. "We painted the horse to look like Cairo. Do you like him?"

"I do."

"It's fun to pretend," Caroline said. "But it's even more fun when our dreams come true."

She looked directly at Tristan, prompting him to lead the way across the bridge she'd built to his children. Taking a breath, he took the first step in what would be a major change in their young lives. "Children, do you know what Miss Caroline wants to be?"

Dora looked at her with grave intensity, biting her lip as if her life depended on the right guess. Freddie looked bored, though Tristan saw worry in his eyes. "She's the governess," Freddie said coolly.

"No," Tristan said quietly. "Keep looking."

When she smiled, Dora's eyes got wide. "She's a... lady."

"She's that," Tristan said gently. "She's also dressed in her everyday clothes, the clothes a mother would wear. Caroline is going to be more than your new governess. We were married this morning. She's to be your new—"

"Friend," she interrupted.

Tristan bristled at the rudeness, then realized she'd saved him from a grave mistake. No one could replace Molly and she didn't want to try. He wished he could touch her foot under the table to acknowledge the correction. That's what he'd have done with Molly, and Caroline deserved the same gesture of apology. He offered a tiny nod, an acknowledgment that she knew best, then waited for her to continue.

She looked from Dora to Freddie. "Your father and I know this is a surprise, but we've given the situation a great deal of thought. We've been corresponding and—"

Dora flung herself into Caroline's arms and hugged her hard. Holding the child close, Caroline kissed the top of her brunette head.

Tears threatened to well in Tristan's eyes. He fought them off, but his heart turned into an aching bruise. He looked at Freddie, saw confusion on the boy's face and realized he had a choice. He could act like his own father and be cold, or he could treat his son the way he'd wanted to be treated at that age.

"Freddie," he said quietly. "Let's speak outside."

His son's frown deepened into a sneer.

Tristan stood and waited. Still Freddie didn't budge. The child was glaring at Caroline with an arrogance

Tristan recognized all too well. He'd seen in it himself. Even more frightening, he'd seen it in his father. Somehow he had to undo the damage done by his months of coldness. He touched Freddie's shoulder and felt bone. Squeezing gently, he eased the boy off the chair and led him down the steps to a patch of weeds. With the sky turning purple, they stood face-to-face.

Looking into his son's eyes, Tristan said words he couldn't recall ever hearing from his own father. "I love you, son."

Freddie look stunned, embarrassed…and like a child. "You do?"

"Yes." He spoke with authority. "I'm proud of your dreams and intelligence, your desire to be a scientist and how you help with your sister. We all miss your mother. I certainly do—"

"But you're marrying Miss Caroline." The boy sounded offended.

"Yes." Peace in the house hung on his next words. "I admire her, Freddie. I respect her and trust her. Dora needs someone, and—" *So do you.* At the defiant look in Freddie's eyes, Tristan held back. His son was still a boy, but his journey to manhood would be fueled by respect. "We *men* need her, too. A woman is a gentling influence. I hope you'll accept Caroline as a member of the family, not as a mother, but as a friend. Perhaps you could call her Aunt Caroline."

In the boy's turbulent expression, Tristan saw grief for his mother, the longing for peace and another time-honored male tradition. Freddie wanted to fight and win. The mask of indifference was gone. In its place was a boy who didn't quite know what to do. "She makes good pies," he finally said.

"She does?"

"She baked them before supper," Freddie explained. "Dora helped and she let me have a taste."

Tristan liked pie. "Then perhaps we better get back for the meal so we can have dessert."

"I guess so."

The boy hadn't agreed to call Caroline "aunt," but Tristan counted the exchange as a start. Wanting to show affection but not sure how, he clapped Freddie on the back the way he slapped privates who'd done a good job. As if something had been jarred loose, Freddie turned and hugged him hard. "I love you, too, Father."

They didn't need to say or do anything else. In the way of men, they went back to the veranda where the females were seated at the table awaiting the arrival of supper. Dora looked like a real princess, and Caroline looked like a real mother, a bit worried but hopeful as they climbed the steps. As soon as Tristan's foot hit the veranda, Dora ran to him and hugged him. The three of them—Tristan, Freddie and Dora—hugged for a very long time, with Caroline watching from a distance, but not joining them.

Just as she'd dreamed, Caroline was sitting at the supper table with a husband and children. The three of them told her stories and she laughed, but it soon became apparent her success in uniting Tristan and his children came with a single failure. The three of them were a family. She didn't belong except as an observer. When Evaline served the pie Caroline had made for dessert, the three of them praised her baking but quickly returned to remembering pies Molly had baked. Caroline didn't mind talking about Molly at all. The children's memories needed to be enjoyed. What hurt was being forgotten.

Tristan had finished his pie and was looking affectionately at Dora. The child had kept her dress clean, but she had a ring of cherry pie around her mouth. With Caroline watching, Tristan dipped his napkin in his water glass and cleaned her face, a bit awkwardly because he wasn't accustomed to such things, then he said, "I believe it's bedtime."

"Will you read to me?" Dora asked.

"Of course." He turned to Freddie. "Are you too old for bedtime stories?"

"I read to myself," the boy answered. "But you can say goodnight. Mother used to do that."

"Then that's what I'll do." Tristan turned to her, his eyes shining with love for his children. "Will you excuse us, Caroline?"

"Of course."

She managed a smile, but disappointment welled in her middle. He'd said nothing about returning to her. She'd wait a bit but not too long. She stood with the three of them, watching as Tristan hoisted Dora to his hip and followed Freddie into the house. The candles burned bright, but the darkness pressed at the edges. She wondered which story Tristan would read to Dora, and if the child had a favorite.

Next she imagined him knocking on Freddie's door. They'd trade a joke or a remark about the meal, then he'd say goodnight. In her dreams he came back to the veranda...he came to be with her.

The door creaked and her eyes opened. Instead of Tristan, she saw Evaline still wearing the crown that made her a queen. Caroline thought of Noah's medals and his desire to be a commissioned officer. Their dreams would never come true. Neither would hers, it seemed. She thanked Evaline for the fine meal, then went upstairs to the little room adjacent to Tristan's suite. In the dim light, she took in the narrow bed, a white chest of drawers and a rocking chair. The room was intended to be a nursery. Caroline couldn't help but think of the children she'd never conceive. She longed to rock a baby to sleep, to hold it to her breast and feel its breathing turn deep.

It was her wedding night.

There would be no children. There would be no love, physical or otherwise. There would be nothing but restless dreams. She scanned the room again, feeling the rise of a lump and the taste of regret. "Oh, Lord," she murmured. "What have I done?"

Dropping into the rocker, she buried her face in her hands and wept. This morning she'd been confident that she belonged with Tristan and the children; now she felt all the pain of being an outsider. Even worse, she'd seen a side of Tristan she deeply admired. As annoyed as he'd been by the dream game, he'd played along. When he saw the wisdom of it, he'd embraced it. He'd hugged his children and they'd hugged him back.

Fresh tears welled in her eyes. "Lord," she whispered. "This is why You brought me here. I know it. But it hurts to be alone."

Alone in a crowd...alone in a family.

She felt the stirrings of self-pity, then the pounding of resentment. Abruptly she lifted her head. "I will *not* be bitter...*I will not be bitter.*" She slid to her knees, laced her fingers in a knot and prayed. "Father God, bless Tristan and his children. Bring them close to each other and close to You. Heal their sorrow and their fear."

Masculine footsteps interrupted her prayer. Already she could recognize the cadence of Tristan's walk. It matched the beat of her heart as she listened, growing louder as he approached her room, then fading as he passed her door. Disappointment welled in her chest, but she pushed it aside. Considering the lines they'd drawn, a private talk in her bedroom would have been too personal. With the silence heavy, she fought the ache of loneliness by counting her blessings.

She was a wife instead of a governess.

The dream game had been a resounding success.

She liked Evaline and Noah, and Jon had befriended Bessie. And Tristan… The quinine had helped already. She thanked God for his improved health.

She had a roof over her head and food to eat, warm clothes and shoes without holes. She'd survived a stagecoach robbery, ridden a horse and not been drowned when she'd fallen in the river. She had much for which to be grateful, and yet she wanted more…she wanted a husband and a baby of her own. She couldn't stop the tears that welled. "Why, Lord?" she murmured. "Why can't I be satisfied—"

A soft knock startled her. Eyes wide, she stared at the door to the storage area between her room and Tristan's. It had to be him… He'd come to her.

Chapter Nine

Until tonight, Tristan hadn't realized how much like his own father he'd become. He'd distanced himself from Freddie and Dora for different reasons, but the effect had been the same. He didn't know his children the way he wanted to, especially Freddie, who was older and learning to be a man. The boy had copied Tristan's every move, every attitude, and until tonight, he'd set a poor example. He wondered what other mistakes he'd been making. He didn't know, but he knew someone who did and he'd left her alone on the veranda.

After leaving Freddie, he went back to the supper table. Someone had cleared the dishes and extinguished the candles, leaving nothing but shadows and the smell of wax. Inhaling the cool air, he realized he'd been gone close to an hour. Caroline had gone upstairs…alone.

It shouldn't have mattered to him, but it did. He very much wanted to include her in tonight's success. Feeling intrepid, he went to the kitchen where he piled a tray with the remaining pie, a knife, two plates and two forks. As quiet as a spy, he carried the tray to his suite, placed it by the fire and lit the logs in the hearth. When the flames settled into a steady dance, he went through the closet and tapped on her door. If she was asleep, he didn't want to wake her. Or maybe he did… Even a wife in name only deserved an acknowledgment on her wedding night.

After a moment, she opened the door a crack and peeked at him. "Hello, Major."

She'd slipped back into formality. What it signaled, he didn't know. "I thought we'd agreed on Tristan."

"Yes," she mumbled. "Of course."

Her hair was down, and she had brushed out the braid. Backlit by the lamp, the dark waves had a translucent quality that reminded him of the ocean at night. His eyes flicked to her hand, and he saw a hairbrush and the unbuttoned cuff of her nightgown.

"Am I too late?" he asked.

"For what?"

"To invite you to my room for more dessert." He suddenly felt silly in the closet. "It's later than I realized. Perhaps in the morning—"

"No!" she said quickly. "I was hoping we'd have a minute together."

He'd been thinking in terms of an hour, maybe two. Deep down, he wanted days with her, maybe longer. If their feelings grew, he'd want fifty years…except he didn't know if he had fifty years. He might not have fifty days.

Leaving the door ajar, she tied back her hair with a ribbon and slipped into a robe. As she punched into the sleeves, he glanced around the room and remembered its purpose. The room was meant to be a nursery. Tristan had purchased the ranch from a man with a young wife. They'd expected to raise a family, but she'd been unhappy and they'd left with their dream unfulfilled. Peering into the nursery, Tristan considered the dreams a woman would have…the dream Caroline had of being a mother. The inadequacy of their marriage struck him as cruel, but it would be crueler still to seek anything more than friend-ship. Not only did he not want a woman to grieve for him, he couldn't risk leaving a wife with a child he'd never see.

"Come with me," he said, issuing an order.

She opened the door wider, saw the narrowness of the closet and hesitated. He stepped back to let her pass and bumped his head on something sharp. Grimacing, he pressed his hand to his scalp and felt blood.

"Are you all right?" she asked.

"I'm fine." He hurried out of the closet, fetched a hand-kerchief from his bureau and pressed it to the cut. Blood quickly saturated the linen.

Caroline came up beside him. "Let me do that."

"I can manage."

Ignoring him, she put one hand on his forehead and the other against the handkerchief. Firm but gentle, her fingers made a vise of sorts. Reconciled to the wound, he bowed his head so she could maintain pressure. "I seem to have been attacked by a nail," he said drily.

"You might need a stitch."

"I don't want a stitch," he grumbled.

"Would you rather bleed all over your pillow?" she re-plied rather haughtily.

As a man who gave orders, Tristan knew when to sur-render. "I suppose not." He raised his hand with intention of taking over the handkerchief. "I'll do that."

"Not yet. We should keep pressure on it."

Pressure on his head put a different kind of pressure on his heart. He'd forgotten how it felt to be the recipient of a woman's touch. Everything Caroline did brought heal-ing of some sort. Tonight she'd made his family whole. He wanted that same wellness for his body, but she didn't have that power. God alone numbered a man's days. In Tristan's experience, He didn't much care about the in-between.

Annoyed, he put his hand on top of hers and pressed. "I'll hold it."

"But—"

"That's an order, Miss Bradley."

Startled, she slid her hand away from his and moved back. Tristan felt like a fool for knocking his head, but he felt even worse about the hurt in Caroline's eyes. She'd moved in front of the fire and was standing with her arms crossed and her hair falling down her back. Through the meal she'd been the picture of poise. Now she looked shaken and he felt like an ogre.

He tried to smile. "Forgive me, Caroline. I didn't mean to be harsh." How could a little cut cause so much trouble? "I asked you to my suite so I could thank you, and instead I end up in your care."

"It's just a cut," she murmured.

"Yes." He put on a rueful smile. "A cut to my pride and to my head. I don't like being in your debt."

"You don't owe me anything."

"I owe you a great deal." With his hand still pressed to his scalp, he indicated the divan. "Please sit down. I thought we could have more dessert."

"You liked the pie?" she asked.

"Very much." He wanted to talk about more than her baking skills. "Tonight you gave my family a wonderful gift. You deserve to hear about it."

She looked suddenly shy. "Perhaps tomorrow would be better. With your head and all—"

"Please don't argue."

"But—"

"Caroline…" He tried to sound firm, but her name came out in a near whisper. "I may be ill, but I *was* an officer in the British Army. People *used* to do what I wanted. Indulge me, please."

Her lips curved into a smile. "Your friends want to take care of you."

"I suppose," he said. "But I seem to have lost all dignity."

"Not to me."

"You're being kind. What you did tonight was remarkable."

Pleasure gave her cheeks a rosy hue. "It went well, didn't it?"

"Very." He risked lowering the handkerchief. To his dismay, blood trickled down the nape of his neck. Annoyed, he put the cloth back in place.

"Sit down," she ordered.

Surrendering to the inevitable, he sat on the divan. With his neck bent and his eyes on the carpet, he heard the swish of her robe as she came to stand behind him. Her fingers combed through his hair to part it, then came to rest on the handkerchief. She blotted the fresh blood, then examined the cut with her fingers. A horrible thought made him cringe. His blood was tainted. Doctors believed the contagion came from swamps and not from people, but exactly how the disease spread had yet to be understood.

"Don't touch the blood," he said, feeling sick.

"I'm being careful." She pressed the handkerchief back in place. "You definitely need a stitch. Hold this while I get a needle and thread."

He did as she ordered, silently wondering what other holes in his life this good woman could mend. She had a gentle way of dealing with wounds and blood and sadness, a quiet acceptance of what had to be done. He admired her greatly, but he had to put a stop to such thoughts. Closing his eyes, he concentrated on the snap and hiss of the fire until he heard her return.

"I'm back," she said coming up behind him. "I'll need

to shave some of the hair. Where do you keep your shaving tools?"

"In the washstand."

She went to the heavy piece of furniture and pulled out the chair for him. "Come and sit."

Tristan shaved standing up, and it felt odd to sit in a spindly chair he never used. Being careful to keep pressure on the cut, he removed his shaving tools from the drawer while Caroline poured water from the pitcher into the basin. The moment should have been awkward, but she had the demeanor of a nurse and he was accustomed to being a patient. She cleaned the cut, then used his razor to gently scrape away an inch of hair.

"This will hurt a bit," she said to prepare him.

"I've endured worse."

"Were you wounded in battle?" she asked as the needle pierced his scalp.

"A few times." A second stitch followed the first. "Malaria has proven to be a more formidable enemy."

The thread pulled the skin tight. She took a second stitch for good measure, made a knot and snipped. "The cut will ooze a bit, but you'll be fine."

He stood and faced her. "Yet again, I'm beholden to you."

"It's just a stitch," she said modestly.

"Yes, but tonight with the children was far more than 'just a stitch.' You opened my eyes, Caroline. I'm grateful."

"I merely put you all in the same room. Your hearts did the rest."

She'd said *your hearts,* meaning Tristan and his children. She hadn't said *our hearts.* After he'd made peace with Freddie and Dora, Caroline had become as invisible as the maid who laid the fire he'd lit. Once the memories had been set ablaze, he and the children had savored the warmth while Caroline had been left in the cold. Not any-more…not tonight. "You belong with us."

"Not really."

She'd restrained her hair with a ribbon, but the unruly strands framed her face. He saw the same spirit in her eyes, but it had been dulled by disappointments like the one she'd suffered tonight. He had no business touching her, but he raised his hand and brushed her jaw with his thumb. Wise or not, he kissed her cheek. The caress held all the tenderness in his heart, but it felt shy and incom-plete. Looking into her eyes, he wondered if she felt the same inadequacy.

He lowered his hand. "Let's have some of that pie."

Slightly flushed, she sat on the divan, cut a generous slice and handed it to him as he sat next to her. She cut a smaller one for herself and picked up her plate. Their forks scraped the china in unison, a sign they were tasting the same sweetness and feeling the same awkwardness.

After a third bite, she set the plate on the tray. "Your children are lovely, Tristan."

"It's only been a day, but you seem to know them."

"Little girls aren't hard to understand. Freddie's more of a challenge."

"For me, too."

"It'll take time," she said. "But I hope you all become close."

"I hope *we* become close." When she looked at him with wide eyes, he realized his mistake. *We* hinted at the two of them. He had to clarify. "I mean the four of us, of course."

"Of course." She echoed his sentiment, but he'd seen the glimmer in her eyes. They'd known each other only briefly, first through letters and now by circumstance, but he felt a connection that went deeper than time. Suddenly restless, he went to the fireplace and jabbed the logs with an iron rod. She'd married him because she wanted to be a mother to his children. He felt an obligation to make her dreams came true. He just didn't know how to truly make her part of the family without the risk of their feelings growing stronger.

She lifted her chin. "I suppose we should discuss what to do when your father arrives."

He should have been pleased with her sensible attitude, but the shift in topic annoyed him. He didn't want to talk about his father. He wanted to sit next to her on the divan and watch the flames shrink into embers. He hadn't asked her into his room to talk about their strategy, but it was a safer topic than figuring out how to be a family.

He stayed on his feet. "With the bridge down, we have some time to prepare. The limited nature of our marriage is no one's business, but it's important for the sake of the children that we appear to be—" *in love* "—united."

"And happy," she added.

"Yes."

"Concerning your father, what do I need to know?" She sat with her hands folded in her lap, a willing student.

"Officially his name is Harold Smythe, Duke of Willoughby. Willoughby is a place. You should address him as 'your grace.'"

"'Your grace,'" she repeated.

"Yes." The title sounded awkward on her American lips and foreign to his ears. "In England, as a third son, I was addressed as Lord Tristan. As heir apparent, I've been assigned a courtesy title from my father's lesser titles. I won't use it in America."

"If you *did* use it, what would it be?"

"Tristan Willoughby Smith, Marquess of Hayvenhurst."

She looked befuddled. "I think I prefer 'major.'"

"So do I." He smiled at her. "You're officially Caroline Bradley Smith, Marchioness of Hayvenhurst."

Her cheeks paled. "I feel like Dora finding out her middle name. I can hardly say it, let alone write it out."

"You'll do fine."

She shook her head. "I know how to be a mother, but a marchioness is another matter altogether. How long do you think he'll stay?"

"I don't know." A day was too long in Tristan's opinion. "I have no intention of returning with him to England, but he'll attempt to persuade me. One of us has to give in. It won't be me."

He thought of the gnarled branches of the Smythe family tree. Some had died of natural causes; others had to be pruned for the health of the tree. In that regard he'd cut himself off from his father, but the roots were very much intact. Freddie was the newest branch on the tree, and he needed protection Tristan couldn't give if he died. To hide his concern and sadness, he turned his back to Caroline and stared into the flames.

He heard the swish of her robe, then felt her hand on his arm. "I've been wondering. What happened to your mother?"

"She died of influenza. I was five."

"I'm so sorry."

"So am I," he said quietly. "The ring I gave you, it was hers."

"I'm honored." She hesitated. "I'll return it when—" She didn't finish. *When he died...when she ended the marriage.*

Tristan's heart clawed at his chest. He cared about the ring, but he cared more about the children. "If I die—"

Her fingers tightened on his arm. "Don't talk like that."

"We have to be realistic. If I die, leave immediately."

Her eyes dimmed. "May I say something?"

She'd speak her mind whether he granted permission or not. "Go ahead."

"Bitterness is a kind of poison. For a time I was bitter about Charles. I only made myself unhappy."

"What are you saying?"

"Perhaps there's another way to deal with your father."

"Such as?"

"Kindness… Charity."

He shrugged off her hand. "Those are lovely sentiments, but you don't know the duke."

"No, I don't. But I know you worry about the influence he may have on the children. The only way to counteract his behavior is through your own. Compassion instead of disdain. Acceptance instead of manipulation. You cannot control the duke's behavior, but you can control your own. You can choose to set an example for Freddie and Dora by treating everyone—even the duke—with courtesy and respect."

Tristan remembered himself in short pants, standing in his father's study awaiting discipline for a mild prank. The duke had caned his bare backside until he was begging for mercy. Could he repay that treatment with courtesy and respect? He doubted it. But one thing he did know about his father's treatment of him, the humiliation had turned him into a fighter. Being a fighter turned him into a soldier. Soldiers fought and sometimes died. They protected those in their care. Tristan thought of his children. He'd protect them and so would Caroline, but who would protect *her?* The duke would belittle her at every turn. He'd insult her and point out her faults. His visit would be difficult for everyone, but especially the woman he would view as a future duchess, particularly if she followed her own advice and returned his insults with kindness. No, if she would not protect herself, he'd do it for her. Tristan knew what he had to do. "We'll begin lessons tomorrow."

"Lessons in what?"

"How to be a marchioness." He didn't want her to change. He liked her the way she was, but he knew the power of symbols and protocol. They could shield her from some of the duke's scorn.

He tried to read her expression but couldn't. In one instant anger flashed in her eyes. In the next, she looked like a nervous child at a piano recital. Being married to a nobleman clearly didn't appeal to her. She hesitated, then stood. "We need to deal with your father's expectations, so whatever you say will be fine. It's late. If you'll excuse me—"

"Of course."

She headed for the door to the closet, pausing before she stepped into the dark. "Goodnight, Tristan."

"Goodnight, Caroline."

He might have approached and kissed her cheek, but she closed the door, leaving him to wonder if their wedding night had seemed as inadequate to her as it did to him.

Caroline closed the door to her room and thought about Tristan's plan to make her into a marchioness. How could a woman like herself—someone who had clerked in a store and liked to bake pies—become a noblewoman? After removing her robe, she blew out the lamp and slid into the narrow bed. The evening had been a peculiar mix of triumph and disaster. She was thrilled with Tristan's connection to his children, and she had dared to hope the four of them would become a family.

Then he'd spoken of his father and titles, and she'd been

reminded that he belonged in England. She'd felt like a fish out of water…a fish about a thousand miles from any water at all. She'd never belong in Tristan's world, not as a wife and not as a marchioness. If he survived the malaria, he'd want an annulment. Whatever hope she had for the marriage to ripen into love had to be denied. She pulled the covers up to her chin.

Lord, where are You?

She closed her eyes against the dark, but her throat tightened with longing. She wanted to be settled and content. She'd wanted to be a wife and mother. She'd been hopeful until Tristan mentioned giving her lessons. Sleep stayed away, but she didn't bother playing the dream game. Instead she wept for what she'd never have and the woman she couldn't be.

Chapter Ten

A week passed with Caroline slipping into a quiet routine. Along with Evaline she planned meals for her family. She baked pies, saw to the children's lessons and made sure they washed behind their ears. Dora happily called her Aunt Caroline, but Freddie didn't call her anything. Whether he resented her place in the family, or whether the resentment came from being ten years old with a dislike of schoolwork, she didn't know.

She'd also slipped into a routine with Tristan. At night he tucked the children into bed, then they met in his suite and sat by the fire. She'd told him more about Charles, and he'd spoken of his life in England, his military accomplishments and the pain of losing Molly. In those quiet hours they became friends...more than friends. She tried to deny her feelings, but she had to admit Tristan was a man she could easily love.

The admission frightened her because his feelings were unreadable. Sometimes he teased and flirted with her. Other times he treated her like a maiden aunt. Did she interest him or bore him? She didn't know, but she disliked what he called her "duchess" lessons. In the droll tones of a professor, pacing as if giving a lecture, he'd schooled her in titles, etiquette and English history, Smythe family lore and the Willoughby holdings. He'd also suggested she learn how to ride, something she steadfastly refused to do. While she enjoyed Tristan's attention, she cringed at his effort to turn her into someone she wasn't, someone she couldn't be.

She was happiest with the children, and that's where she was now. She and Dora were pinning a hem on a new pinafore.

"Aunt Caroline?" the child asked.

"Yes, Dora?"

"Do you think Daddy will get well?"

Caroline's breath caught in her throat. "I hope so."

"I want to know for sure." Her voice came out in a squeak.

As much as Caroline wanted to hide behind easy assurances, the child deserved the truth. "He's getting better thanks to the medicine." She inserted another pin. It pricked her finger and drew blood. "Miss Bessie is hopeful and so am I."

Dora stood on the box like a statue, her shoulders straight and her chin firm. "Mommy said God would look out for us."

"He does."

"I'm glad," she said simply.

The faith of a child...Caroline envied it. She'd once believed with the same ease, but she'd learned that not all prayers were answered the way she wanted. Instead of a family of her own, God had given her this precious child and her troubled brother. As for their troubled father, she didn't dare hope for more than she had.

A terrified cry came from downstairs "Miss Caroline!" The voice belonged to Evaline.

Caroline imagined Tristan lying in a heap in his study,

delirious with fever. He seemed well last night, but he hadn't joined the family for breakfast. She assumed he'd gone for an early ride on Cairo, but now she worried. She lifted Dora off the box and set her on her feet. "Wait here."

"No!" The child clutched Caroline's skirt. "I'm scared."

Caroline didn't dare bring her downstairs. Seeing Tristan passed out would only frighten the girl more. She settled for giving Dora a firm hug. "Wait here, sweetheart. I'll be back as soon as I can."

"I want my daddy!"

"Of course you do." Caroline smoothed back the child's messy braid. "Let me see what's happening, then I'll come back. Okay?"

With her bottom lip trembling, Dora nodded. Caroline kissed her forehead and hurried to the stairs. What she saw from the landing made no sense at all. Evaline was fanning the face of a woman lying in a heap on the floor. She was on her back with her head in Evaline's lap. Her dark hair was curled on the housekeeper's white apron and her gown made a puddle of black silk. A young woman, presumably a lady's maid, stood in the corner with her back pressed against the wall.

Evaline looked up at Caroline with wide eyes. "This woman fainted!"

"Who is she?"

"My daughter-in-law." The voice was male, unfamiliar and distinctly British. Caroline looked at the door, where she saw a tall man in an expensively tailored coat and a top hat. He had blue eyes that matched Tristan's, blond hair threaded with gray and Tristan's nose and chin. Instantly she recognized the Duke of Willoughby. With a woman unconscious, she had no time for introductions. "Good afternoon, sir."

Belatedly she recalled Tristan's instructions. She should have called him 'your grace.'"

He looked at her as if she were a bug. "You must be the children's nanny."

"No, your grace," she said, still coming down the stairs. "I'm Tristan's wife."

"Molly?" He gaped at her. "I thought you were dead."

"I'm Caroline," she answered. "And I suggest we save the explanation for later. Your daughter-in-law needs medical attention."

Crouching at the woman's side, she put her hand on her forehead. As the duke's daughter-in-law, she had to be Louisa, Andrew's widow. Tristan had detailed the family tree in their late-night talks, but he'd said little about Louisa except that she'd married Andrew. The heat of fever instantly dampened Caroline's palm. "She's burning up."

The woman moaned but didn't open her eyes. Caroline turned to Evaline. "Do you have smelling salts?"

"In the kitchen."

"Fetch them." She looked back at the unconscious woman. Not only was she burning up, but blisters also were erupting on her forehead and neck. Bessie had a better eye for disease, but Caroline knew contagion when she saw it. With a chill running down her spine, she looked at the duke. "Has your daughter-in-law been exposed to smallpox?"

"Heavens no!"

His denial was too quick to be trusted. "But you took the train from the East Coast. Was it crowded?"

"Yes, but—"

"So you don't really know. She could have—"

"She has a name." The man stood even taller, glaring at her with an intensity that unnerved her. "This is Marchio-

ness Andrew Smythe. I don't care that we're in America! She's to be addressed as 'Marchioness Andrew.'"

"Formalities can wait, sir. I'm concerned for her health." *And the health of my family.*

"I assure you," he said coldly. "The marchioness did *not* contract smallpox. I wouldn't allow it."

Did this man think he could control a deadly and infectious disease? Tristan had described him as difficult. Caroline had to agree. Unwilling to argue with him, she spoke to the lady's maid. "Do you know if she's been exposed to anyone who's been sick?"

"No, ma'am." The girl couldn't have been more than seventeen.

Caroline felt sorry for her. "Would you see to her trunks, please? They'll need to go upstairs."

"Yes, ma'am."

The girl curtsied and slipped through the door. Caroline removed a handkerchief from her pocket and wiped Louisa's brow. If the woman had smallpox, the entire household would be in danger. The disease killed nearly half the people who became infected, and it left the survivors badly scarred. Silently Caroline gave thanks she'd told Dora to wait upstairs.

Evaline arrived with the ammonia carbonate. "Stay back," Caroline said quietly. "It could be smallpox."

"Lord, have mercy!" Evaline cried.

"I'm not sure." Caroline indicated the line of bumps. "But the blisters are worrisome. We need Bessie."

Evaline wrung her apron. "She and Mr. Jon went riding today. They're looking for those healing herbs she talks about."

"Send Noah to find them. And summon Tristan, please."

"Yes, Mrs. Caroline."

"And Evaline?" She looked at the housekeeper with a silent plea. "Dora's in the sewing room. She's frightened."

"I'll go to her." The housekeeper headed up the stairs.

"Speak to her, but don't open the door," Caroline called after her. "Whatever you do, keep her upstairs."

When Evaline reached the landing, she turned and the women locked eyes. They both knew what an illness, even a mild one, could do to Tristan. Swallowing hard, Caroline went back to tending her patient. The more information she had, the more she could help Bessie. Before uncorking the smelling salts, she took Louisa's pulse. It was strong and steady.

Without looking up, she spoke to the duke. "Did she have breakfast this morning?"

"How should I know?" He grumbled. "I had eggs and toast in my room. The eggs were cold, and the toast was dry. The hotel in that little town is deplorable. I barely slept."

The man was a self-obsessed fool, a benefit if he'd stayed in his room and not asked anyone in town about Tristan or the children. She uncorked the smelling salts and held the vial under the woman's nose. Louisa inhaled once, twice, then startled into consciousness.

"What happened?" she said in a weak voice.

"You fainted," Caroline replied.

"I'm so sorry to be a bother."

She tried to sit up, but Caroline nudged her flat. "You need a few minutes to recover. My sister's a nurse. She'll be here soon."

The woman's eyes lit up. "Are you Dora's nanny?"

"No," Caroline answered for the second time. "I'm Tristan's wife."

"Molly?"

The poor woman looked as if she thought she'd died

and really was seeing Molly. Caroline took pity on her. "I'm not Molly. My name is Caroline. Tristan and I married just recently."

"Oh, I see." Sorrow filled her eyes.

The duke grumbled behind them. "I should have been informed."

Louisa glanced up at the duke, her eyes shiny with fever or sudden tears. Caroline couldn't discern the difference, but news of her marriage to Tristan had saddened this woman. Perhaps the circumstances had renewed her grief for her own husband. Caroline spoke in a hush. "I'm very sorry about Andrew."

Something knifelike flicked in her sparkling blue irises. "Thank you."

The duke interrupted. "Where is the marquess?"

"Who?" Intimidated, Caroline forgot her lessons in titles and etiquette.

"Lord Tristan, of course!" the duke bellowed.

The pomposity irked her. "We're in America, your grace. He goes by 'major.'"

Louisa arched a brow, whether out of shock or pleasure Caroline didn't know. The duke said nothing, but his silence carried a threat. Caroline looked back to the ailing woman. "I'm sure Tristan will express his regrets for your loss."

Louisa's eyes filled with longing, then she squeezed Caroline's hand. As their fingers touched, her gaze went to the ring on Caroline's finger. The pink diamond spoke far louder than words, and Louisa looked up. "I wish you and Tristan nothing but happiness, Marchioness. We were good friends, you know. We grew up together. We were… close." Fresh sorrow dimmed the woman's eyes.

Judging by her obvious melancholy, this woman and Tristan had been more than childhood playmates. What exactly did "close" mean? And why hadn't Tristan done more than mention Louisa's name in passing?

Louisa managed a tiny smile. "Does Tristan still love horses?"

"Very much."

"He wanted to breed Arabians," she murmured.

Louisa closed her eyes, leaving Caroline to weigh the unexpected information. Louisa, it seemed, had known Tristan extremely well…well enough to know his hopes and dreams. She'd come to America expecting to find him widowed. What else had she expected? It seemed to Caroline Tristan had left out more than a few important details about his sister-in-law. Why hadn't he spoken of her? He'd schooled Caroline in the names of his brothers and cousins, his grandparents and servants to whom he'd been close. He'd described everyone except Louisa, who was beautiful, poised and gracious, even while lying on the entry floor. The woman was clearly born to be a duchess, while Caroline had been born to bake pies.

She studied Louisa's flushed face. "How long have you been ill?"

"A few days, I suppose."

"Have you had headaches?" Caroline asked. "Perhaps nausea?"

The duke interrupted. "What kind of question is that?"

Caroline looked over her shoulder, raising her chin until her eyes met his cold stare. "It's a necessary one, your grace."

He lowered his chin. "A *lady* doesn't speak of such things," he said, implying Caroline wasn't a lady.

Her temper flared, but she held it in check. Turning back to Louisa, she saw that more bumps had emerged at her hairline.

Evaline came back to the entry through the back hall,

an indication that she'd spoken to Dora and used the back-stairs to send Noah in search of Bessie. "Dora's quiet now," she said to Caroline. "I sent Freddie to get his father. Noah's going after Jon and Miss Bessie."

"Good."

Lady Louisa spoke in a hush. "What's wrong with me?"

"I don't know yet." Caroline thought of all the things the rash could indicate. Smallpox was the biggest worry, but other diseases—measles in particular—had to be considered.

"I'm so sorry," Louisa murmured. "I should have stayed at the hotel. The children—" She sealed her lips, then implored Caroline with a bleak stare. "If something happens to Dora or Freddie, I'll never forgive myself."

She'd used the children's everyday names, a sign she cared about them. "Let's wait and see," Caroline replied.

With another look, the two women moved from acquaintances, and possibly rivals, to allies. No matter the cost, the children had to be protected. When Louisa's eyes fluttered shut, Caroline knew she was praying the same prayers that had run through Caroline's mind for the past five minutes.

The duke cleared his throat, an unnecessary gesture used solely to gain attention. Caroline looked up and over her shoulder. He had a gaunt face, a liver spot on his neck and a critical arch to his bushy brows. Her initial reaction to the man was distaste, but she couldn't ignore the concern in his eyes. Whether the concern came from a fatherly affection for Louisa or from what he hoped to gain by using her, Caroline didn't know.

She had expected to be challenged by Tristan's father. She hadn't expected to compete with a beautiful woman from Tristan's past. In Denver Caroline had always been second-best. In Louisa's company, she was second-best yet again. Considering Tristan's silence, it seemed possible, even likely, that he had feelings for Louisa. They shared a past, and it had been romantic enough to bring Louisa to Wyoming. With Andrew gone and Tristan widowed, nothing stood between them—except his unconsummated marriage to a lowly American.

The front door swung open and Tristan strode into the entry hall. His gaze whipped from the duke to Louisa. He didn't see Caroline at all. She'd become invisible to him. He had eyes only for the woman lying on the floor, looking up at him with such adoration Caroline could hardly breathe.

Ten minutes ago Tristan had been in the barn grooming Cairo when Freddie had come running through the double doors.

Grandfather's here! I want to meet him!

The use of the name shouldn't have troubled Tristan, but it did. Approaching the house with Freddie at his side, he'd told the boy to mind his manners and wait outside. Climbing the steps, he'd mentally rehearsed his first words to his father in fifteen years. *Good afternoon, your grace. Shall we speak in my study?*

He planned to tell his father he'd do his duty when the time came, but that he wouldn't be returning to England until necessary, the implication being he wanted nothing to do with his father, living or dead. He hoped the insult would send the old man packing.

Tristan had been ready for the duke. He hadn't been at all prepared to see Louisa. The sight of her paralyzed his lungs. He'd once loved this woman. He'd been hurt when she rejected him and confused when she refused to see him. The tender feelings had faded with time, but he had wondered for years why she left him, if he'd somehow failed her or if she'd truly loved Andrew.

Watching her now, he could feel his plans for his father derailing.

Louisa lying prostrate on the floor complicated the situation. Molly had filled his heart completely and he'd recovered from being jilted, but the wound had closed over a knot of guilt. For years he'd wondered if he'd failed to rescue her from a plot of some kind, or if her love for Andrew had been sincere. Her dark clothing indicated mourning, so he stepped forward to offer condolences.

"Stop!" Caroline cried.

He didn't appreciate being ordered around in front of his father. "What is it?" he said coldly.

"Louisa is ill."

The ramifications chilled him as surely as the fever heated his blood. With his weakened system, he couldn't afford another infection. His brow furrowed. "How ill?"

"I don't know," Caroline said in a hush. "We're waiting for Bessie, but the pustules indicate a pox of some sort."

Fear for himself turned to terror for his children. He'd seen outbreaks of smallpox in the West Indies. He'd been vaccinated, a privilege of being an officer, but his children had no such protection. He was familiar enough with the disease to know the symptoms. He looked down at Louisa's face, forcing himself to see the blisters on her hairline rather than her pleading eyes. The bumps were scattered and small. They didn't look like smallpox to him, but he knew a sure sign of the disease.

He looked at Caroline. "Does she have pox on her hands?"

"I didn't look."

Louisa looked at her hands herself, then held the one she'd offered to him palm out. "Both hands are clear."

"Then it's not smallpox." Crouching at her side, he clasped her hand. "It's most likely chicken pox, which, as I recall, I had and you didn't."

"That's right," she murmured.

Time had changed her appearance, but she'd only become more beautiful. It had changed Tristan, too. While he treasured the gold of pleasant memories, he hadn't forgotten the pain of unanswered questions or the immediate problem of his father looming behind him. "This is quite a surprise," he said to her.

"For me, too." She wrinkled her nose as if she were still a little girl. "I seem to have fainted in your entry hall."

"I can see that."

"It reminds me of the day I fell off Bonfire."

Bonfire was the mare she'd ridden when they'd explored his father's estate as adolescents. An excellent horsewoman, Louisa had fallen just once but she'd landed in a stream and gotten covered with moss. It had been a silly accident, one where they'd ended up laughing and kissing for the first time. It had been his first such experience... hers, too. A smile curved on his lips. "That was quite an event."

"Yes." Averting her eyes, she withdrew her hand. "Your wife is taking good care of me."

Caroline... He'd forgotten her in his relief over the pox, but he looked at her now. Her eyes were full of questions, dark and guarded in a way he'd never seen before. In their late-night talks he'd barely mentioned Louisa, yet here he sat holding the woman's hand, speaking in a jaunty tone and trading memories like the old friends they were.

"Caroline," he said too boisterously. "This is my sister-in-law."

"We've met," she said.

"Yes, of course." Feeling foolish, he stood and looked

down at Louisa. "I employ a nurse for the children. I'm sure she's well versed in chicken pox."

He looked to Caroline, both for confirmation and to include her, but she focused her eyes on Louisa. "Evaline went to get her. She's my sister. Her name's Bessie and she's far more knowledgeable than I am. I'm sorry to have given you such a scare."

"Nonsense," Louisa replied. "I fainted in your entry hall. If anyone owes an apology, it would be me. You've been sweet and exceptionally understanding."

Caroline looked more ill at ease than ever. Tristan wanted to intervene, but she found her tongue first. "We'd planned for the duke and his companion to stay in the guesthouse, but you should be near Bessie. Can you climb the stairs?"

Louisa tried to sit up. "I'm a bit wobbly…"

Tristan offered his hand. "Allow me to assist."

Louisa took it and he pulled her upright, keenly aware of his father's eyes on his back. If his sister-in-law's presence was an indication, his father was already attempting to manipulate him. The old man had known of Tristan's infatuation with Louisa. Tristan strongly suspected she was being used to lure him back to England. The manipulation made Tristan sick. If Andrew had been a pampered pet, Louisa had been reduced to bait.

He felt sorry for her. "Caroline will take care of you," he said gently.

"Of course," his wife agreed.

He wished Evaline were present so he didn't have to treat her like a servant. "Do we have a guest room ready?"

"Yes, Major."

He didn't blame her for the formality, but it irked him. He'd schooled her in etiquette, but he hadn't expected her to treat *him* any differently. It also put a chink in the united front he wanted to present to his father. The lapse worried him. He could only imagine how insulting the duke had been to Caroline upon his arrival. And now she had to deal with chicken pox. Louisa would be well mannered, but Freddie and Dora would likely fall ill and be irritable.

Even as he explained away her attitude, Tristan knew he was ignoring the obvious. A woman from his past had just walked into his life, and he'd reacted like a smitten adolescent. No wonder Caroline had put up her guard. He'd insulted her and belittled their vows. He felt inept and wanted to explain, but he couldn't follow her up the stairs. Their talk would have to wait until tonight, both for the sake of appearances and because he had to deal with his father.

When the women reached the top of the stairs, he turned to the duke with deliberate slowness. "Good afternoon, your grace."

"Good afternoon, Marquess." The duke drawled out the title. "You look well."

"I go by 'major,'" he said coldly. "And I'm quite fine, thank you." The malaria had stayed away for more than a week. He'd been feeling much better since Bessie increased the quinine, but he felt edgy from lack of sleep and his temper tended to flare.

The duke arched a bushy silver brow. "You've forgotten your manners, Tristan. Not only did you fail to advise me of your marriage, but you also didn't introduce me to your bride."

"I assure you, I didn't forget. Subjecting my wife to your scrutiny was less important than caring for Louisa. You should have stayed in Cheyenne until she was well."

The man huffed. "She's not that ill."

"I beg to differ." Tristan spoke as if he were dressing down a soldier. "She fainted and she's contagious. Two children reside in this household. How long has Louisa been ill?"

"How would I know? I have concerns of my own."

"You haven't changed a bit, have you?" Tristan wasn't surprised. The duke always put himself first.

"Neither have you," the man retorted. "But the circumstances *have* changed. You'll return to England immediately."

"No.

"You have no choice in the matter."

"Yes, I do," Tristan said mildly. "I can't stop being your son, but I won't return to England to be at your beck and call. I'll assume my responsibilities when necessary and no sooner."

"It's necessary now."

"It will be necessary when you pass on." Refusing to argue, Tristan crossed the entry to the door and turned the knob.

His father bellowed at him. "Tristan!"

As if he were a boy, he stopped. Like the officer he'd become, he made a slow turn that demanded respect. When he didn't receive it, he glared at his father. "What is it?"

"I want to meet my grandson."

Such a meeting was inevitable, but Tristan dreaded it. "You'll meet Freddie at supper." Of course there had been no mention of Dora.

"I want to meet him now," the duke insisted.

Tristan bristled. "You might have authority in Willoughby, but you have none at The Barracks."

At that moment, the front door flew open. Freddie burst into the entry hall, proving yet again that no one, not even his children, followed Tristan's orders.

Chapter Eleven

"Grandfather!" The boy had eyes only for the old man, and the old man had eyes only for him. Tristan could have been a coatrack for all that he mattered.

Looking ridiculously pleased, the duke offered Freddie his hand. "Frederick! It's a pleasure to meet you at last."

The boy beamed at the attention. "Hello, Grandfather."

Tristan's first instinct was to wedge himself between Freddie and the older man. If Tristan succumbed to the malaria, Freddie would replace Andrew in the duke's "affections." He'd be turned into a pet. Tristan couldn't allow his son to become spoiled, but intervention would exact a price. Freddie might become rebellious, and the duke would certainly be indignant. Tristan also understood Freddie's hunger for family. The boy had no cousins, no uncles or aunts aside from Louisa, whom Freddie had never met. A grandfather should have been a welcome addition to the boy's world. Sadly, Tristan had no illusions about the kind of love Freddie would receive from the duke. The roots of the Smythe family tree had been infected with selfishness, scheming and manipulation. The duke cared far more about his legacy than he did about the needs of a child. Even now the man was studying Freddie as if he were livestock.

"Look at that blond hair!" he declared. "You're clearly a Smythe."

Yes, but Freddie had his mother's nose. He also had Molly's inquisitiveness. Freddie was…himself. He was also a child and susceptible to flattery. "Freddie, you're excused," Tristan said firmly. "You'll see your grandfather later."

The duke huffed. "Come now, Tristan. Allow the boy to stay. We have much to discuss. After all, he's a future duke."

Freddie's eyes popped wide. "I am?"

Tristan had told his children nothing of his title and family. It had been irrelevant until his brothers died, then he'd felt the weight of his illness. "We'll speak later," he said to the boy.

"But Father—"

"Freddie—" His voice held a warning. To his relief, his son held back an argument. Tristan softened his tone. "We'll speak later. Find Noah and see if he needs help putting up the horses and carriages."

The duke raised his brows in seeming shock. "Surely you have servants for such tasks?"

Freddie liked helping on the ranch. He never argued about chores, but he was looking at Tristan quizzically. "Do I have to?"

"Yes, you do."

The duke smirked. "You'll love England, my boy. We have an entire staff just for the barns. You won't have to lift a finger."

Freddie looked at him, wide-eyed. "No chores?"

"Not a one."

Tristan interrupted. "That's quite enough, your grace."

The man's plan couldn't have been more obvious—undermine Tristan's authority and steal Freddie's affection. As much as Tristan wanted to walk away from his father, he had no choice but to sit down with the man and lay down some rules.

The duke smiled possessively at his grandson. "Do what your father says, Freddie. We'll have plenty of time together."

The boy seemed to grow six inches. "I'm glad you're here, Grandfather."

"So am I, Freddie."

Tristan couldn't say the same. As the boy left, Tristan indicated the hall leading to his study. "We need to talk."

"Yes, we do."

Ramrod straight, the duke paced down the hall. Tristan followed until they reached the study. He indicated the duke should enter first. As the man passed him, Tristan thought about what his father would see. Paintings of Arabian stallions covered the walls. The carpet had been imported from Persia, and military memorabilia decorated a dozen mahogany shelves. He had hundreds of books, everything from poetry to mathematics. Burgundy drapes hung from the windows, and comfortable chairs and a divan made a half circle in front of a stone hearth. The room told Tristan's story, though he felt certain his father would show no interest.

Predictably the duke crossed to Tristan's desk without once turning his head, then without asking permission, he helped himself to a cigar from a crystal humidor. The cigars were a gift from the men in the West India Regiment, and they'd become a treasured souvenir.

Ignoring his father's presumption, Tristan sat behind his desk. The duke dropped down on the chair across from him, causing the leather to squeak. It squeaked again as the man rolled the cigar in his fingers, silently ordering Tristan to light it.

Tristan wouldn't do it. He enjoyed a good cigar, but he didn't enjoy his father's company. The fact saddened him. Just as Freddie longed for a grandfather, Tristan wanted a father who'd offer advice and understanding, someone who'd care that he was struggling with malaria and had lost his wife, that he was raising his children and trying not to fall in love until he could claim a small piece of the future. The duke was his father by blood, but the family tree was diseased in a way that made them strangers.

The duke continued to roll the unlit cigar between his fingers. "Again you've forgotten your manners—"

"Not at all."

"—*and* your responsibilities." His eyes narrowed. "You can't possibly remain in America. I raised you to do your duty."

"You didn't raise me at all." Tristan had been closer to the groomsmen in the stable, even the cook, than he'd been to his own father. Now the man acted as if he owned him.

"You're my heir," the duke insisted. "You'll do what I say."

Tristan showed Cairo more respect. "I'll do what I believe is best for everyone involved."

The duke rolled the cigar between his fingers, daring Tristan to be a gentleman and light it. It was a trap of sorts. Lighting it was an act of compliance. *Not* lighting it made him a petulant child. Either way, his father was pulling the strings as if Tristan were a puppet. Those strings had to be cut, so Tristan smirked. "I don't recall offering you a cigar."

"You didn't."

"They're Cuban. A gift from my men."

"Then I'll take another for later." The duke opened the

humidor, took two cigars to make a point and put them inside his coat. Staring at Tristan, he removed a match from his pocket, struck it against his shoe and lit the cigar clamped between his lips.

Tristan smelled sulfur and thought of the battlefield. He'd fought for his country and he'd been willing to die for it. He would do no less to protect his family. It was too soon to send Caroline away with the children. Their departure would alert the duke to the problem of his health. Neither could Tristan stand to give up even a minute with them. He and Freddie were just getting to know each other, and Dora wouldn't understand at all. She'd feel abandoned and rightly so.

If his father wouldn't leave and the children had to stay, Tristan had only one choice. He'd live in close quarters with his enemy. As a military man, he could do it. The boy who'd longed for his fathers' attention had grown up and become a father himself, one who'd protect his children at any cost.

Tristan took a cigar of his own, lit it and blew a ring of smoke, watching it dissipate to suggest he was bored. Finally, he said, "I'm sorry about Andrew and Oscar."

"Thank you."

"Pennwright provided the details." Tristan thought of the note in the secretary's familiar hand. His own father hadn't told him of the deaths of his brothers, and even now the duke accepted sympathy without offering it in return. Tristan hadn't seen his brothers in years, but the three of them had shared the rituals of childhood, pulling pranks and wrestling with each other. They hadn't been close, but they shared the same blood.

His father puffed heavily on the cigar, causing the end to burn hot before it withered to ash. When the tip looked ready to break apart, he tapped it into a candy dish not meant for ashes. "I'm going to be blunt, Tristan. Andrew was the finest son a man could have. His death left me in shock…and somewhat unprepared. Oscar, as you know, was a terrible disappointment."

And what was I to you?

The question stayed unasked, in part because Tristan knew the answer. If Andrew had been a pampered poodle and Oscar a cur, Tristan had been a puppy wagging for attention.

Suddenly far away, the duke looked admiringly at the signet ring that never left his finger. "Andrew was a mirror image of myself. He exceeded every expectation I had… except for one." He raised his gaze to Tristan with the suddenness of a bullet. "Your brother failed to produce a son, but that no longer matters. You've given me Freddie. He looks like me, don't you think?"

The man's vanity knew no bounds. "Freddie looks like himself."

"Yes, but he's clearly a Smythe."

So was Tristan. Again he'd been overlooked as a branch on the family tree. "And your point?"

The man's gaze sharpened with the intelligence that made him dangerous. "We've had our differences, Tristan. When you failed to reply to my letter, I came expecting you to be as rude as you've been. I was hoping, however, that duty alone would prompt you to return immediately to England."

Even if he'd been healthy, Tristan would have delayed returning to England. He had a duty to fulfill, and he'd been born and bred to be loyal, but he didn't want his father to have any control whatsoever over his children. His illness made the obligation treacherous, and he didn't want the duke to know about it. The old buzzard would circle until Tristan died, then he'd take Freddie for his own.

Tristan blew another ring of smoke. "I'll meet my obligation when it's time. You seem well enough to me."

He man harrumphed. "Of course I'm well enough."

"Then there's no hurry," he said lazily. "As you can see, I have responsibilities here."

"None that matter," the duke declared. "Sell this ridiculous ranch at once."

"No."

"I insist."

Tristan knew better than to argue with the duke. Stalling offered the wisest course. "I'll consider a trip in the spring. There's no point in a winter voyage."

The older man's brows knit together. "I can't stay until spring."

"Of course not." The sooner his father left for England, the safer Freddie would be. "I imagine you and Louisa are eager to return home."

"Louisa." He spat her name. "She's useless to me now. She's nothing but a mannequin, always has been."

Inwardly Tristan balked at the insult. The girl he'd known in England had been good-natured and fun. She'd also been intelligent. Calling her a mannequin said far more about the duke than it did about Louisa. He couldn't stop himself from defending her.

"I'd hardly call Louisa *useless*."

The duke gave him a speculative stare. "You ruined my plans by marrying that American woman. How long has it been?"

There was no point in hedging. "A little more than a week."

The man tapped the cigar on the candy dish. "If I didn't

know better, I'd think you married her to embarrass me. She'll never be accepted, you know."

Tristan thought of the reasons for their marriage and the option of an annulment. He enjoyed the duchess lessons because of Caroline's good humor, but she clearly had no desire to assume the role. He wished she did. The more time he spent with her, the more he appreciated her natural goodness. If he hadn't been ill, he'd have viewed the limitation of their marriage in a very different light. As things stood, he couldn't allow the marriage to go beyond friendship. If they fell in love and he died, she'd grieve. If he lived, she'd become the Duchess of Willoughby, a fate with other costs.

The duke leaned back in the chair, his eyes narrowing like a sleepy cat. "In their own way, women are useful. Louisa's still quite lovely, don't you think?"

Tristan heard his father's sly tone and recoiled. If he denied noticing Louisa's beauty, he'd be a liar. If he agreed with his father, he'd be disrespectful to women everywhere. He answered by silently puffing on the cigar.

The duke mirrored his actions. "As I recall, you were once in love with her."

"I also enjoyed sardines for breakfast. I outgrew that habit."

"Nonetheless, a man never forgets his first conquest."

Tristan had kissed Louisa, but she hadn't been a conquest. He'd been with just one woman, his wife. He refused to let the insult stand. "Louisa wasn't a conquest. She deserves respect."

"But you wanted her."

Tristan had heard enough. "What are you suggesting?"

The duke set the stump of the cigar in the dish. "Divorce your worthless American wife and you can have Louisa."

"I have no reason to divorce Caroline." *And every reason to love her.* The thought sobered him. He couldn't love Caroline, not yet. Maybe not ever. But neither could he deny the hope that he'd recover and that someday she'd want to be his duchess. He had to stop his father's criticism now. "I care deeply for my wife. She's a good woman."

"No, she isn't." His father huffed with disgust. "She's unsuitable. She's crass and rude and—"

"That's enough."

The duke frowned. "You always were intractable. Suit yourself. Don't divorce her. You can keep Louisa as your mistress."

Tristan had expected such a remark. The duke kept one mistress in London and another in Paris. Even when Tristan's mother had been alive, he'd broken his vows. Tristan believed in marriage and he'd honored Molly with his fidelity. He'd give Caroline the same respect. "I'm not interested in a mistress," he said drily.

"You will be."

Tristan held in the retort. If his father sensed weakness, he'd move in for the kill. "This is none of your concern."

"I'm the duke," he said, matter of factly. "You're my heir. Everything you do is my concern. When I give an order, you'll follow it."

"No, sir. I will *not*."

"Why you—" the duke clenched his teeth. "You're an abomination! If Andrew had lived, I wouldn't have to put up with you!"

What did a son say to such outward disdain? Tristan didn't know, but a realization slowly dawned... As a boy he'd cowered in his father's presence and feared his punishment. Looking at the duke now, he saw a pompous fool, a man with an inflated notion of his own importance and the inability to care for others. The duke wasn't infallible. He wasn't God. He wasn't even close.

Tristan had to wonder... If God didn't have anything in common with the Duke of Willoughby, what was He like? Tristan thought of Caroline's dream game and how she'd seen into the hearts of his children. He recalled the gentle way she stitched the cut on his head and how she'd cried with him over Molly. In spite of losing her husband, she had a childlike faith in God's goodness and it sustained her. That kind of faith could sustain him, too.

Tristan felt as if he were shedding a too-tight skin, but he instantly went on alert. No matter what he felt, or didn't feel, for his father, Freddie had to be protected. That required all his attention and complete vigilance. He kept his voice mild. "Is there anything else, your grace?"

"Yes." The duke waited, silently commanding Tristan to kowtow to him. As an officer, Tristan had the patience to wait all day.

Finally the duke spoke. "Freddie is a future duke. He should begin training."

As if he were a dog. His military control kept Tristan calm. "Freddie is a boy. He doesn't need *training*."

"Of course he does."

"He's not a pet, your grace. He's an active, happy child. I won't allow you to influence him."

"But I'm the duke."

"And I'm his father."

The old man seemed not to hear. "The boy has my build, don't you think?"

Tristan said nothing.

"And my coloring, too." The duke's eyes gleamed. "My hair was as blond as his until it turned gray."

Tristan also had light hair, not that his father ever noticed. "Is there anything else, your grace?"

His father stood. "I expect my accommodations are ready?"

"Yes. You'll be staying in the guesthouse." Jon usually occupied it, but he'd moved to the bunkhouse for the duration of the visit.

Tristan rose and came around the desk. He followed his father out of the study to the entry hall, then stepped in front of him and opened the door. His father's valet had been waiting outside, and together the men went to the guesthouse.

Shutting the door, Tristan thought about the tactics his father would use to gain Freddie's affection. He'd spoil the boy with gifts. He'd praise him until he was barking like a trained seal. Tristan's blood burned in his veins, a reminder of his illness. He had to stay healthy, and he had to hide his condition from his father.

He also had to protect Caroline. If he didn't school her properly, his father would flay her alive. She'd also seen him take Louisa's hand. His feelings had been tiny embers from the past. They'd flared in an unexpected breeze and immediately died, but Caroline would recall the sparks. He hadn't told her about Louisa because the episode embarrassed him. No man liked being jilted. But after what Caroline had witnessed, she deserved to know what had happened.

The memory raised old questions. Had Louisa left him because she loved Andrew? Or had he failed to rescue her from some sort of trouble? If he'd failed to help her, he didn't want to repeat the mistake. He wanted to speak with her, but she was ill. He'd have to wait for answers from Louisa, but tonight he'd give answers of his own to Caroline.

"I'm sorry to be such trouble," Louisa said to Caroline as she climbed into bed. "My lady's maid can tend to my needs when she returns."

The girl had gone downstairs to fetch tea and a bowl of broth. Caroline had sent her. "I don't mind helping."

Louisa sighed. "If I'd known I had chicken pox, I'd have never left Cheyenne. I hope you don't come down with it."

Caroline had no such worries. "I've had it and so has my sister." Even more important, Tristan had had it as a child, though Caroline was still reeling from how she'd learned that small fact. He'd been close to this woman, even closer than she'd first thought. Had he loved her? Judging by how easily he'd taken Louisa's hand, it seemed more than possible. It seemed likely.

Louisa pulled the covers over the nightgown Caroline had loaned her because her trunk hadn't yet been delivered to her room. Bessie hadn't returned, but Caroline expected her any minute. Until the nurse arrived, she felt duty-bound to stay with Louisa.

She dipped a cloth in cool water and squeezed it nearly dry. "This will fight the fever."

Louisa slumped against the pillow. "I've been a terrible disruption to you."

Caroline put the folded cloth over Louisa's brow. "Don't worry about the children. If they get sick, we'll manage."

"You're too kind," Louisa said gently. "I wasn't apologizing for the chicken pox. I want you to know, I respect your marriage. In no way do I want to interfere—"

"It's all right," she said too quickly.

"No, it's not." Louisa removed the cloth from her brow. "How much has Tristan told you about his father?"

"Quite a bit." It was Louisa he'd neglected to mention.

"Then you know he's a conniver." She averted her eyes. "He had…expectations for Tristan and me."

"I wondered," Caroline murmured.

"Tristan must have told you about us."

He hadn't, but Caroline was too embarrassed to admit

her ignorance. She took the cloth and dampened it again. "You're ill. We should speak later."

"No," Louisa insisted. "I have to get this off my chest. Would you give Tristan a message for me?"

Caroline stopped wringing the cloth. "What is it?"

"Tell him I'm sorry."

"For what?"

"Everything…" Louisa closed her eyes. "You're right. I'm too ill to think clearly. I shouldn't have said anything. I'm sorry, Caroline…so sorry." Tears leaked from her eyes.

Questions swarmed in Caroline's mind, but she couldn't quiz an ailing woman. It was Tristan who needed to explain, but what right did she have to confront him? He'd promised her nothing but respect. If he chose to keep secrets, he had that right. More troubled than she wanted to be, Caroline studied Louisa's face. The woman was pretty, even beautiful with her delicate nose and wide eyes. Her dark hair made a cloud on the pillow, and her figure had womanly curves any man would desire. She had poise, grace, intelligence and honor. She'd make a fine duchess, a position Caroline had no ability to fulfill.

It wasn't the first time she'd felt second-best to another woman, but it was the first time she'd felt that stab of inadequacy as Tristan's wife. If they hadn't already been married, what would he feel for Louisa? The noble thing to do—the honorable thing—was to immediately offer Tristan an annulment. If he had feelings for Louisa, she didn't want to stand in his way. Neither did she want to wait around for *him* to reject *her*.

Only the children stood as a barrier. She couldn't stand the thought of losing her adopted family, but neither could she return to being a governess after more than a week of being a mother. As she worried about the future, Louisa slipped into a restless slumber. Several minutes passed, then a soft knock sounded on the door.

"Come in," Caroline said.

Bessie stepped into the bedroom and closed the door behind her. "I hear we have a guest with chicken pox."

"We do." Caroline told her about Louisa's symptoms but nothing about Tristan's reaction to the woman...or her own. She needed time to sort her thoughts, but she also needed to know if Freddie and Dora had already had the childhood disease. "I need to speak to Tristan about the children. Do you need anything before I go?"

"I'm fine," Bessie said. "Jon's taking care of the herbs we collected."

"Did you find what you wanted?"

"I had an amazing time." Bessie's cheeks were pinker than usual, presumably from time in the sun, but Caroline had to wonder if Jon's company had something to do with the spark in her sister's eyes. The two of them often walked together after supper. Caroline wanted to hear more but not in front of Louisa.

"We'll talk later," she whispered.

Excusing herself, she headed downstairs to look for Tristan. He was nowhere to be found, but she learned about the duke's whereabouts from Evaline. He was safely tucked into the guesthouse.

"That man is full of himself," the housekeeper complained.

"I know," Caroline said. "But we have to put up with him. Louisa is much nicer."

Evaline sighed with sympathy. "That woman's going to be itching very badly. I hope the children don't get sick."

"I do, too," Caroline replied. "Have you seen the major?"

"He left a while ago."

She thought of the places he could be. Most likely he'd gone to the horse barn. She didn't want to be around horses, but she needed to speak with him. "Thank you, Evaline."

As she headed for the door, the housekeeper called after her. "Do I need to do anything special for dinner? The duke seems very hard to please."

Caroline thought a minute. She and Tristan had been eating supper on the veranda with the children. She loved their meals, especially the tone of Tristan's voice as he offered grace. She'd felt a new gentleness in him, a new hope. Tonight he had duties as his father's heir. "Tristan and I will eat with the duke in the dining room. If you'd see to the children, I'd appreciate it."

"Yes, ma'am."

Evaline returned to the kitchen, and Caroline paced through the front door and into the yard. In the distance she saw Jon approaching with a basket in each hand. They were full of stems, grass and flowers, an indication Bessie had indeed been successful in her hunt for medicinal herbs. Judging by Jon's dashing smile, they both enjoyed the expedition.

Their paths crossed in a patch of sunlight near the guesthouse. Caroline greeted him with a smile of her own. "You don't look like a man who's been ousted from his home."

"I'm not," he replied. "I gave it up willingly."

"That was kind of you."

He shrugged. "The less Tristan sees of his father, the better. Who's the woman he brought?"

"She's Andrew's widow."

Jon's brow shot up. "Louisa is here?"

"You know her?"

"Not personally, but—" He paused, clearly weighing his words. "Tristan will have to explain."

"No, he doesn't," she said quickly. He didn't owe her anything at all. They had a legal agreement for the purpose of protecting his children. Apart from that common concern, they were from different worlds. Tristan read Shakespeare. Caroline read her Bible, but little else. She'd grown up cooking for her father and sister. Tristan had grown up with servants who tended to his needs. He'd distanced himself from his father, but his feelings for Louisa were another matter entirely. Caroline's mind went down a sad and familiar road. How many times had she been interested in a man to have him set her aside for someone else?

"Caroline? Did you hear me?"

Jon's voice pulled her back to the sunlight. "I'm sorry. What did you say?"

"I asked how Tristan handled the initial meeting."

"With Louisa?"

He gave her a sad, patient look. "I was asking about the duke, but it seems Louisa upset you even more."

"Oh, no," she protested. "I'm fine."

"You don't look fine."

"I am." She gave an offhand laugh. "Why wouldn't I be fine? You know as well as I—my marriage to Tristan is a formality. Louisa is a lovely person. And she's English. If he cares for her, that would be—" Suddenly tears welled and she had to bite her lips.

"That would be utterly stupid," Jon said.

Caroline wished she hadn't spoken to him. She wished she'd stayed in her room until she'd sorted her thoughts. She waved off his concern. "Tristan and I have a legal commitment. Nothing more. If you'll excuse me, I need to ask him if the children have had chicken pox."

"He's in the horse barn," Jon answered.

They walked in opposite directions, leaving Caroline alone with her worries. She was halfway to the stable when Tristan emerged from the building with a man she didn't recognize. Presumably the fellow had arrived with the duke. He wore a stylish frock coat and had ramrod posture. Sideburns made his face plump and cheerful. Even from a distance she could see Tristan enjoying himself. The stranger seemed to be telling a joke with arm gestures and odd posturing.

When Tristan doubled up with laughter, her heart sank. He had bitter feelings toward his father, but he fit comfortably into his father's world.

Caroline didn't.

But Louisa did… She fit perfectly.

With her chest tight, she turned and walked back to the house. She didn't want to lose the children, but neither would she stand in the way of Tristan's happiness. If he had genuine feelings for Louisa, she'd remove herself from his life. She'd accept being second-best…again. Feeling like a moth in a bevy of butterflies, she hurried back to the house.

Chapter Twelve

Tristan had enjoyed a spirited reunion with Pennwright, but the rest of the day had been impossibly irritating. It was now late into the night. Alone in his bedroom, waiting for Caroline to come upstairs, he thought about his father's obnoxious behavior.

The misery had started with the duke's arrival at the dinner table. He'd walked into the dining room with his own valet, as if he were going to ask the man to taste-test the food for poison. He'd complained about Evaline's cooking and had demanded his own pitcher of gravy. The children had eaten earlier with Bessie, and Jon had joined them rather than endure the duke. To Tristan's consternation, Freddie had come into the dining room and announced he'd been invited by his grandfather.

Tristan didn't have the heart to deny his son, though he now regretted the decision. The duke had fawned over the boy, flattering him with as much intensity as he insulted Caroline. Her conduct was impeccable, but he belittled her table manners. He had inspected the water goblets for spots and the silverware for tarnish. He'd even berated her for interrupting him when she'd merely taken a deep breath.

Tristan had intervened, but he couldn't control his father's tongue. When the man wasn't making rude comments, he droned on about himself and England, excluding Caroline while enticing Freddie.

The meal had ended two hours ago, and the duke had retired to the guesthouse. Bessie had long ago seen to the children and Louisa. Caroline seemed to have disappeared. He'd been expecting her for an hour now, but still she hadn't come upstairs. Not only did he want to apologize for his father's rudeness, but he also had to tell her about his former feelings for Louisa.

When the clock on the mantel chimed eleven times, he wondered if she'd slipped into her room without him noticing. With his father staying in the guesthouse and Louisa bedridden, she didn't have to use the main door to his suite, as they'd planned. Frustrated, Tristan paced through the storage room and tapped on her door.

No answer.

He tapped again more forcefully. "Caroline?"

Hearing nothing, he opened the door and stepped into the cubbyhole of a room. In the moonlight coming through the window, he saw the untouched coverlet on her bed and a Bible left open on her desk. He wondered when she'd read it and if she'd been seeking wisdom or comfort. He didn't know, but words he'd memorized as a child came to him.

Our Father, Who Art in Heaven
Hallowed be Thy name

The verse had made him angry as a boy, but now he felt a longing to understand God the way Caroline did. She didn't see Him as a distant commander-in-chief. She saw the kind of father Tristan had never known but wanted to be. Tonight she'd also seen the illness in the Smythe family tree. She'd been belittled by the duke the way Tristan had been belittled as a boy. He had to find her.

To signal he wanted to see her, he left both doors to the closet open, then stepped into the hall. He glanced at Bessie's door, saw no light and figured she'd gone to sleep. He walked ten paces to Louisa's room, paused and listened to the silence. She, too, seemed to be sleeping. Dora's room was dark, and so was Freddie's. Caroline wasn't in the house.

Wondering if she'd been cornered by the duke, Tristan reconnoitered the downstairs as if searching enemy territory for a prisoner of war. Every room was empty, so he headed to the veranda. With still no sign of Caroline, he walked to the railing and found her at last. She was alone in the garden, thirty feet away and walking through the fallow rows. Moonlight rained down on her, giving shape to a shawl covering her shoulders and the neat arrangement of her hair. She reminded him of the deer that came and nosed the dead plants, scavenging for food when there wasn't any.

He thought of Molly and her request that he remarry. He'd kept his promise, but he hadn't fulfilled it completely. Molly would have wanted him to honor Caroline with all the love a wife deserved. She'd have wanted Freddie and Dora to have brothers and sisters. With the moon bright on Caroline's face, Tristan admitted to wants of own.

He wanted to be free of the malaria.

He wanted to love again.

He wanted to honor his duty as the future Duke of Willoughby and be the best husband and father a man could be. He wasn't sure how to do all those things at the same time, but he knew what *not* to do. Keeping his emotions in check wasn't the answer. He'd learned the lesson playing the dream game.

"Help me, Lord," he murmured. "I want to be well again. I want—" He felt like Dora asking for a cookie or Freddie dreaming of becoming a scientist. Like his children, Tristan had visions for a future that seemed beyond his grasp, but just as *he* was capable of giving Dora a cookie and paying for university for Freddie, his heavenly Father had the ability to handle the problems beyond Tristan's control. With a hopeful heart, he prayed. "Father God, I want Caroline and the children to be happy and safe. I want to love them as a husband and father."

It had been more than a week since he'd had a bout of fever. The daily quinine was helping. Tonight he felt good. He felt strong…and he very much wanted to be the husband Caroline deserved. Only he didn't have that right. Until he could be sure of his health—at least *more* sure— he had to convince her of his loyalty without overstepping the lines they'd drawn. He'd start by telling her about his past with Louisa.

He ambled down the path to the garden, deliberately kicking a pebble so she'd hear him and wouldn't startle. Deep in thought, she still didn't notice him. When he was five feet away, he spoke in a hush. "Caroline?"

Gasping, she faced him. "Tristan!"

"I've been looking all over for you." He didn't mean to scold her, but he was disappointed that she'd been avoiding him.

"I'm sorry," she said. "I—I needed air.

"So did I."

He saw no reason for small talk. "I'd like to tell you about Louisa."

"You don't owe me an explanation," she said hurriedly. "In fact, I've been thinking. There's something I need to say."

A gentleman acquiesced to a lady. Caroline had endured

a difficult day and deserved to vent her spleen. "I'm listening."

"Today was...challenging."

"Very."

She ambled down the row, looking at the sky as she gathered her thoughts. He wouldn't rush her. After an evening with his father, she could take all the time she needed. He stayed at her side as she walked, her skirt brushing the ridges of empty earth. With her face tilted up to the stars, she finally spoke. "I'm wondering if perhaps we were too hasty to get married."

He'd been expecting her to complain. Instead she'd taken the duke's insults to heart. "What are you saying?"

"You don't need me, Tristan. I saw how you looked at Louisa—"

"Caroline, stop." He clasped her arm. "It's true that Louisa and I were once in love. She jilted me for Andrew and I still don't know why. I stopped loving her years ago. There's nothing between us."

"But there could be," she murmured.

"I'm not married to Louisa," he said with authority. "I'm married to *you*."

"Not really."

"We took vows," he reminded her.

"Yes, but it's the physical union that truly binds a man and woman. As long as we haven't consummated the marriage, you're free to obtain an annulment. Perhaps we should consider it."

He didn't want to consider an annulment. He wanted to be a healthy man with a future. But he wasn't. "Is that what you want? To end our marriage now?"

She didn't answer, leaving him to weigh the events of the day. His father had harassed and belittled her. She'd also come face-to-face with a woman from his past. Even sick with the chicken pox, Louisa was English and aristocratic, kind, educated and poised. She'd been born and bred to be a duchess, whereas Caroline's talents went in other directions. He could understand why she felt dispirited, and he wished he had the words to soothe her anxieties.

Finally she spoke to the sky. "Your father is a cruel man, but that doesn't mean he isn't right about certain things."

"Such as?"

"I'm not fit to be your wife."

"That's utter nonsense. My father's impossible. You shouldn't listen to him."

They were near the end of the row. The branches of a tree cast a tangled shadow and she stopped. "Your father spoke the truth tonight. I'm not schooled in English ways. Like he said, I'm a lowly American. You could do better."

"I think not."

She looked into his eyes. "Please don't patronize me, Tristan. You hired me to be a governess, not your wife. You come from a world I don't understand. Someday you'll be the Duke of Willoughby—"

"If I live."

"You will," she said with confidence. "Every day you're stronger. Earlier I saw you with a man down by the barn—"

"That was Pennwright," he interrupted. "My father's secretary."

"You were at ease."

"Yes. He's an old friend."

She took a breath. "So is Louisa. Don't you think you should give your feelings a chance?"

"No!"

He didn't know what to make of her willingness to step

aside. She loved his children, yet she was willing to sacrifice herself for the happiness of others. The offer struck him as generous, noble...and pathetic. He wanted her to fight for what she wanted, not give it up in a misguided act of martyrdom. He understood why she'd be reluctant to be a duchess, but did the gesture mean she didn't have feelings for him? There was a sure way to find the truth. If he kissed her as sincerely as he wanted, he'd know her heart. But they'd also set foot on a rickety bridge to the future, one missing planks and strung with old rope. With his health precarious, he had no business leading her into that kind of danger. At the same time, he had to convince her of his loyalty.

"I want to tell you more about Louisa," he said. "Let's go inside."

"You don't have to explain—"

"Caroline." He clasped her biceps. "I *want* to explain, though I'm not sure I can. I was twenty. She was seventeen. We'd spoken of marriage and had an understanding. Out of the blue, she became engaged to Andrew."

"I'm sorry."

"I tried to speak to her, but her family sent her away. To this day I don't know if I somehow failed her or if she failed me."

Caroline touched his cheek. "That must have been devastating."

"It was, but it happened a long time ago. I haven't thought of Louisa in years. I'd like to know why she married Andrew, but I'm very aware that I'm married to you. You need to know that I honor my commitments, especially when they pertain to marriage."

They were back where they'd started, leaving Caroline with the same question. Just how much of a commitment had Tristan made to her? She couldn't help but wonder if his feelings for Louisa were as dead as he indicated. She didn't expect them to pick up where they left off. Fifteen years was a long time, but she could imagine them falling in love all over again.

She'd experienced Louisa's graciousness for herself. Before supper she'd checked to see how the woman was doing. At least a hundred more pustules had erupted, including one on the tip of her nose. Louisa had joked about having polka dots and had entertained them by making funny faces. Not only did Caroline like the woman, she admired her. Louisa was Tristan's equal, his mirror image with feminine beauty in the place of male strength.

It hurt to face facts, but Caroline refused to deny the obvious. She was second-best. They both knew it. She turned to Tristan. "Louisa admires you greatly."

"And I admire her," he said with British aplomb.

"You were good friends. You could be friends again, even more than friends. Don't you think you should give those feelings a chance?"

He waited so long to answer that she knew she'd asked a hard question. "That's what I thought," she said. "You need time."

"I certainly do *not!* I know my own mind, and I don't love Louisa." He looked into her eyes. "Time is the one thing I may not have."

He meant the malaria. "You're much improved. Bessie's optimistic that you'll make a full recovery."

"I hope she's right."

"So do I." Watching him in the moonlight, she saw a hesitation that matched her own. "You could be missing something wonderful because you're afraid. Give Louisa a chance. Be brave."

It hurt to speak the truth, but she refused to look away.

She had loved Charles and seen him murdered, but she cherished their time together. She'd lost her mother as a child and her father to a heart ailment, but she had an abundance of happy memories. During the war, she'd seen women bury sons, brothers and husbands. Life was precarious for everyone. Love had to be cherished.

Hoping to share her courage, she smiled at Tristan. "I'm right, you know."

"Yes," he agreed. "But not about Louisa."

"About what then?"

"About us…"

In his eyes she saw the desire for a kiss. He cupped her jaw with his palm, his thumb brushing her cheek with a tenderness that could have been given to a child…or a wife. She stayed as still as the fallow ground, waiting, wondering, hoping…until footsteps on the path to the house caused them both to pull back.

Get 2 Books FREE!

Love Inspired® Books,
a leading publisher of inspirational romance fiction, **presents**

Love Inspired **HISTORICAL**

A series of historical love stories that will lift your spirits and warm your soul!

FREE BOOKS! Use the reply card inside to get two free books by outstanding inspirational historical romance authors!

FREE GIFTS! You'll also get two exciting surprise gifts, absolutely free!

GET 2 BOOKS

IF YOU ENJOY A HISTORICAL ROMANCE STORY that reflects solid, traditional values, then you'll like *Love Inspired® Historical* novels. These are engaging tales filled with romance, adventure and faith set in various historical periods from biblical times to World War II.

We'd like to send you two *Love Inspired Historical* novels absolutely free. Accepting them puts you under no obligation to purchase any more books.

HOW TO GET YOUR
2 FREE BOOKS AND 2 FREE GIFTS

1. Return the reply card today, and we'll send you two *Love Inspired Historical* novels, absolutely free! We'll even pay the postage!

2. Accepting free books places you under no obligation to buy anything, ever. The two books have combined cover prices of $11.50 in the U.S. and $13.50 in Canada, but they're yours to keep, free!

3. We hope that after receiving your free books you'll want to remain a subscriber, but the choice is yours—to continue or cancel, any time at all!

EXTRA BONUS
You'll also get two free mystery gifts!
(worth about $10)

FREE!

▲ If offer card is missing, write to: The Reader Service, P.O. Box 1867, Buffalo, NY 14240-1867 or visit: www.ReaderService.com ▲

BUSINESS REPLY MAIL
FIRST-CLASS MAIL   PERMIT NO. 717   BUFFALO, NY

POSTAGE WILL BE PAID BY ADDRESSEE

THE READER SERVICE
PO BOX 1867
BUFFALO NY 14240-9952

NO POSTAGE
NECESSARY
IF MAILED
IN THE
UNITED STATES

Chapter Thirteen

Tristan pulled Caroline under the cottonwood at the end of the garden. The shadows hid them from view, but he could hear the whisper of her breath in the darkness. Had his father stepped outside for a late-night cigar? Tristan had no desire to deal with the duke. He'd been about to kiss Caroline and he resented the intrusion.

Drawing her close, he heard the drone of conversation. He recognized Jon's voice and relaxed. He couldn't make out the words, but Jon sounded buoyant. When Bessie's laughter drifted in their direction, Tristan knew his friend was up to his charming ways. Looking over his shoulder, he saw the couple heading for a stone bench at the other end of the garden.

Caroline whispered, "We should make our presence known."

"Or we should leave," he said quietly.

They turned together, bumping arms as he gripped her hand. They'd taken a single step when a feminine gasp caught Caroline's attention and she stopped. When she turned to look at the couple, so did Tristan. Jon was kissing Bessie, and he wasn't being shy about it. Neither was Bessie reserved in her response.

Caroline pressed her hand to her mouth. Her fingers tightened in his and she started to shake with a suppressed giggle. Tristan had to clench his jaw to keep from letting out a laugh of his own, a reaction that would put an ignoble end to a kiss that was getting longer…and longer… and longer. He needed air. So did Caroline. Gripping her hand, he led her to the path and they hurried to the house while Bessie and Jon were lost in the kiss.

Tristan guided Caroline to the veranda where they gasped for air, laughing until she slumped against him. They were closer than they'd ever been. Closer than when she'd ridden with him on Cairo… Closer than when she'd stitched his head and he'd kissed her cheek.

Until now he'd held back because of the malaria, but tonight it seemed right to match his mouth to hers and that's what he did. The kiss was tender but wise, a mix of questions and promises that tasted sweeter with each passing moment. He imagined a future bright with love, a house full of children and a porch with rocking chairs where they'd grow old together.

The thought stopped him cold. He felt better than he'd felt in weeks, but the malaria still lurked in his blood. Kissing Caroline was a promise of sorts, one he feared he couldn't keep. Suddenly tense, he stepped back. "Go upstairs."

She put her hand on his chest. "Are—are you coming with me?"

Neither of them was ready to go beyond a kiss, but they both understood the potential. He shook his head. "I'm staying here."

"Then I'll stay, too."

"No, don't."

"But—"

"Please, Caroline. Just go."

She stepped back, her head down and shoulders hunched. He knew she felt rejected, even inadequate. Sending her away after a kiss was a terrible thing to do, but allowing their feelings to grow before he could be sure of his health could cause the worst pain imaginable.

"It wasn't the kiss," he said without touching her. "It's—" He didn't know what *it* was. He only knew he'd gone too far too soon. For Caroline's sake, he had to win the war raging in his blood before he gave in to the feelings he could no longer deny. He loved her, and he wanted their marriage to be far more than adequate. He wanted it to be…spectacular.

Caroline fled through the house to her room. She lit the lamp and turned it low, but even the soft light was harsh after kissing Tristan in the dark. Blinking, she saw the open doors between her room and his and closed them. Even if he knocked, she wouldn't answer. She'd been wounded tonight, like a bird that had flown bravely from a cage only to smack into a window. Beyond the glass she'd seen a glorious future. She'd dared to believe Tristan had feelings for her. She'd been sure of it when he kissed her…then he'd set her aside.

She no longer thought he still loved Louisa, but something was keeping them apart. Either he doubted her ability to be a duchess, or he expected to die from the malaria and didn't want her to grieve. With either choice, the facts stood. He'd kissed her and rejected her. The kiss had been soft and tender and so sweet she'd believed they were falling in love. But then he'd pulled back. Dropping down on the rocker, she looked at the ring on her finger. The diamond sparkled with a pinkish glow, but it didn't belong to her, not really. She'd always be second-best to women like Louisa.

Fighting tears, she pressed her palms to her cheeks. "Not again, Lord," she whispered.

How much rejection could a woman take? Tonight she and Tristan had crossed a line. She couldn't imagine going back to being his friend, a wife in name only, when she'd experienced his kiss. She needed to ask God to guide her, but the prayer choked her. She'd never felt so unwanted and unworthy in her entire life. He denied feelings for Louisa, but what man wouldn't be attracted to a woman of Louisa's perfection?

A knock on the hall door startled her. Rather than come through the storage room, it seemed Tristan had put more distance between them by approaching from the hall. "Go away," she said in a low voice.

"It's me," Bessie whispered. "I have to talk to you."

Caroline had no desire to speak with anyone, especially not her sister who'd just been thoroughly kissed. She couldn't bear to think of the excitement in Bessie's tone, but they were sisters. "Come in," she said, rising to her feet.

Bessie slipped inside, her face flushed and her eyes bright. "I hope I didn't wake you, but if I don't talk to someone I'll go crazy."

Caroline reached around her and closed the door. "I think I know why."

"How—"

"I saw you with Jon."

Bessie pressed her hands to her face. "This is awful!"

"Why?" Caroline would have given a year of her life to have Bessie's problem.

"I'm too old to feel this way!"

"No, you're not." Her sister was forty-one. "Who says you have to be young to be in love?"

"I do."

Caroline laughed, but it hurt. "I imagine Jon disagrees."

"He's impossible!" Bessie closed her eyes. "But the way he kissed me... Oh, my!"

Caroline laughed again. It hurt even more than the first time, but she was happy for her sister. She only wished Tristan hadn't held back. She couldn't allow herself to love him, not when he didn't love her back. But it was impossible not to dream of a future with him. With the malaria, Louisa and his obligations in England, their situation was complicated. Bessie had no such impediments. There wasn't a reason in the world she and Jon couldn't fall in love, except for Bessie's silly notion that she was too old.

"I'm happy for you," Caroline said simply.

"Happy?" Bessie plopped down on the rocker. "How can you be happy? I'm *terrified!*"

Caroline laughed. "Trust me, sister. That terror turns into something good. I've been in love before. You haven't."

Gripping the arms of the chair, Bessie pushed off. The rockers creaked like a runaway wagon. "I'm too old for this silliness."

Caroline sat on the bed across from her. "That's a lame excuse and you know it. How old is Jon?"

"He's a year older than I am."

"Do you think *he's* old?"

"No."

"Then neither are you." For once Caroline had more experience than her older, wiser sister. "Trust me, Bessie. You won't regret taking a chance with Jon. Even if you get hurt, it's worth the risk."

Bessie inhaled deeply. "That's good advice. I hope you take it for yourself."

"What do you mean?"

"I've seen how the major looks at you. I understand the

limitations of the marriage, but anyone can see he has feelings for you."

Caroline didn't want Bessie to see the defeat in her eyes, so she turned her attention to the window. She thought of that uncaged bird hitting the glass. Beyond it lay everything the bird wanted, but it had no way of escape. "If Tristan has feelings for me, he regrets it."

"What do you mean?"

"He kissed me tonight—"

"Oh!" Bessie declared. "Then I'm right."

"No, you're wrong. He sent me away without a word of explanation." In quiet tones, she told her sister about Tristan's past with Louisa. "Either he's afraid of the malaria, or he's confused about Louisa. I don't think he still loves her, but I think he *could* love her again. She'd be a far better duchess than I'd be."

"That's rubbish!"

"It's true." Caroline stood and went to the window. It overlooked the garden. The moon was higher now, visible but too small to cast any meaningful light. The cottonwood had lost its leaves a week ago, and now the branches were empty and fragile. She touched the glass.

Bessie stood and came to stand beside her. "If I didn't know what you'd been through with Charles, I'd call you a coward."

Caroline's fingers curled on the cold glass. She considered herself brave when necessary, but some fights were lost before they started.

Bessie kept her voice low. "I don't blame you for giving up on Tristan. You're right about Louisa. Even with the chicken pox, she's the picture of grace. She's smart and pretty. I'm sure the kids will love her. Why, she's just plain old perfect. No wonder Tristan had feelings for her. You know, she—"

"Stop!"

"I was about to say that she reminds me of someone."

"Who?"

"You." The women turned at the same time. They were eye to eye, but what caught Caroline's attention was the mirror on the wall behind her sister. It reflected Caroline's pale face and Bessie's hair, mussed from Jon's touch. Fear and risk collided on the silver glass. The uncaged bird refused to be fooled again.

"I'm not that strong," Caroline said firmly.

"I think you are." Bessie lowered her hands. "For someone who just gave me a lecture on courage, you're acting like a mouse."

"I'm being cautious."

Considering her first marriage, she had to weigh the costs. When she'd married Charles, she'd claimed to be brave enough for anything, and they'd both suffered. She didn't want to go down that road again, but neither could she imagine *not* going down it. Hope and fear went hand in hand. She wanted to choose hope, but her insides were shaking.

Mustering her faith, she smiled at Bessie. "You're right. I'm being timid. I don't really know what Tristan's thinking, and I'm not sure he even knows."

"He probably doesn't," Bessie went back to the rocking chair. "He's recovering from malaria, but it's a long road. As for Louisa, I don't believe for a minute he's still in love with her."

"Maybe not," Caroline agreed. "But he could fall for her again, I'm sure of it. Even *I* like her."

"I do, too," Bessie admitted. "You two don't have to be rivals, but you *do* have to fight for Tristan."

"How?"

Bessie's eyes took on a silvery glint. "You have to prove

to yourself that you can be the wife he needs, and you have to be willing to go to England. He's already teaching you what you need to know. The problem is that you don't believe you can do it."

"I know I can't," she insisted. "I like being ordinary, and I can't stop being an American."

"That's true," Bessie acknowledged. "But you're also a woman of faith. You dared to love Charles against the odds—"

"And look what happened."

Bessie's eyes shimmered. "You just told me love is worth the risk. Is it?"

"Yes, but—" Caroline bit her lip. "What if I embarrass Tristan? He can do better than me. Look at Louisa—"

"I'm looking at *you,* and I'm seeing a woman who needs to fight for the man she loves. We've both trusted God through good times and bad. We're scared right now, but don't you think God knows what's happening?"

"Yes, but—"

"You're still afraid."

"Yes! I'm terrified," she admitted. "You make my situation sound simple, but it's not."

"I think it is," Bessie countered. "God put Esther into the king's court for 'a time such as this.' He brought you to Wyoming for a purpose, and He brought me. I have to believe He'll give us both the strength we need to live in a way that honors Him."

Caroline had said similar things to Tristan when she'd urged him to be brave. The thought of being his duchess completely unnerved her, but she had the faith to take the first step of the future God had planned just for her.

"What should I do?" she said to Bessie.

Her sister smiled. "I think you should learn to ride a horse."

"A *horse!*"

Bessie chuckled. "Why not? Tristan would love to share that part of his life with you."

"That's true," she admitted. "But I'm terrified—"

"Which scares you more? Learning to ride or losing Tristan forever?"

She whispered, "Losing Tristan."

"That's your answer," Bessie said quietly. "It's my answer, too. Not only did Jon kiss me, he asked me to marry him."

"He did!"

Bessie's cheeks turned bright pink. "I didn't give him an answer, but I will tomorrow. And it's going to be yes."

"Are you sure?" Caroline asked. "You haven't known him long."

"We've waited our entire lives for each other. We're too old to waste another minute. What do you think of a June wedding? Perhaps Adie and Pearl and Mary could come?"

"That would be wonderful." Caroline hugged Bessie tight. She couldn't have been happier for her sister, but she had to admit to a bittersweet moment. With Bessie's engagement, Caroline would soon be the only woman from Swan's Nest who wasn't happily married. A marriage in name only was no marriage at all. But she didn't have to settle for so much less than what God intended marriage to be. If Tristan had feelings for her, she could learn to be a duchess. She could be brave and get on a horse.

Releasing Bessie, she shared a smile with her sister. "I'm happy for you. Jon's a lucky man."

"So is Tristan," Bessie said quietly. "But you need to—"

"Fight for him," Caroline finished.

"Yes."

She managed a tiny smile. "Do you think he'd give me riding lessons?"

Her sister smiled. "I'm sure of it."

They talked about a wedding dress for Bessie and a riding outfit for Caroline. When the clock chimed midnight, they hugged and said goodnight. Tomorrow she'd ask Evaline to help her sew a riding habit. The outfit would take time to complete, but she didn't mind the wait. She'd be praying for courage. More than anything, she wanted to prove to herself and Tristan that she could be the wife he needed.

Chapter Fourteen

❦

Kissing Caroline changed everything for Tristan. By mutual agreement, she'd stopped coming to his room for duchess lessons. He missed her, but he couldn't continue the charade of a loveless marriage until he came up with a plan. He'd withdrawn from the war zone in order to size up the enemy. The war wasn't with Caroline or himself. It was with the malaria. After four days apart from her, he decided on a strategy. If he could go a full month without a fever, starting now, he'd court his wife properly. If the kiss they shared was an indication, and he believed it was, her feelings were as strong as his. He had to get well. It was that simple.

He also had to convince her that she'd make an excellent duchess. They wouldn't return to England immediately, maybe not for years, but someday he'd take the mantle of authority and he wanted her at his side. His father felt otherwise, and he'd made his objections clear.

He'd also continued to show a keen interest in Freddie, and the boy had eaten up the attention. Tristan understood all too well. Pampered poodles did tricks for treats, and the duke was doling out praise with a heavy hand.

Tristan wanted his father to return to England, but he

couldn't broach the subject as long as Louisa was ill. According to Bessie, Louisa had the worst case of chicken pox the nurse had ever seen. Louisa had conveyed through Bessie that she wasn't ready for visitors, but she hoped to speak with Tristan as soon as she recovered. Considering he'd lived with the mystery of their parting for fifteen years, he didn't mind the delay.

He was far more concerned about Caroline, who was looking at him from across the breakfast table with a pensive expression. She had finished her meal except for her coffee, which he now knew she drank with one heaping spoonful of sugar. After lowering the cup, she put her napkin on the table but didn't excuse herself, a sign the wall between them was about to come down.

He set down his cup of tea and waited.

Caroline put her hands in her lap.

He smiled.

She smiled back. "I have a favor to ask."

"Of course," he answered. "What can I do for you?"

"I want to learn to ride."

He couldn't have been more surprised if she'd announced she could fly. "You do?"

"Yes." She sat straighter. "Evaline finished my riding habit last night. We can start today if you're free."

"I'm free, but—" He felt like he had water in his ears. "Why are you doing this? You don't like horses."

"You do."

"Yes, but there's no need for you to trouble yourself."

She looked deflated, but then she bucked up. "If you don't want to teach me, I could ask Jon—"

"No," he said quickly. "I'm just surprised."

"In a bad way?"

"Not at all." He was surprised in a good way…a very good way. Since he'd started counting the days without a fever, he'd marked four days off the calendar. He had moments of feeling poorly, but he hadn't been pasted to his bed like a corpse. He'd gone even longer if he counted back to the trip from the river, but on his mental calendar he had twenty-six days before he could open the doors between their rooms.

Teaching Caroline to ride gave him a welcome excuse to be with her. "I assume you'll want to ride sidesaddle?"

"Actually, no."

She stood and he saw her riding costume, a tailored jacket with a split skirt. The garment was unusual, and he wondered how she'd come up with it. It would preserve her modesty but he knew how his father would react. He'd call her a hoyden. Tristan thought she looked both lovely and practical. For a rancher's wife, riding astride made perfect sense and he'd have suggested it himself. She could have worn a pair of his trousers for all he cared about propriety, but he worried that his father would mock her without mercy.

"A split skirt is…unusual," he said.

"Evaline made it for me." Looking at him, she held out the sides. "You don't approve?"

"Quite the contrary." He skimmed her with his eyes. "It's very practical."

It was pretty, too. The fawn color contrasted with her dark hair and made her eyes light brown. He also saw the stubborn tilt of her chin and recalled taking her across the river. He wanted to make the lessons a resounding success, and he had an idea. He rose to his feet. "Shall we meet at the barn in an hour or so?"

"That would be fine."

He dismissed her with a nod. "I'll see you there."

As she left the room, he watched the sway of her skirt. He didn't know what the future held, but he planned to enjoy every minute of the morning. He admired Caroline's courage. He also knew that making her comfortable around animals in general would go a long way to making the lessons a success. He left the table and headed for the front door.

As he reached for the knob, his father stepped into the house. "I'm here for Louisa."

Tristan had heard from Evaline that she'd recovered enough for an outing. "Where are you going?"

"I thought we'd see some of this land of yours. Pennwright tells me it's quite impressive."

Tristan knew better than to trust the duke's praise, but for a moment he was a boy again, hungry for his father's attention. Wiser now, he addressed his father as a man. "If you'd like a guide, I'll ask Jon to show you around."

"I was hoping you'd accompany us."

"I have a prior commitment."

"I see." The duke looked speculative. "I suppose a guide won't be necessary. It'll be a short ride."

Tristan's neck hairs prickled the way they did before cannon fire. He had the feeling he was missing something, but a direct challenge to the duke would only lead to subterfuge. If he hadn't made plans with Caroline, he'd have gone with his father to keep an eye on him.

The rustle of skirts drew his gaze to the stairs. "Good morning!" Louisa said brightly.

With a sweep of his eyes, Tristan took in her royal-blue skirt and jacket, a lace jabot and a black top hat with a swathe of tulle to hide her face, no doubt still bearing marks of her illness. It was a tribute to her poise—and perhaps her need to get out of the house—that she'd decided to go for a ride in spite of her imperfect complexion.

"Good morning," Tristan answered. "You're looking well."

"I feel wonderful." She beamed a smile at him. "I was hoping to run into you this morning."

The duke reached for the doorknob. "Don't let me interrupt, my dear. I'll meet you on the porch."

The duke was never considerate. He'd left them alone for a reason, and Tristan feared he knew what it was. The duke wanted Louisa to tempt him so he'd return immediately to England. The ploy wouldn't work, but he welcomed the chance to speak with her.

Graciously she tipped her head to the duke. "Thank you, your grace. This won't take long."

"Take all the time you need, Marchioness." The duke used the title naturally, though Louisa was officially a dowager and the title belonged to Caroline. His departure left Tristan alone with Louisa for the first time in years.

She lowered her voice. "Could we speak in your study?"

"Certainly." He indicated the hall, waited for her to pass and then followed her to his office. When she stepped inside, he indicated the divan. Instead of sitting, she shut the door he'd intentionally left open. He, too, wanted privacy but not at the risk of provoking curiosity or worry for Caroline. There was no reason to think she'd come looking for him, but he couldn't ignore the possibility.

"I'd prefer to keep the door open," he said quietly. Already the meeting felt clandestine.

"I don't trust the duke," she whispered. "His valet could be lurking."

Tristan had to agree. Leaving the door shut, he stood directly in front of it. He'd open in it in a heartbeat if anyone approached, especially if he recognized the tap of Caroline's boots. Being alone with Louisa was a potential insult to his wife, and he didn't want to hurt her feelings.

Instead of sitting, Louisa stayed on her feet. With her chin high, she lifted the veil from her face so that he could see her eyes along with polka dots left by the fading chicken pox. She held her chin high. "For fifteen years I've prayed that you'd forgive me for what I did."

"I have," he answered. "Though I have to admit, I'm not sure what I'm forgiving."

"Oh, Tristan—" Her voice broke.

He'd once loved this woman. He still did—but only as a sister. Protective instincts compelled him to comfort her, but he stayed by the door. Until he could be sure she wasn't being used by the duke, he'd keep a firm and polite distance. "You left me for Andrew."

"I had no choice."

Caroline had used the same words about crossing the river. "There's always a choice, Louisa. And there's always a cost. I bear you no ill will, but I'd like to know why you did it."

"You know my father gambled."

"Yes." So did the duke, the difference being the duke could afford to lose and Louisa's father couldn't.

Louisa steadied herself with a breath. "My father ran up a terrible debt. Your father offered to cover it, but only if I married Andrew."

"Why would he do that?"

Louisa bit her lip. "I'm ashamed to tell you."

She turned and went to the window, giving Tristan a moment to consider the facts he'd evaluated a hundred times before. He'd been in love with Louisa, but she hadn't been highly sought after. Her father had a lesser title than the duke, and her family was known to be in debt. Her one asset was her beauty. If she and Andrew had produced children, they would have been lovely to behold. And that, Tristan realized, was why his father had essentially bought Louisa for Andrew. She'd been no better than broodmare.

He felt sick for her. "My father gave you to Andrew because you're beautiful."

"Yes."

"But you had no children."

Louisa turned abruptly to the window. "I didn't know about Andrew until our wedding night."

"Know what?"

She continued to speak to the window. "Andrew preferred the company of his male friends in London. He was a homosexual."

"I see." Tristan had heard rumors about his brother, but he'd written them off as gossip.

Louisa still had her back to him. "That's why we failed to produce an heir. He had no interest in me."

"He had no interest in *women*," Tristan corrected. "That's why my father forced the marriage. Andrew needed a push, and you were the perfect pawn."

At last Tristan understood why she left him. If she'd refused to marry Andrew, the duke would have ruined her father and her two sisters would have suffered. The conversation answered one question but raised two others. Had the duke deliberately picked Louisa because he knew Tristan would be hurt? Not likely, Tristan decided. The duke hadn't cared about him at all.

The second worry had burdened him for fifteen years. "I should have found a way to speak with you. I should have helped you—"

"Oh, Tristan..." She turned away from the window but didn't approach him. "There was nothing you could have done to stop your father. We were young. Even if I'd come to you, we couldn't have run away. I had a duty to protect my family, especially my sisters."

"You paid a high price."

"Yes, but I'm done paying my father's debt. Your father

brought me on this trip as your reward for returning to England. Your American wife disrupted that plan, but he has another one and it's despicable. I will tell you now that I will do *nothing* to come between you and Caroline. I've hurt you enough already."

"It's over and done," he replied. "I married Molly and had a wonderful time of it."

"I'm glad."

So was Tristan. "You've had a far harder life, I'm afraid."

"Yes, but I'm done being used. The duke instructed me to break up your marriage, but I won't do it."

She couldn't have done it even if she tried. His feelings for Caroline grew with each passing day. If the malaria stayed away as he hoped, he'd be free to tell her he loved her.

Louisa's expression turned wistful. "Please don't misunderstand, Tristan. It's not that I don't care for you. If you'd been free to marry, I'd have been glad to test the waters. But you're not free. You're married to a charming woman who loves you very much." She lifted one brow. "And If I'm not mistaken, you're being neglectful."

"What do you mean?"

"Husbands and wives often choose to maintain separate bedrooms, but a wife rarely chooses to sleep in a tiny little room that's clearly meant to be a nursery."

"How do you know it's a nursery?" he said, scowling. "Is it?"

He said nothing, which told Louisa everything.

"That's what I thought," she said cheekily. "I caught a glimpse of the tiny space when your housekeeper left the door open while cleaning. Something's amiss. I don't know why you're not showing your wife proper attention, but it's plain you're keeping her at arm's length. I've been watching her, Tristan. She cares for you, and I believe you care for her. What's wrong?"

Old friend or not, Louisa didn't have the right to such an intimate observation. "My marriage is none of your business."

"Yes, but I consider Caroline a friend, and I know how it feels to be a neglected wife. Don't make that mistake."

He didn't want to neglect Caroline at all. He wanted to spend the rest of his life with her, but he had to be sure he had a future. "I have my reasons."

"Whatever they are, you're hurting Caroline."

Tristan said nothing. If he told Louisa about his illness, she might accidentally reveal the information to the duke. "Thank you for your concern, Louisa. The circumstances are complicated."

"As are mine," she said. "Which leads to the other reason I wanted to speak with you in private. I need your help."

"In what way?"

"I need a husband." She gave him a winsome smile. "Since you're not available, I'm considering Stuart Whitmore. Do you know him?"

"I do." Whitmore owned a ranch thirty miles from The Barracks. Like Tristan, he was the youngest son of a duke. Unlike Tristan, he had a reputation as a rake. Rumor had it his father had banished him to America.

"He's an interesting fellow," Tristan acknowledged. "A bit of a scoundrel, but he's done well for himself."

"He's also in need of a wife." She lifted one brow. "We met in Cheyenne. I thought perhaps you could hold a house party and invite him?"

Tristan had failed to rescue Louisa once before. He saw a chance to help her now, but he had to consider the cost. A gathering meant having his father stay longer at The Barracks, and it would require Caroline to test her mettle as a hostess. If the party failed, he might lose her completely. But if it succeeded—and he was sure it would—she'd gain some of the confidence she needed to be a duchess. Battles weren't won by being timid. "That's a grand idea," he said. "I'd like to get to know Whitmore better myself."

"Excellent!" She smiled. "He has family visiting from England. We can invite them all."

Tristan nodded in agreement, but his protective instincts began a backbeat of caution. Whitmore's father was Darryl Whitmore, the Duke of Somerville. He was known to be an impressive man, and the Duchess of Somerville could be as haughty as Tristan's father. Entertaining Whitmore and some Americans would have presented a challenge to Caroline. Providing entertainment for English nobility was far more daunting.

"Who exactly is visiting?" he asked.

Her eyes sparkled. "The Duke of Somerville passed away two years ago. The dowager doesn't care for her daughter-in-law, so she decided to visit her youngest son in America. She's traveling with her two nieces."

"The dowager is quite formidable," Tristan acknowledged.

"She is," Louisa agreed. "I'll need your help to impress her."

"We'll also need male guests for the two nieces."

"I'm sure Mr. Whitmore has friends."

"No doubt," Tristan agreed. "I'll speak to Caroline later today. In fact, I'll suggest she invite friends of her own."

Before he'd ended their late-night talks, she'd told him about her friends in Denver and a place called Swan's Nest. He knew that Adelaide Clarke had married a Boston preacher named Joshua Blue, and Mary Larue had recently married a famous gunslinger. Even Tristan had heard of

J. T. Quinn. She'd also visited Pearl and Matt Wiley in Cheyenne before arriving at The Barracks. Not only did Tristan want to meet the people Caroline loved, he also saw an opportunity to finish what they'd started at the courthouse in Wheeler Springs. If he stayed healthy, they could repeat their wedding vows in front of people she loved, with Reverend Blue presiding.

Louisa's eyes twinkled with hope that had nothing to do with him. "I know Stuart's a rake, but he quite charmed me in Cheyenne. Your father disliked him intensely."

Tristan laughed. "All the more reason to invite him to a party."

"I'm afraid the dowager might be difficult," she said apologetically. "She's quite willing to speak her mind."

Tristan thought of Caroline. He could teach her etiquette and history, but she'd need more than knowledge to contend with a cranky dowager. She'd need confidence with a touch of audacity and a sprinkling of wit. He'd help her as much as he could, but the battle would be hers. He considered begging off the house party, but he saw a benefit to Caroline facing the dowager in their own home surrounded by friends.

Louisa interrupted his thoughts. "I should be leaving for that ride with your father. I detest the man, but I'm pitifully dependent at the moment."

"Not for long, I hope."

He opened the door and guided her into the hall. She paused to adjust the veil on her hat, then she tugged on the black gloves she'd had in her pocket. As he crossed the threshold, he saw Caroline in the entry hall. Her back was to them and she was opening the door. Had she come to his study first? Had she heard them talking? Tristan refused to allow even the faintest stain on his loyalty to her.

"Caroline!" he called in a loud voice.

She faced him with an eager expression. At the sight of Louisa, her eyes widened with surprise then narrowed with dismay.

"Hello," she murmured to them both. "Louisa, you're looking well."

"Thank you." She went to Caroline and gripped her hands. "You have a wonderful husband, Caroline. Treasure him."

She gave a last look to Tristan, one he knew was a goodbye, then she left him alone with his wife.

Caroline watched Louisa slip through the door in a cloud of royal-blue linen. As the door creaked shut, she turned back to Tristan and saw both a challenge and an admission in his eyes. He'd been alone with Louisa in his study. She'd expected the old friends to have conversations, but the moment had a secretive air. She felt excluded and forgotten.

Turning back to him, she forced a smile. "I'm sorry to interrupt."

Tristan strode across the entry hall and took her hands in both of his. "You didn't interrupt a thing."

"But—"

He looked as if he wanted to kiss her. Instead he gave her a stern look and let go of her fingers. When he stepped back, she felt utterly foolish for imagining a kiss and averted her gaze to the floor. She saw boot prints, wondered who'd left them and wished she'd left the house five minutes sooner.

Tristan cleared his throat. "Louisa has asked us for a favor."

Caroline lifted her face, but she still felt foolish. "What is it?"

"She'd like us to hold a house party." Tristan described

how Louisa had met Stuart Whitmore and explained about the man's family. The thought of entertaining a dowager duchess nearly sent Caroline running to her room. She'd mustered her courage to learn to ride. Having a house full of women as poised as Louisa was more than she could imagine.

"I'm not ready for that much company," she said to Tristan. "I'll embarrass you."

"That's not possible."

She managed to laugh. "I think it is."

Both commanding and imperial, he held her in place with a piercing blue gaze. The air smelled of his shaving soap, and his freshly scraped jaw remind her of a marble bench in the garden at Swan's Nest. She'd often sat there to pray, smelling roses and dust and wishing for a man like Tristan to love her. Upstairs she heard Evaline speaking to Dora. Footsteps charged down the hall and she looked up. The little girl was nowhere in sight, but Caroline felt all the ties of being a family. If she wanted to keep her adopted family, she had to fight for them. She had to prove her abilities to herself and a house full of English nobles.

"All right," she said. "We'll give that party."

"Very good." He sounded like an officer praising a private who'd managed to properly shine his shoes. "Louisa can help you with the invitation for the Whitmores. She knows their names and titles. I thought you'd also like to invite your friends from Denver."

Caroline very much wanted to see Adie, Mary and Pearl, but they didn't know she'd gotten married and she didn't want to explain the circumstances. Neither were her friends accustomed to the ways of people like the Duke of Willoughby. "It would be awkward."

"Nonsense." Tristan frowned. "They're your friends and they're welcome here. Invite them."

"I'd rather not."

A peeved expression crossed his face. She'd disregarded his request, something a good soldier didn't do, but she couldn't face her friends. They'd want to hear about the courtship that hadn't happened and the marriage that existed solely for legal reasons. Just as problematic, they'd come if she asked and the trip to The Barracks was long and difficult. Pearl was expecting a baby in a couple of months. Just before Caroline left Denver, Mary had whispered that her monthly was two weeks late.

She could see Tristan's dissatisfaction, but she wouldn't change her mind. Instead she changed the subject. "When should we send the invitations?"

"Immediately," he answered. "We've had excellent weather, but it won't last. I'll have the invitations hand delivered to the Whitmores. I imagine the guests will stay a week. We'll need entertainment...music and games, maybe charades. And for course, there will be riding for everyone."

"Riding?" she said meekly.

"Absolutely. Nothing strenuous for the women, just an easy tour of the ranch. For the men, we'll have a hunt, perhaps jousting."

"Jousting!"

"Only for the men," he said, laughing. She loved the sound of it, but she had more doubts than ever that she could be the wife he needed. He gave her another stern look. "Let's begin those riding lessons."

"Yes," she murmured.

Mustering her courage, she walked with Tristan out the door and to the stable where a very large and intimidating horse awaited her, a fitting reminder of the challenges to come.

Chapter Fifteen

They walked side by side to the barn, with Tristan talking about the house party and Caroline wondering if he'd lost his mind. The more he said, the more worried she became. She had no idea how to entertain in the fashion he seemed to expect. He assured her Evaline and Noah would see to the accommodations and food, but as Tristan's wife, she'd be accountable.

So far Evaline had yet to serve a meal that didn't give the duke a bad case of indigestion. With an additional six people visiting—Whitmore, the dowager duchess, the two nieces and two gentlemen who had yet to be determined—Caroline would have her hands full. The women would bring lady's maids, and Whitmore and the gentlemen would possibly have valets. Caroline counted bedrooms and decided to ask Evaline and Sophie Howe, the foreman's wife who helped with cleaning, to prepare every available bed. The servants would have to double up, but she didn't think they'd mind.

Suddenly nervous, she glanced at Tristan's profile. His blond hair was combed back into a peak, and his skin had a healthy glow. Dressed in a blue chambray shirt, dark trousers and shiny black boots that came to his knees, he had the air of the nobleman he was. No one would ever guess he had a potentially fatal disease, but it could still be in his blood. A new worry twisted through her mind. If he became ill during the party, it would be impossible to hide.

"I'm worried," she said suddenly.

"About what?"

"If you become ill while we have guests, what will happen?"

His jaw stiffened. "I don't plan on becoming ill."

She wanted to press for an answer but didn't. No man liked being reminded of weakness, and Tristan especially disliked it.

He gave her a friendly smile. "I'd much rather focus on your riding lessons."

Caroline would have preferred playing dolls with Dora or even catching frogs with Freddie, but she put on a brave face. When they reached the barn, Tristan indicated the door to the tack room. He guided her inside, then shut it behind them. Without the sunlight, the room turned into a palette of grays and browns. They were standing so close she could smell his shaving soap over the scent of hay. She'd been prepared to walk into the barn where she'd see Cairo and Grandma. She didn't know what to think when he crouched down and reached into a wooden box.

"What's going on?" she asked.

"I have a surprise for you."

She couldn't imagine what it would be. "I'm not fond of surprises."

"You'll like this one." Standing tall, he held a ball of butterscotch fur against his chest.

"It's a kitten!" she declared.

"Take it." He turned to give her room to lift it. As she grasped the tiny creature, her fingertips grazed the cotton of Tristan's shirt and she looked up. He seemed not to react to her touch, but he inhaled softly as he slid the kitten into her palms. Snuggling the cat against her chest, she looked down at its face. The tiny thing had a black dot of a nose, pale green eyes and a tail that swished with feline nonchalance. She guessed it to be six or seven weeks old and eager to get on with life. She also discerned the cat to be female. "She's adorable."

"She's yours."

"Really?"

"We can use a mouser in the house." His lips quirked. "But mostly she'll be a pet. Dora loves kittens."

"So do I." Caroline lifted the tiny thing and rubbed noses with it, then she looked at Tristan. "I thought I was here for a riding lesson."

"You are." He took back the kitten. "In fact, you've just had the first one."

"I have?"

"I've discovered you like animals...and animals like you." He scratched the kitten's tiny head with his index finger. When it stretched, Caroline thought of a flower opening in the sun. "Let's call her Daisy."

"Whatever you'd like."

He put Daisy back in the box with her mother and siblings. "We'll leave her here until you go back to the house. It's time for the second lesson."

He opened the door into the barn, indicating she should lead the way. Breathing deep, she followed him into the cavernous space. The smells took her back to Wheeler Springs and the carriage house where she'd agreed to become his wife for the sake of the children. She'd been accepting of the limitations and she still was, but today she felt longings she couldn't deny. She cared about Tristan for a hundred different reasons.

He loved his children.

He was respected by his friends.

He was loyal, kind and courageous. How could she not have feelings for this man who'd been so understanding of her fears? Just as he'd probably hoped, the kitten had given her a bit of confidence. Feeling brave, she walked with him to the center of the barn. A horse stomped its foot. Another chuffed so loudly she jumped. Instinctively she reached for Tristan's hand.

He clasped her fingers and smiled. "This way," he said, indicating a stall at the end of the barn. She glimpsed a carved sign above the door. Instead of letters, she saw strange shapes. Pointing to it, she asked, "What does that mean?"

"It spells 'Cairo' in Arabic."

She stopped in her tracks. "I can't ride Cairo. He's too big. He's—"

"You're not riding Cairo," he said gently. "I am. But there's someone else for you to meet."

She dug in her heels. "I thought I'd be riding Grandma. Bessie says she's gentle."

"She is." His eyes twinkled. "We'll get to Grandma."

"But—"

He stopped in the aisle and faced her. "Trust me, Caroline." He took her other hand, again stroking her knuckles with his thumbs.

She'd become accustomed to the caress. It calmed her... It pleased her. Finally she nodded. "All right."

He led her to the stall at a leisurely pace. The top half of the gate was open, and she expected Cairo to stick out his giant head and look down at her. The horse didn't appear. Feeling brave, she let Tristan tug her close enough to peer over the half door. Instead of the fearsome stallion, she saw another animal altogether. "That's a goat!"

"Her name is Hannah." Tristan sounded pleased. "She's Cairo's best friend."

"My father kept a nanny goat in Charleston. It was my job to milk it." She looked up at Tristan and smiled. "Goats have a bad reputation, but they're rather sweet if they know who's in charge."

He opened the door to the stall. "Go on in."

She went up to Hannah, who gave her a friendly push with her head and bleated at her. Laughing softly, Caroline rubbed the goat's ears as she looked over her shoulder at Tristan. "Hannah's sweet. Why is she with Cairo?"

"Goats have a way of calming skittish horses."

"And skittish women?"

"I hope so," he replied. "Is it working?"

"I believe it is."

"She helped Cairo quite a bit," Tristan explained. "He didn't take kindly to being shipped across the Atlantic and again from the West Indies to here. Hannah keeps him company. I thought you'd enjoy getting to know her."

"I am," she admitted. "I'm having a good time."

Sunlight glinted through the window at the top of the stall, turning Tristan's straw-colored hair into shining white. Once pale, his cheeks were brown with the sun and his eyes were the brightest blue she'd ever seen. If she'd been seeing him for the first time, she'd have never guessed he'd been ill. Any doubts she had about learning to ride vanished at the sight of this brave man who'd fought for his country, his health and his family. If he could face an uncertain future, she could learn to ride.

She looked into his eyes. "I'm ready for the third lesson."

"Good." As he gave Hannah a last pat, Caroline stepped out of the stall. Tristan closed the gate, then led her to the stall directly across from the one holding the goat. She looked over the gate, saw a pony and laughed. "Now that's a horse I could ride!"

"This is Biscuit.

He was light brown with a whitish mane and tail. "Because of his coloring?" she asked.

"I suppose. Dora named him."

"Does she ride him?"

"Yes, she does. Quite well as a matter of fact." A father's pride rang in his voice. "Let's give him some carrots."

Tristan fetched the treats from a crate. He showed her how to feed the pony by gripping the carrot and then flattening her hand to avoid a mishap involving teeth and fingers. Biscuit took the carrot from his hand and chewed happily. When he finished, Tristan handed her a carrot. "You do it."

Caroline followed his example, laughing as Biscuit's lips tickled her palm. When the pony pulled back his head to chew, she looked up and saw Tristan leaning on a post, watching her with frank appreciation. He looked both pleased and proud, and she blushed. "You've been wonderful, Tristan. I thought today would be hard, but you've made it delightful."

"Do you feel ready for Grandma?"

"I do."

"She's saddled and waiting in the corral." He held out his arm. Taking his elbow, she fell into step at his side. Together they passed the stalls, most of them holding horses that even she could see had excellent bloodlines. Tristan ran a cattle ranch, but he had the heart of a horseman. It was easy to imagine his horses being prized as the finest mounts in America.

She looked at him and smiled. "Your Arabians are beautiful."

"I think so," he said without modesty. "I had plans for breeding them, but—" He shook his head, unwilling to go down a road that led to uncertainty.

She tightened her grip on his bent elbow. "Bessie says you're doing well. You haven't had a fever in days."

"That's no guarantee that it's gone."

She expected him to pull away, but he drew her closer as they walked through the barn, their paces matching until they reached the door. Breaking away from her, he lifted a wide-brimmed hat from a nail and pulled it low. Side by side, they stepped into the yard where sunlight fell from the sky, warming the day with the start of an Indian summer. As relaxed as a cat, he led her to the corral where Bert Howe was holding Grandma. Next to the horse she saw a mounting block. She thought of how Tristan had pulled her onto Cairo and how she'd held his waist.

Today she'd be alone. Shivering with nerves, she told herself to be brave.

"You'll do fine," Tristan said with assurance.

He stopped her at the gate to the corral. In short sentences, he gave her basic instructions for mounting, holding the reins and positioning her feet. The next thing Caroline knew, she was sitting astride Grandma, clutching the saddle horn and feeling wobbly.

Tristan adjusted her stirrups. "Think of Grandma as a rocking chair with legs."

"She's a very *high* rocking chair!" Caroline almost hiccupped. "*And* she has a mind of her own."

"Move with her and you'll be fine," he said calmly. "Now take the reins and hold them like I showed you."

She did as he said, but her stomach felt queasy.

Satisfied with her posture, he swung up on Cairo with a grace she envied. Sitting next to him, she felt awkward and stiff.

"Are you ready?" he asked.

"I am."

When he instructed her to lift the reins, she obeyed. So did Grandma, and they took off at a leisurely walk. It was more than leisurely, Caroline decided. It was so slow she felt silly. Tristan didn't seem to mind, but Cairo chuffed in irritation until his master spoke to him. Riding along the fence, Tristan spoke to Caroline in the easy tone he'd used on Cairo. They talked about nothing in a way that relaxed her. As if it were just part of the conversation about the weather, Tristan told her how to urge Grandma into a faster walk. The mare perked up and so did Caroline.

For the next half hour they stopped and started, walking slow and then fast. Tristan gave instructions, and she gave the commands to Grandma. When she noticed him admiring her, she beamed a smile. "You're a good teacher."

"You're an excellent student."

"Could we go faster?"

"We can," he said, hesitating. "But trotting is quite different from walking. I suggest we do it tomorrow."

"I can handle it," she said, feeling confident.

"Very well." He told her how to work her knees to do something called posting, and to expect some bouncing until she found the rhythm, then he backed Cairo away from her. "Watch me."

He urged the stallion into a trot. Man and horse looked like a single creature, moving in perfect time. He made riding look easy and her confidence rose another notch. When Grandma shifted her weight, Caroline felt the roll in her back and swayed easily. The horse really did feel like a rocking chair.

Tristan rode up next to her. "You've done well today. Are you sure you're ready for more?"

"I'm positive."

Following his instructions, she put Grandma into a trot. To her horror, the comfortable rocking chair turned into a bone-jarring, teeth-rattling monster of a horse.

"You're doing fine," Tristan called from atop Cairo. "Use your legs."

"I-I-I'm t-t-trying!"

"You'll get it."

She straightened her spine and attempted to use her legs the way he'd instructed, but she was still bouncing like a ball on a string. Gritting her teeth, she focused straight ahead.

Tristan stayed beside her. "That's enough for today. Rein in Grandma."

Relieved to have the lesson over, she slowed the horse to a walk. Her legs ached so badly she wondered if she could stand, but she was smiling with pride as Grandma followed Cairo to the gate. Tristan climbed down from the stallion with a natural grace.

She expected him to help her off Grandma, but he was staring at something in the distance. She followed his gaze and saw the duke, Louisa and Freddie riding toward them, each one sitting tall and looking at ease, especially Louisa. Perched on a sidesaddle, she was the picture of grace. She was exactly the kind of woman Tristan deserved, and she had his full attention.

With her head high, Caroline prayed the house party would be a success. If she failed Tristan, she'd insist on the annulment. She'd lose everything and everyone she'd come to love, but she couldn't imagine a life of daily failure. The children, especially Freddie, would suffer because of her. In a way she'd already lost Bessie. With her engagement, her sister would stay with Jon.

With all the courage she could muster, Caroline squared

her shoulders as Louisa, the duke and Freddie reined their mounts to a halt at the fence.

Louisa smiled back with warmth.

The duke ignored her.

Freddie stared at her with such dislike she felt a chill. Something had happened with the duke. She felt sure of it and braced herself for an unpleasant situation.

Chapter Sixteen

"We have company," Caroline said in a high voice.

Tristan immediately sensed her nerves. "Yes, we do."

He had noticed Louisa first. It was impossible *not* to see that bright-blue riding habit, but it was Freddie who had his attention now. The boy usually wore dungarees like the cowhands. Today he was sporting black pants and a miniature frock coat, most likely stitched by the duke's valet. He'd also chosen an English saddle and was sitting ramrod straight, a living picture of the boy Tristan had once been.

Tristan shifted his gaze to his father. He and Freddie were wearing the same haughty expression. The roots of the family tree ran deep, feeding even the youngest, most tender branches. Looking at the two of them, Tristan made a silent vow. Where the duke had sowed tyranny, Tristan would plant a desire to serve others. Where his father had been severe, he'd be gentle. And where the duke condemned others for no reason, Tristan intended to plant seeds of love for God, family and country.

Looking at Freddie, he realized that coping with malaria had changed him. In his weakness, Tristan had been reduced to a child again, and this time he'd felt a Father's love in the concern of his friends, his children and especially Caroline. In some ways he'd been as petulant as Freddie, issuing orders that no one followed, and yet no one had stopped caring for him. It seemed to Tristan that God had a very difficult job. Not only did his children need love, they needed to be protected from themselves and others.

Right now, Freddie needed to be protected from the duke. No matter how much the boy balked, Tristan could not allow him to mimic his grandfather's arrogance. If Freddie spoke rudely to Caroline, Tristan would correct him immediately.

Louisa spoke first. "What a lovely ride we had! Tristan, your ranch is spectacular."

"I'm glad you enjoyed the ride," he said mildly.

"Yes," Caroline echoed.

The duke pretended to stifle a yawn.

So did Freddie.

Tristan's hackles rose, but he wouldn't go to war over a yawn. Louisa lifted the veil from her hat, giving him a clear view of her eyes. "I've had a lovely day, but I'm quite tired. If you gentlemen will excuse me, I'll return to the house."

"Of course," Tristan replied. "Freddie will see to your horse."

The boy huffed. Freddie never huffed. He occasionally whined, but he didn't put on airs. Today he had the nerve to look down his nose at Tristan, then he said, "Don't we have *servants* for that, Father?"

Tristan said nothing for a full ten seconds. The pause was to give Freddie the opportunity to obey on his own and save his pride. When the boy huffed again, Tristan spoke with deceptive mildness. "At The Barracks, a man tends to his own horse. He also tends to a lady's horse without being asked."

Still Freddie didn't move.

Tristan's voice dropped lower. "And when I give an order, it's followed. You'll take care of all three horses, or you'll be confined to your room for three days."

"But *Father*—"

The duke interrupted. "Come now, Tristan. My time with the boy is limited, and we're quite ready for lunch. Perhaps Jon—"

"No." Tristan clipped the word. Next to him Grandma bobbed her head, a reminder that Caroline was silently observing the exchange. He wondered what she was thinking, but he didn't want to trade a look in front of Freddie. Louisa watched him with sympathy, as if she understood too well how it felt to be undercut by the duke. The next move was Freddie's.

The boy stayed in the saddle, unaware that he'd become a rope in a game of tug-of-war. Tristan watched as Freddie feigned disinterest. Silently he willed his son to slip from the saddle and do as he'd been told. Instead Freddie locked eyes on Caroline. "You're riding like a man," he said with disgust.

Tristan erupted. "Freddie! That's enough."

Caroline wisely stayed calm. "Yes, I am. It's quite practical."

Louisa broke in. "Caroline, you'll have to share the pattern for your split skirt. Don't tell anyone, but I, too, ride astride on occasion. It's far more practical for jumping."

The duke laughed out loud. "Jumping! She can barely stay on that nag of a mare."

"That's uncalled for, your grace." Tristan kept his tone civil but just barely. Caroline deserved respect, and Grandma was far from a nag.

"It's true," Freddie said pompously. "We saw her trying to trot. Grandfather said she looked like a broken doll."

"Freddie!" Tristan's voice boomed. "Apologize this instant."

"Why should I?" the boy whined. "She was supposed to be the *governess,* not my mother. If she wasn't here, you'd take us to England. We could live in Grandfather's house and we'd have—

"That's enough," Tristan said. "It's also a lie."

Caroline stayed quiet. It wasn't her place to defend their marriage. It was his. "Caroline is my wife. For that alone, I insist on respect."

"Grandfather says she's common." The boy sounded smug.

"Your grandfather's opinion is both unwanted and incorrect." Tristan was speaking to Freddie, but he directed his gaze to the duke. He wanted to order the man to leave The Barracks immediately, but he'd promised to help Louisa. Seething inside, he aimed his gaze at his son and spoke with deadly calm. "Frederick Willoughby Smith, you will apologize *this instant* or face punishment."

"Tristan—" Caroline spoke so softly he barely heard her. "Perhaps Freddie and I should speak in private."

"No."

"But perhaps—"

"Caroline!" He regretted snapping at her, but he couldn't allow his authority to be questioned in front of his son…or his father. "I'll discipline my son, thank you very much."

"Of course." She sounded compliant, but he heard the tremor in her voice. Should he have said *our* son? That claim would have fueled Freddie's resentment, however, and it went against the honesty Caroline herself advocated. Whether the quaver in her voice had come from anger or hurt, he didn't know. Later he'd apologize for snapping, but first he had to finish with Freddie.

He stared at the boy until he saw the start of a crack in his resolve. Just when he thought Freddie would give in, the duke let out a petulant sigh. "I've had enough of this silliness, Tristan. It's time you—"

"Gentlemen!" Louisa raised her voice. "Perhaps you can agree to disagree."

Tristan said nothing.

The duke snorted but didn't argue.

"Good." Louisa turned to Freddie. "I'm feeling quite tired. If you'd tend to my horse, I'd be most grateful."

Freddie looked positively smitten. "I'd be honored, Aunt Louisa."

On the surface the situation had calmed, but Tristan felt a riptide of disrespect pulling them into deeper waters. Freddie had been invited to address Caroline as "Aunt" several days ago, and he hadn't used the endearment. Louisa had defused a tense situation, but she'd badly upstaged Caroline. To add to his wife's sense of inferiority, Louisa performed a gracious dismount while Caroline sat perched on Grandma. Freddie and the duke climbed off their horses. With Tristan already on the ground, Caroline alone was on her horse. She'd have to dismount with an audience.

Hoping to give her dignity, he explained the situation to the three onlookers. "This is Caroline's first time alone on a horse."

"How wonderful!" Louisa exclaimed.

The duke wore a smirk. "We saw *that* from afar."

Caroline looked at the duke, then at Louisa and finally at Tristan. He gave her careful instructions for the easiest dismount, which unfortunately was inelegant. "Remove both feet from the stirrups," he said. "Then lean forward and swing your right leg over Grandma's rump."

With a surprising grace, she swung her leg over the horse and slid to the ground. She did just fine until her feet hit the dirt and her knees buckled. In a tangle of stockings and split skirts she fell against him. He circled her waist with his arm. If they'd been alone, he'd have enjoyed holding her close. They'd have laughed about the stumble and he'd have praised her courage. With Louisa and his father watching, the moment was simply embarrassing.

When she wobbled, he wondered if she'd twisted her ankle. "Are you hurt?"

"Only my pride." And her confidence, he feared.

She steadied herself then looked defiantly at the duke. Louisa had stepped to the fence and was standing with her gloved hands laced on the top rail. "You did wonderfully, Marchioness."

She'd used the title to show respect. Tristan appreciated the gesture, but he feared Caroline would feel mocked. He arched a brow at Louisa. "We're informal at The Barracks."

"Of course," she said. "Forgive me."

Caroline had regained composure. "There's nothing to forgive. I hope you enjoyed your ride."

"Very much," Louisa said quickly. "The land is—"

The duke intruded. "*I* found the landscape rather tedious. England is much greener, and we don't have this miserably hot weather in October."

"Wyoming and England are lovely in their own ways," Louisa said diplomatically. "I understand you call this time of year an Indian summer?"

"Yes," Caroline said to Louisa. "Tristan tells me we're hosting a house party in a few weeks. The warmer weather will be ideal."

Louisa smiled her gratitude. "I'm quite excited. I hope you and Tristan will take the opportunity to celebrate your marriage."

Caroline shook her head. "There's no need—"

"Oh, but there is." Louisa gave Tristan a meaningful look, one meant to remind him of his obligation as a husband. She meant well, but Caroline could easily misinterpret Louisa's look as a shared secret, which it wasn't. When Tristan didn't speak up, Louisa continued to make her point. "You've been married such a short time. A celebration is in order…a grand one, I think."

The duke harrumphed. "That's hardly necessary."

His implication was clear. He didn't think the marriage warranted public acknowledgment, and he wanted to snub Caroline. This was no time to be timid. Tristan spoke with complete calm. "Not only is it necessary, your grace, it will be an honor to introduce my new wife to a family as distinguished as the Whitmores."

He put his arm around her waist, felt the tension in every muscle and knew she'd have preferred riding Cairo to facing a house full of English nobles.

Caroline tried to appear nonchalant, even haughty, but her voice betrayed her nerves. "I hope you all enjoy the visit with the Whitmores."

"I'm sure we will," Louisa said gently. "Thank you, Caroline."

"It's our pleasure," she said evenly.

Tristan loved Caroline and he wanted her to succeed. A public acknowledgment of their marriage would make a quiet annulment impossible, but he didn't care. He had no intention of annulling the marriage or allowing Caroline to fail so badly that she'd insist on it.

He looked into her eyes. "The party is going to be a resounding success. I'm sure of it."

When she lifted her chin, he saw the woman who'd pulled a gun on him in the canyon. She'd been shaking inside, but she hadn't showed her anxiety. He sensed the same reluctant determination now, and he knew without a doubt his American bride had the courage to be a duchess…only she didn't know it.

Tristan did some mental calculations and decided to hold the party in three weeks. With a little luck, the good weather would hold. They had to move fast, so Tristan started giving orders.

"Caroline will write the invitations. I'll see that they're delivered to the Whitmores by one of my men.

She looked pale but nodded.

"Louisa, if you'd help with the entertainment, I'd be obliged."

"Of course." Her cheeks turned rosy. "Do you have a piano?"

"No, but we have some talented musicians in the bunkhouse. I'll arrange for music." He'd heard impromptu concerts. The men were enthusiastic if not classically trained, and he rather liked the idea of the duke having to cope with a fiddle-playing cowboy and zealous banjo player. Bert Howe played the guitar and he did it well. Tristan thought of whirling Caroline around the room in a waltz. By the end of the house party, he'd know if he'd beaten the malaria. He could ask her to dance without guilt or fear. In the middle of a waltz he could kiss her and confess that he loved her.

"We'll have dancing," he said firmly.

Caroline inhaled sharply but said nothing.

Tristan looked at his father. Considering how he'd mocked Caroline, he deserved a comeuppance and Tristan knew how to give one. No one gave the duke orders, but

Tristan had no reluctance. "Your grace, you'll be in charge of the hunt for the men."

The duke looked peeved, then sly. "Perhaps another form of entertainment is in order... Something the ladies would enjoy."

"Such as?" Tristan asked.

"An American horse race." He looked pointedly at Caroline. "Your wife can show off her new skills."

Tristan clenched his jaw. His father was cleverly setting a trap. "I don't think that's a good idea."

"Why not?" The man's eyes were marble-hard. "Louisa would enjoy it, and I believe the Whitmore nieces are quite skilled. Your wife is learning, isn't she?"

"Yes, but—"

Caroline interrupted. "A race is a fine idea, your grace. My skills aren't up to such a test, but our guests will enjoy it."

The duke gave her a pitying glance. "For once, the marchioness and I agree. She's not up to a ride."

Despite the veneer of agreement, his words were meant to demean. Louisa gave Caroline a sympathetic look. The duke gloated. To Tristan's pride, Caroline kept her chin up as she answered him. "I'm looking forward to entertaining your friends, your grace. I hope they enjoy themselves."

"So do I," he said in a deadly tone. "The Dowager Duchess of Somerville is an impressive woman and an old friend. I don't want her inconvenienced."

"Of course," Caroline agreed.

Tristan vaguely remembered the dowager as a woman with thin platinum hair, a taste for emeralds and an acerbic sense of humor. As an ally, she was superb. As an enemy, she was lethal. For Caroline, the house party would be ripe with opportunities for both triumph and humiliation.

The duke excused himself with a curt nod. Louisa

smiled sympathetically then followed him, leaving Tristan alone with his wife and the painful awareness that she'd just been thrown to a pack of aristocratic wolves. His father was the alpha male, the leader who'd run her off if she couldn't compete. If Louisa rode in his silly race, Caroline would be forced to ride, as well. Her riding lessons, it seemed, were just getting started.

Caroline had had her fill of riding lessons, Louisa's perfection and Tristan's insistence that she could be someone she wasn't. She had no desire to celebrate their nonexistent marriage, especially not in Louisa's shadow. The woman couldn't have looked more elegant in her riding costume. Even with the marks on her face, she was lovely. Her beauty came from the inside, along with the poise of a woman born to nobility...a woman who could ride sidesaddle without the slightest wobble.

In her split skirt, now dusty and wrinkled, Caroline felt like a gawky schoolgirl. Only a bit of pique had enabled her to stand up to the duke. Tired and saddle-sore, she wanted to go to her room. Recalling Tristan's lecture to Freddie about caring for his horse, she turned to him. "Do I need to tend to Grandma?"

"Not today." His eyes were gentle on her face, but she felt as if he were scouring her for a likeness to Louisa.

With a nod, she left him with Grandma and Cairo and turned to the gate. Tristan clasped her arm and she turned. "What is it?"

"That race," he said quietly. "My father's going to torment you with it."

"I expect so."

"I could insist on a traditional hunt. He'll still make remarks, but you wouldn't have to resist as strongly."

Was he making the offer to protect her? Or was he

afraid she'd embarrass herself and him? If Louisa and the duke wanted to showcase Caroline's inadequacies, he'd found the perfect stage for an inept performance. She couldn't ride, and she didn't know very much about fine clothing or art and the symphony. Her favorite meal was chicken and dumplings, not pheasant. She liked to bake pies and eat supper as a family. She also had her pride, and she'd come to love this man who couldn't stop being an English noble anymore than she could stop being average.

"You don't have to protect me," she said quietly.

"I do. It's my duty."

Feeling clumsier than ever, she started to walk away. He called after her, "Another riding lesson tomorrow?"

She'd never be an accomplished rider, but she wanted to be adequate. She faced him. "That would be fine."

He dismissed her with a nod, but she saw pride in his eyes. She also saw hesitation. Was he worried she'd embarrass him? Or was he afraid for his health? She wanted to ask him, but she had worries of her own. If she failed to hold her own with the Whitmores, she'd ask for the annulment to protect them both.

Sick with dread, she entered the tack room and fetched Daisy. With the kitten against her chest, she walked to the house with thoughts of Hannah, Biscuit and the way she'd stumbled into Tristan's arms. Her legs ached, and her ears echoed with insults from Freddie and the duke. Cuddling Daisy, she circled to the back of the house to the veranda. She wanted to take refuge in her room, but Dora saw her and came running.

"Aunt Caroline!" she cried. "Let's play the dream game!"

She couldn't bear the thought of repeating the game, not with her own dreams dying, but she neither could disappoint Dora. Crouching down, she cradled Daisy in her hands. "Look what I have."

"A kitten!"

"She's going to live in the house."

Dora stroked the tiny feline while it meowed. After a time Caroline shifted Daisy to the crook of her elbow and stood. Gripping Dora's hand, she walked with her to the divan and pulled her into her lap. They played with Daisy until Dora remembered her original request. "I want to play the dream game."

Fortified, Caroline stroked the child's hair. "Do you still want to be a princess?"

When she shook her head no, Caroline knew something was wrong. She raised Dora's chin with her fingertip. "You look sad. What's the matter?"

"Freddie says we're going away."

Caroline could imagine the dreams the duke had planted in the boy's mind. "Where did he say you were going?"

"To England with Grandfather." She flung herself against Caroline's chest. "I don't want to go to England. I want to stay here with you and Biscuit…and my kitten."

Caroline held back a frown. What kind of person manipulated children? Until now she'd held the small hope that Tristan and his father would reconcile. He hadn't asked for her opinion, but she would have counseled him to be respectful in the spirit of "honor thy mother and father" and to pray for the ability to forgive the man who'd hurt him. She believed in those principles, but respect and forgiveness didn't require Tristan to put his children in the hands of a selfish manipulator.

She held Dora close. "Your daddy won't let anyone take you away."

Her lip quivered. "Is he still sick?"

"Yes, but he's getting better."

Dora snuggled closer. "I don't like Grandfather, but Aunt Louisa is nice. We played dolls last night."

Was there *anyone* who didn't think Louisa was perfect? Caroline couldn't possibly compete with her.

Dora snuggled closer, petting the kitten as she looked up at Caroline. "I like Aunt Louisa, but she talks funny."

"She's from England. I like how she sounds."

"I like how *you* sound." Dora's eyes blurred with angry tears. "I don't want two aunts. I want you to be my mama."

Caroline had no business encouraging such a deep attachment until she could be sure of the future, but how could she deny Dora this simple request? She couldn't. "I'd like that very much."

"Mama." She spoke firmly, as if stamping the word on her heart. She said it again, stamping it on Caroline's.

"I love you, Dora."

"I love you, too."

The child snuggled in her arms. Daisy was wedged between them, a ball of soft fur while Caroline's nerves twitched with worry. She had deep feelings for Tristan. She loved her borrowed children and didn't want to lose them, but neither did she want Tristan to look at her as second-best. With Dora's love fresh in her heart, she had more reason than ever to overcome her fear.

Silently she prayed. *Help me, Lord... I don't want to hurt this little girl, but I'm not capable of being a duchess.*

No comfort came in the silence, only a sure and quiet stretching of her faith. God had so loved the world that He'd given his only Son for the benefit of all mankind. When a father loved his children, he sacrificed for them. When a man loved a woman, he fought for her. And when a woman loved a man, she waged the same battle.

With her eyes shut tight, she thought of Tristan's arm

around her waist. She remembered the kiss in the garden and the look in his eyes when he handed her the kitten. She also heard the bitterness in his tone when he mentioned his illness and saw his pride when she'd done well on Grandma. Every instinct told her his feelings were as deep as hers, which left a single solution to her dilemma. She had to make the house party a resounding success.

Chapter Seventeen

The next three weeks passed in a blur of riding lessons, menu planning and visits from the Wheeler Springs dressmaker. To her surprise, Caroline enjoyed the riding lessons in particular. With Tristan's help, she learned to post with some gracefulness, and she enjoyed galloping Grandma around a grassy meadow. She had no fear of the gray mare at all, and she'd made friends with Cairo thanks to dozens of peppermints.

The riding lessons gave her a pleasant break from the house party preparations. If it weren't for Louisa, Caroline would have been overwhelmed. She hardly knew where to start, but Louisa had planned far more elaborate occasions and was taking delight in having a purpose and a protégée. She gladly schooled Caroline in titles and etiquette, laughing when Caroline professed utter confusion. She'd also insisted that Caroline have a completely new wardrobe. Her lady's maid had provided patterns for the latest fashions, and the two women had spent hours selecting fabrics and styles.

With the Whitmores scheduled to arrive any minute, Caroline took a last look at herself in the mirror, then breathed a prayer of thanks for Louisa. The hours together had made them confidantes who were rooting for each other. If Louisa didn't win Stuart Whitmore's heart, she'd be a worthless member of the duke's household, a hanger-on unless she returned to her family, an option that would render her dependent on the good graces of a penny-pinching brother-in-law. Even more important, Louisa had been taken with Whitmore's charm and physicality. Having been trapped in a loveless marriage, she wanted a husband as full of daring as she was.

Caroline hoped her friend would be successful. Any minute Stuart Whitmore would arrive with his mother, her nieces and two English gentlemen. As hostess, Caroline was wearing the fanciest day dress she'd ever had. It was fit for a duchess, but it made her feel like someone she wasn't. She touched the curls piled on her head. Louisa's maid had done her hair in a style that was elaborate, to say the least.

"Mrs. Caroline?"

She turned to the open nursery door and saw Evaline. The housekeeper looked stately in her new uniform, a black dress with a crisp white apron.

"Yes?" Caroline replied.

"The first guests have arrived."

"Thank you, Evaline."

Caroline went down the stairs with a stomach full of butterflies, silently rehearsing the formal greetings she'd practiced with Louisa. The dowager duchess was a stickler for such things. Praying she wouldn't make a fool of herself, she stood aside as Noah opened the door.

Instead of the dowager, she saw Adie Blue. Behind Adie she saw Josh holding the hand of their toddler son. Caroline burst into tears. Just seeing the Blues would have been a joy, but Mary and Jonah "J.T." Quinn walked in behind them. Most surprising of all, she saw Pearl heavy with child. Her husband, Matt, was holding their son on one hip while guiding their six-year-old daughter with his other hand. When Bessie walked into the fray from the hall, the flock from Swan's Nest was complete.

Behind them all, Caroline saw Tristan watching the reunion with a smile. He'd done this to surprise her, and she was grateful.

"How did you get here?" she said to Adie between tears. "How did you know—"

"Your *husband* sent invitations," Adie said pointedly.

Caroline hadn't told them about her marriage. Now she wondered how much they knew and felt nervous.

Bessie touched her arm. "Tristan asked for my help. I wrote the letters and Jon delivered them."

"And it's a good thing!" Always bold, Mary pulled her into a hug. "How dare you get married without us!"

"It's not— It's—" She bit her lip. "It's not that simple."

"We want to hear all about it," Pearl declared. "I say we crowd in your bedroom and you tell us everything. It'll be just like Swan's Nest."

Maybe, but her bedroom would reveal more than she wanted. Bessie interrupted, "Come to my room. I have news, too…something I didn't put in the letter."

Adie, Pearl and Mary waited expectantly, but Bessie had the patience of Job. "Let's get you settled, then we'll visit."

Caroline turned to Evaline. "You knew they were coming, didn't you?"

"Yes, ma'am." The housekeeper beamed. "The major asked me to prepare the third floor. It'll be a bit crowded up there, but we'll manage." With the arrangements they'd made for the Whitmore contingent, the house would be overflowing.

In a flurry of skirts, the women went upstairs with Evaline leading the way and Caroline bringing up the rear. She wanted a word with Tristan, but he'd been joined by Jon and was speaking with the men. She'd have to thank him later.

It didn't take long for the friends to settle into their rooms. In less than an hour, the five women were together in Bessie's room with Pearl on the bed propped on pillows, Adie and Mary in side chairs, Bessie perched next to Pearl and Caroline at the foot of the bed in the rocker she'd carried from the nursery.

"I want to hear everything," Adie insisted. "Why didn't you write to us that you'd gotten married?"

"Because it's a marriage in name only," Caroline said quietly.

Mary raised a brow. "That's not what it seems like to me. He went to a lot of trouble to send for us, and he did it for you."

Pearl nodded in agreement. "I was worried because of the baby, but he offered to pay for a doctor to accompany us. I told him no." She rested her hand on her belly. "The baby's not due for two months, but he offered because he cares about you."

"It's complicated," Caroline said.

Adie's gaze traveled from her face to her coiffed hair to the dress trimmed with more ribbon then she'd owned in her entire life. "You're dressed like a queen. What aren't you telling us?"

Caroline hesitated. "I'm not a queen, but in a strange way, I could someday be a—" She couldn't say *duchess* because she didn't believe it.

Bessie stepped in. "Caroline's trying to tell you that she's the future Duchess of Willoughby. Tristan is more than a retired army officer. He's the third son of a duke. When his brothers died, he unexpectedly became his father's heir. The house party is Caroline's chance to prove she's worthy of such a position."

"Of course she's worthy!" Mary declared.

"I know that." Bessie smiled. "So does Tristan. The person who doesn't believe it is Caroline."

Pearl gave her a sympathetic look. "It's a big step, isn't it?"

"It's huge," Caroline acknowledged. "And I'm so...ordinary."

"You're far from ordinary." Adie spoke with confidence. "You're the woman God made you to be. This gathering is going to be huge success. Not only do you have your husband pulling for you, you have all of us."

"That's right," Pearl agreed. "But you have to stay brave."

Coming from Pearl, the words had authority. The blonde had been the victim of a violent crime and had overcome her fears to find love. The baby in her belly was a testament to sorrow enduring for a night and joy coming in the morning.

Caroline looked next at Mary. She'd lived with a terrible secret. In his mercy, God had turned her shame into redemption for a hardened gunslinger. Caroline thought of the news Mary had whispered when they'd said goodbye. She raised her eyebrows with the question. "Are you—?"

"Yes." Her smile lit up the room. "Jonah's been wonderful. He's running the café so I can rest. The smell of bacon—" Mary winced. "Just thinking about it makes me sick!"

"Me, too," Pearl offered.

The women all looked at Bessie. Adie spoke for them all. "Tell us your news."

The oldest of the women, Bessie never expected to marry. She loved being a nurse and considered it her calling. She looked from friend to friend, her cheeks growing pinker by the moment. "I met a man," she finally said. "His name is Jon."

Pearl spoke up. "He delivered the invitations. I like him."

"So do Josh and I," Adie replied.

Mary chimed in. "He and Jonah traded stories for half the night. He served in the British Army, didn't he?"

Bessie blushed harder. "He was a captain."

Caroline prodded her. "And?"

Suddenly shy, Bessie looked more like a girl than a middle-aged woman. "He asked me to marry him."

The women leaned forward, holding their breath for Bessie's answer until she smiled. "I said yes."

Hugs and questions abounded. Bessie and Jon had planned to have a spring wedding, but when the questions were over, Bessie agreed to ask Jon about moving the wedding up to the end of the house party so that her friends could attend and Josh could perform the ceremony.

"Oh!" Pearl cupped her tummy with both hands. "The baby kicked."

Adie put her hand on Pearl's belly. So did Mary and Bessie. They were all close enough to touch without standing. Caroline felt a million miles away until Pearl met her gaze. "Come here and feel the baby."

Rising to her feet, Caroline rested her hand on Pearl's tummy. The baby rolled under her touch, filling her with an old longing to bear a child of her own. She blinked and thought of the dream game. This dream could come true, but only if Tristan overcame his fear of dying and she proved herself worthy of being a duchess.

She closed her eyes. *Please, God. Keep him healthy and help me succeed.*

When the baby settled, the women broke apart and talk

turned to plans for the house party and the other guests. No further mention was made of Caroline's troubled marriage, but she knew the women of Swan's Nest would be praying for her.

Tristan didn't like being surprised, but he greatly enjoyed surprising Caroline with the arrival of her friends. The entire day had been one victory after another. The Whitmores had arrived two hours later, and she'd welcomed them graciously. The evening meal—home-style American food—had been flawlessly prepared, and Caroline had made the dessert herself. Predictably, his father had complained about the raspberry pies, but the Whitmore crowd had been polite. Even the dowager duchess, a woman known for her sharp tongue and atrocious wigs, had refrained from comment.

Tristan had been proud of his wife and grateful to her friends. Reverend Blue was particularly erudite. Either his faith or his Boston upbringing—maybe both—gave him the ability to defuse the duke's snobbery. Matt Wiley and Jonah Quinn entertained everyone with stories about outlaws and bank robbers, a subject of great interest to the Whitmore nieces and the two men Stuart Whitmore had brought to round out the numbers. Terrence Pierce and Reggie Blackstone were Englishmen considering investments in the beef market. Jon and Bessie completed the table, along with Louisa and the duke.

Best of all, Tristan had been free of fever for twenty-six days. In four more days—less than one hundred hours—he could declare his love for Caroline. By then the house party would be a resounding success, and she'd have the confidence to be a full partner in his complicated life. Just four more days without fever… Just a dozen or so successful meals, a few rides through the hills, a dance and then they'd be free to venture into new and uncharted territory. First, though, he had to get through the remaining one hundred hours.

With the meal complete, he was bantering with the men in his study, watching the minutes tick by on a mantel clock. The men were enjoying cigars and talking about everything from cattle prices to American firearms. The women were in the front room, speaking of babies and whatnot. The evening would have been perfect if his study hadn't been so warm. Sweat was beading on his brow, an uncomfortable reminder of the fevers.

He moved away from the group. Turning his back to them, he looked out the window. The Indian summer filled the day with summer heat, but the evenings usually had a crisp chill. Tristan cracked open the window and felt the draft, but it failed to cool his brow. A shiver raced down his spine and settled in his bones. He was aching from head to foot, and his head was pounding with the familiar threat of delirium.

Dear God, no! Don't let this happen... Not now.

He couldn't deny the return of the malaria. He'd been so close to victory. Now he saw defeat as plainly as the shiny glass keeping back the night.

Where was God? Why hadn't He answered Tristan's prayers? No answer came, only chills that made him as weak as a child. But he wasn't a child... He was a man with duties, children and a wife. He had to beat the malaria. If God didn't see fit to heal him of the disease, Tristan would fight it by himself.

He had to speak to Caroline in private. Instead of sharing today's success, he'd remind her of the promise she'd made to hide Freddie and Dora from his father. With a house full of guests, his illness would be noticed. They could buy time with vague excuses, but the risk of his father learning of the malaria grew with each passing hour, and with that knowledge came increased danger to Freddie.

The duke was in the study now, attempting to dominate the conversation but being ignored by Quinn and Wiley, who were immune to his sense of privilege. Chills shot down Tristan's spine, a reminder he'd soon be nauseous. He closed the window, then he ambled to the group by the hearth. "Gentlemen, please stay and enjoy yourselves. I have some personal business to tend to."

Caroline's friends and the Whitmore contingent nodded and went back to their cigars.

The duke watched him like a hawk.

Jon put out his cigar. "I could use some air. I'll step outside with you."

Trying to appear steadier than he felt, Tristan left the study with Jon trailing him. When they were out of earshot, Jon stopped him. "It's back, isn't it?"

"Yes."

"I'll get Caroline."

"Thank you." Tristan had to speak with her about the children, but he had no intention of accepting her care as a patient. Tonight he'd planned to praise her for the start of the house party. He'd imagined kissing her goodnight before she went to the nursery. Instead he'd be ordering her to prepare to leave The Barracks. He turned his back on Jon and went up the stairs to his suite. Sweating profusely, he took off his coat and flopped faceup on the bed. Staring at the ceiling, he waited for the fever, the delirium, the nausea. Worst of all, he waited for Caroline with the intention of issuing the hardest order of his life.

Like the rest of the women in the front room, Caroline saw Jon motion to her through the door. She made apologies and they stepped into the hall.

"It's Tristan," he said quietly. "The fever is back."

"It can't be…" She could hardly breathe.

"He's upstairs," Jon explained. "He wants to see you."

"Of course." Her mind went in a dozen directions. She had to protect the children, but she couldn't leave Tristan. As long as he was alive, she'd be at his side.

Jon held her gaze. "I'll advise Bessie after the women retire for the night. She'll come to his room."

"Thank you."

"Stay brave, Caroline. Tristan's a fighter."

"I know." She also knew God alone numbered a man's days. Silently, she prayed for mercy, then she went back to the front room and spoke to the women. "Ladies, if you'll excuse me. I'm needed upstairs."

"Of course," Louisa said graciously. "I hope the children are all right."

"They're fine," she answered. "The problem is nothing new." Sadly, she'd spoken the truth.

The Whitmore girls offered understanding. The dowager raised a brow but said nothing. Adie, Mary and Pearl knew better than to quiz her in front of the others. Later she'd explain and ask them to pray. Bessie answered with a raised brow. *Do you need me?*

Caroline shook her head no. She'd leave informing her sister to Jon.

With her stomach in a knot, she hurried up the stairs. She'd been worried about Tristan since supper, but she'd taken the sheen in his eyes for pride. Now she recognized the start of a fever. She went to his room and entered from the hall, cracking open the door without knocking. A lamp tossed a circle of light against the wall and onto the floor. It spread to the bed, a monstrous thing that seemed to swallow Tristan alive. He raised his chin and looked at her. "We have to talk about the children."

"We will," she said. "But only if it's necessary."

"It is."

"Maybe not." Perching on the edge of the mattress, she put her hand on his forehead. "You're feverish, but you're not burning up."

"It just started." His jaw clenched. "In an hour or so, I expect to be delusional."

"You don't know that."

He heaved a sigh. "This could be it, Caroline."

"You're borrowing trouble."

He reached for her hand. "Promise me you'll hide Freddie from my father. Jon will help you—"

"I'll keep my word."

She squeezed his hand, released it and went to the washstand to fetch water. He couldn't die. He simply couldn't. She loved him and hadn't told him. If he died, she'd have to flee with the children, fulfilling her marriage vows in the saddest of ways. "We need to keep you cool. Have you taken quinine today?"

"I took a dose before dinner."

She returned with the washbowl, set it on the nightstand and dampened the hankie stashed in the pocket of her fancy gown. If she needed more cloth to cool the fever, she'd tear the garment into rags. She put the hankie on his forehead then filled a glass with water from a pitcher. She carried it to him then issued an order of her own. "Drink this."

"It won't help," he muttered.

"It won't hurt," she countered. "Sit up and drink."

He gave her a harsh look, one she welcomed because it showed he was strong enough to fight. He sat up and took several sips, avoiding her gaze as she plumped his pillows. When he finished the water, he propped himself up. "You can leave now, but send Bessie."

"No."

"Caroline—"

"Don't you dare boss me around!" She was tired of being polite. She'd been walking on eggshells for hours, worrying she'd misspeak or trip on her gown. She wanted to shout at Tristan to fight the malaria. Instead she silently begged God to heal the man she'd married…the man who didn't know how she felt.

"I love you," she blurted to Tristan. "Don't you dare die on me!"

Awareness flickered in his eyes. He smiled, but feebly. "I love you, too."

"You do?"

"Yes, very much." He reached for her hand. "That's what makes this night so hard. If I could have gone a month without fever, I'd have asked you to marry me again, this time simply because I love you and want you for my wife."

"A month?" She didn't understand. She'd been in Wyoming five weeks and he hadn't been bedridden once. "When did you start counting?"

"Twenty-six days ago. We had a hundred hours to go."

"A hundred hours!" Tears welled in her eyes. "I don't care about a hundred hours. We love each other. We can fight the malaria together."

"And if I die?"

She cupped his feverish face. "I'd rather love you for a single day than not at all."

"I wanted to protect you," he said quietly. "I didn't want you to grieve—"

She wanted to shake him. "I would have suffered more not knowing you loved me and *still more* if I hadn't said the words to you."

It occurred to her that like Tristan, she'd drawn a line

for herself, a mark in the sand that could be erased as easily as it had been made. Whether the house party succeeded or failed, she loved him. By testing herself, she'd acted out of fear, not faith.

"We're a couple of fools," she said meekly.

"What do you mean?"

"We've wasted days when we could have been together."

His jaw tightened. "It wasn't a waste, Caroline. I'm determined to protect you. I couldn't risk leaving you with child—"

"I'd welcome your baby!" She wanted a baby from the man she loved more than anything.

His eyes glinted. "Aside from that," he continued, "there's also the matter of my obligations. If I live, are you saying you'll come with me to England?"

She knew the cost. As an American, she'd never fit in. At best she'd be a curiosity. At worst, an embarrassment. But if she said no, she'd be something she couldn't tolerate. She'd be a coward. And she'd be giving up what she wanted most in the world—the chance to be a wife to the man she loved, and mother to his children. The same faith that required Tristan to fight the malaria would give her the strength to be the wife he needed.

"Yes," she answered. "I'll go with you to England."

As soon as the words left her lips, her insides tightened into a knot. She'd taken a chance when she'd married Charles, and he'd paid with his life. She couldn't stand the thought of failing Tristan, especially when he was looking at her with such hope. The moment called for a kiss, but neither of them wanted the tenderness to be held back by illness.

Tristan spoke first. "I suppose I'm in God's hands now. I can't say the thought is comforting."

"I understand." She knew too well that God didn't answer every prayer the way she wanted. "We'll just have to wait and see."

"Yes."

And so they waited…

Chapter Eighteen

With Caroline at his side, Tristan closed his eyes and relished the coolness of her hand. He'd been down this road before, but he'd never gone down it with so much at stake. If he died, Freddie would be the next Duke of Willoughby. Moreover, Tristan's death would break Caroline's heart, and she'd have to flee with the children. He had a house full of guests who'd all be gossiping about her sudden departure.

An hour passed.

Then two hours.

Caroline stayed at his side, making small talk as she cooled his brow with the cloth. When his shirt became damp with sweat, she helped him into a dry nightshirt. They were married. She had the right to tend to his needs, and that's what she did. It felt as natural as breathing, and he dared to hope that God wouldn't leave him in this bed to die.

A knock sounded on the door.

"That must be Bessie." Caroline stood and headed for the door. Before she reached it, the duke strode into the room. If his father smelled death, he'd circle like a buzzard.

Tristan whipped the cloth from his brow and sat up. "What do you want?"

Caroline gasped. "How dare you walk in here!"

Ignoring her, the duke eyed Tristan. "So it's true. You're in poor health."

He said nothing.

"I've been watching you, *Marquess*." The duke used the title to control him, but Tristan refused to react.

"What have you seen?" he asked casually.

"My valet overheard you speaking to Jon." He studied Tristan's face with the indifference of a man judging the health of prize bull. "I gather you're quite ill."

If he hid the facts, he'd appear weak. "It's malaria."

His father's expression shifted from haughty to grim. "I'm sorry."

"Are you?" Tristan asked.

The duke glared at him. "Of course I'm sorry. I don't want the future Duke of Willoughby to be a sickly invalid."

There wasn't an ounce of sympathy in his father's countenance. No compassion whatsoever for Tristan's suffering or his fears. To the duke, he was a commodity, someone— even a *thing*—to be used for selfish gain. Tristan thought of his feelings for Freddie and Dora. He'd die for his children. The duke wouldn't give his life for anyone. Until Tristan had value, the duke hadn't given him a second thought…but God had. Thanks to Caroline, he'd come to see that a father's love wasn't distant and commanding. A father disciplined and he taught, but he also played the dream game and he encouraged his children to love and laugh and be themselves.

Nothing could excuse the duke's coldness, but Tristan had been wrong to put God in the same camp. Perhaps the duke had been as poorly treated as Tristan. How deep did the twisted roots of his family tree go? And what did a man do to ensure that future trees—his sons and daughters—would grow straight and tall?

He loved.

He loved his children the way God loved mankind. He listened to them. He protected them. He forgave them for their weakness. In that moment, Tristan saw his father not as the Duke of Willoughby, but as a damaged child. The words he blurted startled them both. "I forgive you, Father."

"You *what?*"

"I forgive you." Peace flooded through his body like a cascading river. It wrapped around old rocks of bitterness, dislodging some and leaving others submerged and forgotten. He glanced at Caroline and saw tears in her eyes. It didn't matter what his father said or did. Tristan was at peace with his past. As for the future, he'd trust Caroline to use her best judgment. Forgiveness didn't mean handing his son over to a tyrant.

The duke's face hardened. "Deathbed confessions don't interest me. If you survive, I expect you to return to England at the end of this silly little gathering."

"And if I die?"

"Then Freddie is mine."

He'd been expecting such an answer, but Caroline inhaled sharply. "How dare you speak like that! You should be worried about your son! He's—he's—" She clamped her lips.

"He's dying."

"No, he isn't," she said more calmly. "The quinine is working. Bessie says—"

The duke huffed. "She's a stupid woman."

"She's a trained nurse!" Caroline shouted back.

Tristan wanted to cheer. If she could stand up to his

father, she could stand up to anyone. He admired her courage. Determined to stand with her, he lumbered to his feet. "Get out."

"Not yet." The duke studied Caroline thoughtfully. "Why did you marry a sick man? Do you think you'll inherit his money?"

She gasped. "That's just plain wicked!"

Tristan's blood heated beyond the fever. "I'm ordering you to leave, your grace. You have authority in England, but you have none in my home."

The duke stayed focused on Caroline. "You married quickly…and privately." He looked pointedly around Tristan's bedroom. "I don't see a single feminine touch. Not a hairbrush… Not a robe to cover your nightgown, my dear."

Tristan's flesh crawled at his father's mocking tone. The man was scheming and Tristan needed to know what ugly snake he'd unleash on them. "What are you suggesting?"

The duke looked at Caroline like a wolf stalking a lamb. "You're not sharing a bed, are you?"

Caroline said nothing.

Tristan glared at him. "I won't dignify that remark with a reply."

"You don't have to. The rumor alone will suffice."

With his eyes glinting, the duke turned to Caroline. "Tristan's progeny will carry my blood. If you're not woman enough to command his interest—"

"Get out!" Tristan roared.

"As I was saying," the duke said to Caroline. "If you haven't consummated the marriage, this sham can be annulled. Your husband once loved Louisa. He moped over her for months. She's far more suitable as a wife."

"Get out!" Tristan bellowed again. If his father didn't leave, he'd send Caroline for Jon and the men from Swan's

Nest. He'd have his father carted to Cheyenne and put on a train to New York. He may have forgiven the man, but that didn't mean he'd tolerate the duke hurting Caroline.

The duke's expression softened, deceptively so. Looking almost kind, he spoke to Caroline. "I suspect my son married you to offend me. You've been used."

"That's a lie," she retorted.

"It's true enough. As such, you're entitled to compensation. If you leave by dawn, I'll instruct Pennwright to arrange for an income for the rest of your life." He named an amount that would impress any woman, even a future duchess.

Caroline put her hands on her hips. "You're more pitiful than Tristan said!"

The duke's eyes narrowed. "You're a fool, Caroline."

"I love my husband. If that makes me a fool, so be it."

If the duke heard what Caroline said, he didn't show it. "You're not shrewd enough to be a duchess. Neither are you beautiful or wealthy, but you *are* entertaining. I'm sure the dowager will enjoy hearing about the scandalous American woman who married for money."

"Don't you dare—" Tristan clenched his teeth.

The duke chortled. "Gossip is entertaining, don't you think? Especially when the stories include, shall we say, a wife's marital inadequacy?"

Looking pleased, the duke headed for the door. As he turned the handle, he faced them. "I expect to be kept informed of your condition, Tristan. And I expect to keep Freddie close at hand."

He left without waiting for a reply, leaving Tristan seething with anger, burning up with fever and alone with his wife. The duke's knowledge of the illness made protecting Freddie even more urgent. The man would be watching the boy like a hawk. He might even try to leave with him. Looking at Caroline, he prayed for his Father in heaven to do what Tristan could not… He asked God to protect his son.

Caroline hated the thought of gossip, especially gossip of such a personal nature. How far would the duke go to make her a laughingstock? She hated being afraid, but his threats were real. She thought of the Bible command to honor one's father and mother. How did a son or daughter honor a man like the Duke of Willoughby? She had no idea, but she knew how to protect Freddie. Glaring at Tristan, she barked an order. "Don't you dare die!"

His eyes twinkled, a response she didn't expect. Neither did she expect him to give her a crisp salute. "Yes, ma'am."

If only the fever would take orders as easily. "Get back in bed. You need rest."

He didn't budge.

"Tristan!"

He stood staring at her, a smile spreading slowly across his face. Half wondering if he'd become delirious, she walked to his side with the intention of putting her hand on his forehead. As she lifted her arm, he took her hand and held it. "Nothing's changed," he said. "The fever's the same, but something else is quite different."

"What?" she asked.

He let go of her hand and grasped her arms instead, holding her gently in place as he looked into her eyes. "I won't kiss you while I'm feverish. Nor will I suggest we make love, but I seem to recall we declared our love for each other."

She blushed. "Yes, we did."

"Which means you no longer need to stay in the nursery. Stay with me, Caroline. We'll hope and pray together.

"I'll stay," she said. "But I have to be honest. Your father scares me. Someday you'll return to England. If he ruins my reputation with lies, you and the children will be affected."

"We won't be returning for years," he said quietly. "By then the rantings of an old man will be forgotten."

"Not by the Dowager Duchess of Somerville." She spoke the name with all the weight it would carry in England. "The nieces are just as pretentious. I've heard them gossiping. Years from now, people will talk. I know this is true because it happened with Charles."

"You're having doubts."

"I'm worried about you and the children. I know what it's like to be scorned. I can't stand the thought of Dora being embarrassed by her American mother."

"And *I* can't stand the thought of my father poisoning your mind." His voice rose with each word. She worried he'd waste his strength on being angry, so she stood on her toes and kissed his cheek. "We won't discuss it now."

"Then when?"

A tap on the door surprised them both. Caroline opened it but just a crack. She saw Bessie and let her inside. "He's feverish," she said to her sister. "What else can we do?"

Looking peeved, he glared at her. "I can speak for myself."

"I know that!"

Bessie looked from Caroline to Tristan and back to Caroline. "If he's well enough to bicker, that's a good sign."

"We're not bickering," they said in unison.

Ignoring them, Bessie felt Tristan's brow for fever. "You're warm, but it's not particularly high. How's your stomach?"

"Fine." The malaria usually caused him to be nauseated. "I imagine I'll be sick later."

Bessie nodded. "It's to be expected. Stay in bed and drink as much water as you can. Take quinine in the morning but no more tonight. Mostly you need to rest so your body can fight the fever."

He wiped his hand through his hair. "Unfortunately, I've done this before."

"I'll check back in the morning." She left, closing the door without a click.

In the sudden quiet, Caroline faced him. Tristan spoke first. "Where were we?"

"We were arguing about your father."

"It's a waste of time."

"But necessary," she replied. "We'll talk when you're well. Maybe there's no reason to worry about what he says. The house party will be over in a week. It *is* going well, isn't it?"

"It's going splendidly." Sadness filled his eyes. "We're back at the beginning, aren't we? I need to survive the malaria, and you need to believe you can be a duchess."

"Yes."

"Come," he said holding out his hand. "We'll sit together by the fire."

"You should lie down."

"So should you."

She blushed.

He smiled. "Shall we?"

"Yes."

As husband and wife in name but not in body, they lay together fully clothed, talking and hoping and waiting to see if the fever would spike.

It didn't.

They slept.

In the morning Caroline awoke. Rising up on one elbow she looked at Tristan's face for signs of illness. His cheeks were still flushed but they weren't as ruddy, and his forehead had a sheen of perspiration...and spots...tiny blisters that looked just like chicken pox.

"Tristan!"

He roused sleepily. "What is it?"

"I have to see your chest!"

He looked utterly undone. If she hadn't been tied in knots with worry, she'd have laughed. "I think you have the chicken pox. When you had it as a child, did you get a lot of them?"

"No," he answered. "Just enough to itch."

"You can get them again if you have a mild case."

"It *was* mild." Fully awake, he checked his torso and started to laugh. "I'm covered with spots!"

He leapt to his feet and went to the mirror. Preening like a vain man, he looked at the rash on his brow, then turned to her. "I've got the pox, all right. And I've never been happier in my life."

She went to his side. "I'm happy, too."

"I'll be absent from the festivities for a few days, but be ready to dance with me on the last night." Even ailing, he had a commanding air. "By then you'll see the woman I see—the very beautiful *and* very poised duchess of Willoughby."

"I hope so."

"I *know* so."

She envied his confidence. She'd been ready to fight for him and she still would, but the duke was a formidable enemy. However, she believed in a formidable God. She'd do her best to stay strong, but under no circumstance would she saddle Tristan with an incompetent wife. Their future still depended on the house party and its success. She had to triumph or leave him. There was no middle ground for a future duchess.

* * *

It wasn't long before Caroline faced her next challenge. With Tristan's chair empty at the supper table, she had to tell a house full of guests they'd been exposed to the chicken pox. She also wanted to end whatever rumors the duke had contrived about Tristan dying from malaria. Before the first course was served, she asked for everyone's attention. Her guests dutifully turned in her direction.

"Some of you know Tristan is ill," she said, focusing on the duke. "I want to assure you it's not serious. He has the chicken pox."

"Oh, dear!" Louisa cried. "It's my fault. I had it when I arrived."

"Illness happens," Caroline said graciously. The disease had also affected three ranch hands. Tristan had probably caught it from one of them. "Frankly we're relieved it's not more serious. As some of you know, he contracted malaria in the West Indies. He's been fighting fevers for several months."

The duke slanted a glance at her. "Malaria is potentially fatal."

"It is," Bessie answered. "But Tristan has overcome the worst of it. As a nurse I've seen many reactions to the fevers. At this point, it's reasonable to assume it's a chronic problem, not a fatal one."

"I see." The man almost looked disappointed.

Whitmore broke in. "Malaria is a badge of honor in my book. The marquess contracted it serving his country." With the duke and the dowager present, Whitmore used Tristan's formal title.

"He has my admiration," Terrence Pierce added.

The guests chattered for a moment about the childhood illness, expressing admiration for Tristan and relating their own stories. The awkward announcement was soon forgotten, and the conversation veered to other topics. To Caroline's dismay, the topics included monologues by the duke that held subtle criticism of her. More than once he gave her the look of a cat hunting a mouse. She managed to remain poised, in part because her friends were protecting her.

Josh and Adie deflected his taunts with kindness.

Matt and Pearl sang her praises.

Mary and Jonah distracted him with endless questions about England.

The Whitmore nieces, Mr. Pierce and Mr. Blackstone looked as tired of his monologues as Caroline, but they said nothing out of inborn respect. The dowager yawned rather deliberately, then gave Caroline a look that demanded she stop the man from dominating the table. Caroline wanted to comply, but she had no idea how to control the man and his runaway tongue. The evening droned on until dessert arrived. Predictably, the duke protested the cherry tarts.

"I don't care for cherry." Pushing the plate aside, he snapped his fingers for his valet. "Go to the kitchen and find something edible."

Caroline turned as red as the cherry filling. Tristan would have cut him off with a barb of his own, but she felt tongue-tied. Forcing herself to be strong, she spoke up. "We also have macaroons, your grace. Perhaps that would satisfy your palate?"

He looked close to gagging. "I want pudding!"

Caroline had no idea how to handle a grown man having a tantrum. It wasn't very dukelike in her opinion, nor was it polite. She had a good mind to tell him he'd eat what he was given, but the dowager interrupted.

"Willoughby, shut up!"

"Duchess!"

"You heard me." She waved her finger at him. "I'm sick of hearing about your palate! We're in America. You can't expect the same *quality*."

Did she mean the tarts or did she mean Caroline as Tristan's wife? Caroline had spoken to the woman only briefly and had been intimidated. With her piercing eyes, the dowager seemed to stare through the elegant gown to the inadequate woman who'd been the governess.

With the duchess's criticism ringing in the air, every face in the room turned to Caroline. Heat rushed to her cheeks, staining them with a telltale blush. At a loss, she looked at Louisa. Instead of speaking, Louisa gave her a look that said, *Speak up! Defend yourself!* Caroline tried to say something—anything—but nothing came out of her mouth.

She cleared her throat.

She smiled.

Finally she found her voice. "Things *are* different in America."

"They certainly are!" said Stuart Whitmore.

"Very," said Mr. Pierce.

"Astoundingly so," said one of the nieces.

Some of the guests lifted their forks and enjoyed the tarts. Others, including the duke and dowager, pushed the plates aside. It was awkward and embarrassing and Caroline hated herself for being so unsure. Every doubt she'd had about her ability to be a good wife to Tristan played through her mind. He said he loved her and had confidence in her, but she didn't have it in herself. She'd failed badly tonight, but she had time to redeem herself, if only she could find a way.

The meal ended with continued awkwardness. She went upstairs hoping to find comfort in Tristan's company, but he'd fallen asleep. She went to the nursery where she collapsed in her narrow bed, praying for the strength to do what was right for the man and children she loved, not just for now, but also for the future. She couldn't stand the thought of being an embarrassment to her family. She desperately wanted to redeem herself in front of the Whitmores, but she had no idea how to do it.

The next morning, she dressed and went downstairs to breakfast. Louisa, the dowager and the duke were already eating. Determined to prove herself, she sat at the table as if she belonged. The dowager and Louisa were talking about fox hunts in England, with the duke describing the plans he'd made for Friday's horse race. Louisa showed boundless enthusiasm, and so did the dowager. As a much younger woman, she'd won prizes.

Her silvery eyes went to Caroline and lingered. "Are you participating, Marchioness?"

The use of her title made Caroline go pale. It was a direct challenge, and the dessert debacle was still ringing in her ears. So was the comment about quality in America. Where she'd find the courage—the faith—to ride Grandma in a race, she didn't know. But the words were out before she could change her mind. "Yes, I'm riding," she said with false calm. "I'm looking forward to it."

Chapter Nineteen

Tristan had been ill with the chicken pox for five days, and he couldn't stand one more minute away from the house party. He had a mild case this time, too, and the fever had broken quickly. The blisters itched, but he'd experienced worse punishment from mosquito bites. He was tired of being ill and tired of being pampered, though he greatly enjoyed Caroline's tender care.

He'd also spent time with his children. The day after he'd fallen ill, poor Dora had erupted in spots. She was far sicker than he'd ever been with chicken pox, so he'd spent hours reading to her. Freddie had remained healthy, and that had been a problem. With Tristan confined, the boy spent hours with the duke. He'd become even more disrespectful to Caroline. Tristan had spoken to him, but Freddie needed more than a lecture. He needed to see for himself how a gentleman treated a lady.

Tristan intended to begin that lesson today at the horse race organized by the duke. The male riders included all the men except Reverend Blue and Jon. Along with Bessie, they were making plans for Saturday's marriage ceremony. Louisa and the Whitmore girls would also ride. Caroline had hinted at participating, but he'd told her no. In his opinion she had nothing to prove. After the race, Tristan hoped to be making arrangements with Josh himself. He and Caroline were legally bound, but it seemed fitting to take vows that reflected their deeper commitment.

First, though, he wanted to run hard on Cairo and win the race. As he approached the horse barn, he saw Grandma saddled and waiting at the mounting block. Next to the horse he saw Caroline in her split skirt. She was feeding a carrot to Grandma and scratching the horse's neck.

Tristan paced to her side. "*What* do you think you're doing?"

"I'm riding today."

"But why?" He could see no benefit from her effort. From everything she'd told him, the house party had been a success. If she rode and fell, she'd be humiliated. Even worse, she could get seriously hurt.

"I don't have a choice," she said to him.

"There's always a choice." They'd had this discussion when she'd climbed on Cairo to cross the river. She'd fallen that day. Today's ride would be even more difficult.

She kept scratching Grandma, looking casual except for a knot in her brow. "Louisa rides and so do the nieces. At breakfast a few days ago the dowager talked about riding in England and how much she enjoyed it. She gave me a *very* deliberate look. If I don't ride, I'll appear weak."

"I don't care," Tristan said irritably. "I want you to be yourself."

"And *I* want to be strong."

She faced him. "This is important to me, Tristan. Please understand."

"I *do* understand," he said gently. On a whim, he kissed her cheek. "You won't change your mind, will you?"

"No."

"Then we'll ride together."

"Don't you dare hang back with me! You and Cairo can win."

"I'd rather keep an eye on you."

Her mouth tightened with dismay. "You don't think I can finish the race."

If he told the truth, he'd damage her confidence. But neither could he offer false assurances. "It's rough terrain, Caroline. Far rougher than anything you've ridden. Yes, I'm worried about you. I love you, my dear."

She blushed. "I love you, too."

"I also believe in you." He kissed her forehead. "Do your best, and I'll do mine. I have to admit—besting my father would give me great pleasure."

"Me, too," she said smiling. She indicated the mounting block. "If you'll excuse me, I have a race to run."

Tristan helped her into the saddle, then went to get Cairo. He hoped the race went well because Caroline's confidence hung on the outcome.

Turning her back to Tristan, Caroline clicked to Grandma and rode to where Louisa and the Whitmore girls were waiting. Louisa had a horse Caroline knew to be fast. The nieces had selected gentler mounts. All three of them were sitting sidesaddle and looking relaxed. Next to Louisa, Caroline saw Stuart. Dressed in jodhpurs, he looked very English and very interested in Louisa. Mr. Pierce was riding a brown bay and Mr. Blackstone was mounted on a pinto. Slightly apart from the crowd, she saw Matt and Jonah on a couple of surefooted mustangs.

Even more removed from the riders, she saw the duke and Freddie on Arabians nearly as impressive as Cairo.

Louisa greeted Caroline as she approached. "Caroline! How wonderful of you to join us!"

"My pleasure," she said amiably.

When the duke gave her an arrogant look, Freddie followed suit. Soon Tristan would join them, and the group would go to the starting point a short distance from the corral. Once she'd decided to ride, Caroline had spoken with Jon. Yesterday he'd taken her over the route at an easy pace. With the exception of crossing a wide but shallow stream, it seemed within her ability. She didn't expect to win. She just had to prove she could hold her own. She didn't have to be first, but neither did she want to be last. She simply wanted to be adequate.

After the conversation with Caroline, Tristan didn't know what to do about the race. If he held back to keep an eye on her, she'd think he didn't believe in her. If he rode to win and she got in trouble, he'd be angry with himself. Climbing on Cairo, he decided to take the race a stride at a time. He'd make the decision on the run, literally.

As he neared the group of riders, he spotted Freddie and the duke on two of his fastest Arabians. Tristan had no doubt his father could handle the horse he'd chosen, but he'd have preferred Freddie to ride his usual gelding, a horse far more manageable than the Arabian mare. Not only would Tristan need to watch out for Caroline, but he also had to keep an eye on Freddie. In his current state of arrogance, the boy could easily go beyond his ability.

Tristan joined the riders, accepting greetings from everyone except Caroline and his father. They both ignored him, adding to the autumn chill threatening to replace the Indian summer. At least for today the sky would be clear, an important fact considering the route his father had selected for the race. The riders would circle the base of a hill, cross a wide stream strewn with boulders and return to The Barracks through a rolling meadow. The recent sunny weather meant the stream would be low and the rocks would be visible. Tristan knew the loop well, but the others would find the terrain challenging.

"Shall we proceed?" the duke said.

Murmuring agreement, the riders turned their horses and went down the trail at a walk. Tristan rode close to Caroline but said nothing. When they reached the meadow where the competition would begin, the riders formed a line. The duke raised his voice. "It seems to me we need a prize for winning and a consequence for losing."

"Here, here," said Stuart.

Jonah and Matt said nothing.

Louisa whispered something to the Whitmore girls and they all laughed. Almost sure to lose, Caroline remained stoic. Tristan couldn't put an end to his father's jabs at Caroline, but he could cover for her. In a jovial tone, he said, "There's to be music tonight. The winner dances with the woman of his choice."

Louisa answered with teasing tone of her own. "And if a lady wins?"

"Fair is fair," Tristan called. "She dances with the gentleman of her choice."

Louisa arched a brow at Stuart Whitmore, who gave her a bold look in return. At least for Louisa, the house party had been a success. She and Whitmore had become inseparable.

The duke raised his voice again. "And a consequence?"

Tristan looked pointedly at Caroline. "The last rider dances with me." He'd given her a reason to be last, and he'd done it with humor. He hoped she'd play along with him, but her jaw stayed tight. The men laughed and agreed, certain they'd best all four of the women.

Tristan had contained the duke with humor, and the

man didn't like it. Looking peeved, he shouted again. "Shall we begin the race?"

The riders formed a line across the meadow. With one eye on Freddie, Tristan lined up next to Caroline. The duke raised his arm high. "On the count of three... One... Two... Three!"

The horses broke at a dead run. Tristan held back, watching as Caroline took off on Grandma. When she dug her heels into the mare's side, he had the terrible feeling she was riding to win, or at least riding not to be last. He stayed with her as she rode with the pack across the meadow. Louisa had the lead and Whitmore was chasing her. The nieces were close to Pierce, and Blackstone seemed interested only in staying in the saddle. Freddie and the duke were riding side by side, strategically holding back because their horses could pick up speed later. Matt and J.T. were also hanging back, no doubt keeping an eye on Caroline. Caroline had friends. She also had an enemy in the duke.

When they reached the first turn, she risked a glance at Tristan. "Go! I want you to win!"

The duke was closing the gap between them. Tristan shouted back. "I'm staying with you."

"Then I'll ride harder!"

To his consternation, she pushed Grandma into a run. They'd galloped before, but without pressure and in a smooth meadow. She didn't have the skill to maintain such a pace, but she was determined to try and equally determined to force him to ride to win. If he left her, she'd slow down.

"You win," he shouted. Reluctantly he dug in his heels and gave Cairo free rein. Stretching into a full run, the stallion shot past the nieces, then by Louisa and Whitmore. Tristan relished the speed, the wind, the beat of Cairo's hooves. As he rounded a wide turn, he saw the stream glistening in the sun. The water sparkled on the scattered rocks and made a ribbon of rustling light. Tristan slowed Cairo to a walk, crossed the stream with care and took off for The Barracks. It felt good to run, and it would feel even better to win.

With the other riders out of sight, he crossed the finish line with the intention of claiming his prize—a dance with Caroline, the woman of his choice.

Still riding hard, Caroline watched Tristan and Cairo disappear around a wide bend. The duke and Freddie were still behind her, and Matt and Jonah were lagging even farther behind. As she rounded the turn herself, she saw the stream that had to be crossed. She'd been expecting it, but the rippling water sent a wave of fear down her spine. She immediately commanded Grandma to slow her pace, but the curve ended in a downhill slope and the horse had more momentum than she'd realized.

Grandma's hooves chewed up the apron of sand, then hit the water with a splash. The horse stopped so fast Caroline nearly flew out of the saddle.

Behind her she heard the rumble of hoofbeats, then a shout to get out of the way. She urged Grandma forward, but the horse balked. One of the Arabians charged past her. It was either the duke or Freddie, she couldn't tell which. As she struggled to calm Grandma, the Arabian stumbled. The rider shot over its head and crashed into a boulder. The horse regained its balance and ran, leaving a body in a black coat in the water. The legs seemed short and the coat seemed too small for a grown man.

"Freddie!" She cried, half climbing and half falling off of Grandma.

As she staggered to the rider, she took in the length of

the legs and size of the boots. They were too big to belong to the boy. She sloshed past a boulder and saw the duke's gray hair rippling in the current. Judging by the angle of his head, he'd broken his neck. And from his open eyes she knew he'd died instantly. To be sure, she knelt in the water and took his pulse. As expected, she felt nothing.

Behind her Freddie was calling for his grandfather. In a final act of respect for a human being, if not for a man who'd been a tyrant, she closed the duke's eyes and stood. Freddie ran up to her. "Is he— Is he—" The boy couldn't finish.

"I'm so sorry, Freddie. He's gone." Instinctively she put her arm around him, but he pulled back.

"He—he can't be!"

"His neck's broken."

"It's your fault! You stopped in the middle of the trail. *You* made him fall!"

Freddie ran across the stream, shouting for help and weeping at the same time. Caroline stood frozen in place with her skirt wet, her heart thudding and her boots sinking into the mud. Matt and Jonah arrived at a gallop, both sliding to the ground before the horses stopped. Matt came to her side and put his arms around her. Jonah went to the body, checked for a pulse, then shook his head. "I'll get a wagon."

He climbed on his horse and rode back the way they'd come, leaving her with Matt and the silent weight of guilt. Louisa came from the other direction at a gallop, followed by Whitmore and the others. Still holding her shoulders, Matt spoke quietly. "I'm going to explain what happened. Will you be all right?"

She nodded yes, but her dreams had just been destroyed. For the rest of her life she'd be the American who killed the Duke of Willoughby with her incompetence.

Even worse, Freddie blamed her for his grandfather's death. She'd never win the boy's affection, nor would she earn the respect of the Whitmores. Her future as Tristan's wife had died with the duke. She'd insist on an annulment.

Still mounted on Cairo, Tristan watched the finish line for signs of the other riders. A minute ticked into three, then five. His nerves prickled with worry then caught fire like dry brush. He was about to go back down the trail when he spotted Jonah Quinn approaching the barn at a gallop. When he reached Tristan, he reined his horse to stop. "It's your father. He's dead."

"Dead?"

"He fell. His neck's broken."

Tristan didn't doubt him. Quinn had seen as much death as he had. In even tones, the man told how he and Wiley had witnessed the accident from the top of the trail. He described Caroline's awkward stop, the duke passing her and Freddie's accusations. Quinn had hard edges, and he spoke with authority. "It wasn't Caroline's fault."

"Does *she* know that?"

"She should, but she's pretty shaken up."

Caroline needed him and so did Freddie. Turning Cairo, Tristan looked back at Jonah. "I'd be obliged if you'd arrange for a wagon."

"Yes, sir."

Tristan left at a gallop, covering the path he'd ridden minutes ago with Caroline. Approaching the stream, he saw a tableau that told the story he most dreaded. Caroline was standing apart from the crowd with only Matt Wiley for a friend. The others were on the opposite side of the stream, crowded together like a mob at a hanging. Louisa had an arm around Freddie, and Whitmore stood at her side. The nieces, Pierce and Blackstone were staring at Caroline as if she were a murderess.

Tristan rode down the hill at a funereal pace, his eyes on the body of the man who'd fathered him. The heaviness in his chest wasn't for what he'd lost but for what he'd never had. He looked next at Caroline, saw the resignation in her eyes and knew that once again his father had come between Tristan and a woman's love. Unless he was misreading Caroline's expression, he knew she'd ask for an annulment.

With every eye on him, he dismounted, walked to his wife and drew her into his arms. She stiffened but he held her anyway. "It wasn't your fault," he murmured.

"Yes, it was."

"Quinn and Wiley saw it. He did this to himself."

Shuddering, she slipped away from him. He let her go but only because he heard someone sloshing across the stream. He turned and saw Whitmore. The man lowered his chin in a sign of respect, then raised it. "Your grace, allow me to express my condolences."

Your grace...

It wouldn't be years before Tristan left for England. It would be days. And judging by Caroline's expression, persuading her to accompany him would be the fight of his life.

Chapter Twenty

Caroline wore black to the duke's funeral, but no one else did. The guests had come for a party, not mourning. Wanting to be respectful, she'd asked Evaline to remove the trim from one of her dresses and to dye the gown black. The dress reminded her of the conversation she still had to have with Tristan. Last night, she'd knocked on his bedroom door, intending to ask for the annulment. When he didn't answer, she went looking for him. She'd heard him in his study with Pennwright, talking about his father's holdings and his political responsibilities. He'd spoken with a new gravity, and she had decided to put off the confrontation. After the burial, she'd tell him she wanted to end their marriage.

First, though, she had to endure the funeral. The duke had died yesterday and was being buried without the pomp he would have wanted. Even the sky was cold to him. Gray clouds leaked rain, enough to dampen the earth but not enough to evoke a sense of tears. Josh spoke eloquently of eternity. By the time he finished, Caroline felt stronger. She didn't know if the duke had made peace with his Maker, but she hoped so.

Josh finished the service with a prayer. At the closing

"amen," Tristan dropped a handful of dirt on the coffin. As the breeze carried away the dust, a single clump hit with a final thud. Tristan stepped to the side of the grave to accept condolences. Caroline joined him and together they greeted the mourners. Tristan invited Freddie to stand with them, but the boy refused to be with Caroline. She offered to give him her place, but Tristan said no. She felt terrible. Of the guests in attendance, only Freddie wept.

He'd chosen to stay with Louisa and Stuart, and he was with them now, glaring at Caroline and fighting tears. He wasn't alone in his criticism of her. All day she'd heard whispers among the Whitmore crowd. The nieces had practically run from her.

The dowager duchess had offered sincere condolences to Tristan, but her remarks to Caroline had been oddly challenging. *You'll be remembered, Duchess Willoughby, for how you handle these next few days.*

Had it been a warning or encouragement? Caroline didn't know, and she no longer cared. She felt responsible for the duke's death. No matter what she said or did, she'd be blamed for this tragic day.

When the last guest departed from the gravesite, she turned to Tristan. "I'd like to speak with you in private, your grace."

Tristan disliked being called *your grace.* He especially disliked Caroline's tone when she said it. They'd done battle about names and titles before. In the beginning he'd wanted her to call him "major." Now he wanted to be called Tristan. Even better, he wanted to be called "darling," or "my love." The last thing he wanted from Caroline was the cold etiquette of a subject or a soldier.

"You know my name," he said. "Use it." It was an order, and he'd accept nothing less than obedience.

She sealed her lips.

"My name…say it."

"I don't want to say it." Her voice cracked. "I'd like to speak in private, perhaps in the barn—"

"All right." They'd arranged their marriage in the stable in Wheeler Springs. The barn at The Barracks was a fitting spot to return to the promises they'd made.

Side by side, they left the knoll that had become the family cemetery and walked to the barn where she'd found the courage to learn to ride. He wanted that brave woman to rise up against the cloud of the duke's death. Instead Caroline had the look of a waif. He didn't want their talk to be interrupted, so he took her to the tack room and closed the door. At the river crossing, he'd coaxed her onto Cairo with peppermint and patience. Today he had nothing to offer except his love.

He took her hands in his. "I love you, Caroline. I want you to come to England with me."

"I can't," she murmured.

"Why not?"

"I'll be forever known as the woman who caused your father's death. It will affect the children. It will affect *you*."

"I don't care, and neither should you. I'm now a ridiculously important man. The title humbles me, but it also gives me the privilege of being stubborn. It will take far more than a beautiful American wife to cause me embarrassment."

"I'm not beautiful."

"You are to me."

She shook her head. "I can't risk it, Tristan. If we don't annul the marriage, you'll be criticized. I'll be a pariah—"

He suddenly understood. "I'm not the one you're protecting, am I? You're protecting yourself."

"No!"

"Don't lie. It's unbecoming."

"I'm not lying!"

"But you are," he countered. "You're lying to yourself. You want to end our marriage because you're afraid. You love me. You love Freddie and Dora. How can you walk away from us?"

"Freddie hates me," she murmured.

"He's a troubled boy. He needs you more than ever. And Dora—" He couldn't finish. The thought of his daughter losing another mother sickened him.

She knotted her hands into fists, but there was nothing to pummel except her own dreams. "You don't understand! I stayed with Charles and he was killed. I shouldn't have married him in the first place. If I'd been stronger, he'd still be alive."

Tristan couldn't see the logic. "Do you really think my *life* is at stake? Even my dignity? I'm a duke. No one will dare question me."

Sadness filled her eyes. "You said that to me before, and it wasn't true."

"When?"

"You told me Cairo would obey you, and he bucked me into the river. Jon ignores your orders. Evaline and Noah overrule you. Even Dora has you wrapped around her finger." With the mention of Dora, her voice softened into a lullaby. "But that's all right because they love you. The people in England will be looking for something to criticize. No matter what you say, Tristan, the fact remains. In England I'll be an embarrassment to you. The children will be ashamed of me, especially Freddie. I came to bring healing to you and your children, not to cause a deeper rift."

"Freddie's a boy." His voice started to rise. "You can't let a confused child guide your decision."

"I have to think of his feelings."

He lowered his voice. "And Dora? What about her?"

A sob broke from her throat. "How does a mother choose when her children have different needs? I hate the thought of leaving her—"

"Then don't."

"She'll miss me, but she's young. She'll be all right. She *has* to be." She shook her head. "Maybe if we had more time—"

"We don't." He considered delaying the inevitable, but his first conversation with Pennwright eliminated that possibility. His father's secretary, now *his* secretary, had given Tristan the details on his father's activities. The sooner Tristan arrived in England, the sooner he could end his father's reign of terror over the people of Willoughby. For years the duke had taken advantage of the locals. Some were living in poverty. As much as Tristan wanted to stay in Wyoming until Caroline found her courage, he had a duty to fulfill. "I'm making arrangements to leave at the end of the week. Come with us."

She shook her head. "I can't."

"Then what will you do?" He couldn't leave without her. He simply couldn't. But neither could he stay in Wyoming when he had responsibilities in England. He thought of God balancing the needs of the entire world. It was an impossible task.

Blinking back tears, she straightened her spine. "I'm going back to Denver. I already spoke to Adie. She thinks I should go with you to England, but she won't turn me away."

He wanted to shout at her, to quarrel and issue orders. Instead he clenched his jaw. "So it's decided.

"Yes."

He turned his back and paced to the door. "If you change your mind, you know where to find me."

"I do," she murmured. "But nothing will change."

With his temper flaring he left the tack room. He wanted to call her a coward. He settled for pacing back to the house alone. As the new duke of Willoughby, he had to meet with Pennwright. They had letters to write and arrangements to make. Unless Caroline found the courage to be his wife, the arrangements would include the annulment of their marriage.

He had tried to influence Caroline and failed. He hoped he'd have better luck with Freddie. The boy's behavior, especially his criticism of Caroline, had to be addressed immediately. Tristan would be patient with Freddie's grief, but he couldn't tolerate arrogance. He needed to speak to his son even more urgently than he needed to meet with Pennwright.

The wind pulled at his coat and whipped through the cottonwoods, causing the branches to rub and squeak. Just as he reached the house, the clouds let loose with a torrent of rain. Refreshments were being served to the guests—he wouldn't call them mourners—in the side parlor, a cozy room that should have been filled with tears and poignant memories. When he didn't see Freddie or Louisa, he went back to the entry hall. He heard voices in the front room, entered and saw them on the divan. Whitmore was seated across from them, listening as Louisa told Freddie about Willoughby Manor, preparing him for his new life.

She meant well, but Tristan had grave concerns about the boy's behavior. The seeds of arrogance had to be removed and replaced with seeds of honor, faith and concern for others. He entered the room quietly. When Louisa looked up, he said, "Would you excuse us, please?"

Whitmore stood and spoke for them both. "Yes, your grace."

Someday Tristan would be accustomed to hearing those words, but today he felt the cost of doing his duty. "Thank you."

Louisa said goodbye to Freddie, then left arm in arm with Whitmore.

Tristan sat across from his son and took in his formal appearance. Dressed in a tailored coat, the one stitched by the duke's valet, he looked like a miniature version of the duke. Only his eyes, red-rimmed and puffy, belonged to a child. Freddie was angry and hurt, and he wanted to blame someone. Tristan understood because he'd grieved his father's love for years. He'd been just like Freddie until he'd made peace with himself and God. Thanks to Caroline, he'd even made peace with the duke. The irony of what he had to say struck him as poignant.

"I know you're angry, Freddie."

The boy shot daggers at him.

"And I realize you blame Caroline for the accident." Tristan paused. When Freddie said nothing, he continued. "She's not responsible for what happened. Your grandfather was riding too fast. He made the decision to cross the stream without slowing down."

"But she was in the way! She made him fall."

"I don't agree," Tristan said reasonably. "But suppose she did. If by accident she made the worst mistake in the world, what do you think we should do?"

"I hate her!"

"Does that solve anything?" Tristan could have been talking to himself. Had resenting the duke done any good? None at all, but he saw a chance to do some good now. "Your grandfather and I didn't get along. In my opinion, he made mistakes. Some of them were as serious as the one you think Caroline made. Even so, I forgave him."

"I'll never forgive her." The boy shoved to his feet. "She's common and she's stupid!"

"Freddie!" Tristan would tolerate anger but not disrespect. "You owe Caroline an apology."

"No!"

The boy ran out of the room and up the stairs. Tristan stood but let him go. He could only hope that time would open Freddie's eyes to the truth. The alternative—that the anger would fester and grow—troubled him deeply. What did a father do with a stubborn child? He knew how an officer disciplined a soldier, but Freddie was troubled and grieving. Patience seemed to be in order, so Tristan returned to the parlor where the guests were waiting for him.

As he entered, he heard murmuring about the accident. The nieces were being particularly critical. So was Blackstone. The dowager sat by herself, listening to the gossip and fanning herself as if the air were stale. She saw Tristan and summoned him. "Your grace!"

"Yes, Dowager?"

"Where is your wife?"

"She's—" Tristan hesitated. Telling the dowager that Caroline was hiding in the barn would do not good at all. "She's indisposed.

"I see," the old woman said. "That's unfortunate."

She'd issued a warning of sorts. Unless Caroline faced the gossip now, the accident would become fodder for rumors for months to come. Tristan wanted to stop the criticism, but despite what he'd said to Caroline, even a duke couldn't control scandalous talk. The only person who could vindicate herself was Caroline. He'd planned to cancel the remainder of the house party, but now he wondered if he should insist she keep her obligations.

He addressed Dowager Somerville. "May I ask you a question?"

"Certainly."

"Would you be terribly scandalized if we resumed the house party as planned?"

She gave him the haughtiest look he'd ever seen. "Your wife is currently an object of scandal. What do *you* think you should do?"

Tristan had no doubt whatsoever. Caroline needed a chance to redeem herself, both in the eyes of their guests and in her own opinion. "Thank you, Dowager. If you'll excuse me, I have an announcement to make."

"Of course."

He cleared his throat for attention. "Ladies and gentlemen!"

The room silenced immediately. He could have been addressing soldiers instead of aristocrats.

Tristan lightened his tone. "You came to The Barracks for a party, not a funeral. As you know, we have plans for a wedding. I see no reason to deny Jon and Bessie a celebration. The ceremony will be held as planned, and there will be a reception with music and dancing. No one is to wear black." He paused to let the order sink in. "I'll pay my respects to my father in England. That was his home, and it's where our grief belongs."

He glanced from face to face, daring people to question him. No one said a word. He'd issued an order and it would be followed. He supposed being duke had some advantages, though the person who mattered most wasn't in the room. "Very well," he said. "The house party will continue as planned."

Two days from now, Jon and Bessie would take vows.

The marriage would be celebrated with a meal and dancing, and Caroline would have a chance to shine. His wife would wear her finest gown and he'd dance with her. He could only hope it wouldn't be the first and only time.

Two hours after supper, Caroline was huddled on her bed, her knees pulled to her chest and her neck bent in defeat. Rain beat on the window in uneven rhythms, and the wind shook the house. The Indian summer had disappeared in a day, and winter loomed on the storm. She thought of the duke's fresh grave and how it would turn to mud. Mud took her back to the day she'd buried Charles. Good friends had refused to stand with her. Bessie alone had stayed at her side. Soon she'd lose Bessie. Her sister would become Mrs. Jonathan Tate, and Caroline would return to Swan's Nest.

A knock sounded on the storage room door. It had to be Tristan. She dreaded another quarrel, but she'd been expecting him. "Come in."

He walked into the room, stood at the foot of the bed and put his hands behind his back as if he were inspecting a soldier's barracks. "Has Evaline spoken to you?"

"Not since this morning." She'd talked to the housekeeper about assisting the Whitmores with their packing. She expected the exodus to begin tomorrow and she welcomed it.

"Then you're not aware of a change in plans," he said firmly. "The Whitmores aren't leaving."

"Why not?" Intimidated, she pulled her knees tighter to her chest. They'd always met on his territory. Tonight he'd invaded hers. "We can't possibly continue with the house party."

"We can, and we are."

"That's scandalous!"

"I don't particularly care." He seemed rather pleased, a reaction that unnerved her even more. "Our guests are staying for Jon and Bessie's wedding. As planned, we'll have a celebration. You will *not* wear black, is that understood?"

When she didn't answer, he went to her wardrobe, flung open the doors and pulled out a pink gown with a draped skirt and gold rosettes. She loved the fabric, mostly because it accentuated the pink tint in the diamond ring on her finger. Common sense told her to slip it off and give it to him, but her hands felt encased in stone.

Tristan held the gown to the side and gave it a shake. The satin whooshed and shimmered in the lamplight. "I like this one."

So did Caroline. She'd expected to wear it to the dance at the close of the house party, but the duke's death made the color inappropriate. "I couldn't possibly wear that gown, not now."

He hung it back in the wardrobe, the wide skirt on full display. "You *can* wear it and you will."

Without another word, he walked out of her room and into his, leaving the doors open with an invitation of sorts. Whether the invitation was to continue the argument or to reconcile, she didn't know.

She stared at the pink dress until her vision blurred into a dream of dancing in Tristan's arms. She thought of the dream game with the children. That night she'd believed their dreams could come true. With her heart pounding, she studied the satin folds. Wearing the gown would take courage…but courage didn't guarantee victory. She'd found the courage to cross a river on Cairo and she'd fallen. She'd dared to ride in a race, and she'd caused an accident. She'd put her fears aside and married Tristan, and now her heart was breaking.

She stared at the door to his room, aching to swallow her pride and go to him now. She wanted to believe he didn't care about gossip or her imperfections, but she knew their marriage would be a constant thorn. Even if she did everything right, Tristan would pay a price and so would she. So would the children.

"Help me, Lord," she murmured. "I don't know what to do."

When no answer came, she decided to go to him. Silently she rehearsed what she had to say. *I care for you, Tristan. But not enough to go with you to England.* She imagined taking off the ring. *This belongs to Dora.* The mention of the child sent tears to her eyes and she wondered if she could even speak. *Someday you'll marry again, and she'll have a mother.* And Tristan would have a wife. He'd be as happy as Jon, who had made Bessie's dreams come true long after she'd given them up.

Caroline had dreams, too. The ring on her finger suddenly felt tight, a reminder that many of her dreams had come true and that she'd lose everything unless she found the courage to stand up for herself.

She looked again at the dress, then at the open door to Tristan's room and she knew… She couldn't wear black to her sister's wedding. If the pretty gown caused ridicule, she'd know where she stood with the Whitmores and all of England. She'd know if she could cope with the pressures of being Tristan's duchess. For now, the ring would stay on her finger.

Chapter Twenty-One

Two days later, the guests gathered in the great room for Jon and Bessie's wedding. It was dusk, and a hundred candles were burning on the mantel and in candelabras throughout the room. Reverend Blue stood tall with a Bible already open. Jon stood at his side, his hands folded in a dignified pose. Tristan was next to Jon. He had the ring in his pocket and his eyes on the doorway where Caroline would enter before the bride. When the bridal march started, he'd know if she'd worn the pink dress.

To his dismay, the Whitmores had ignored his implied request to wear their colorful finery. The dowager had chosen a dark gray silk with black buttons, and the nieces were wearing navy-blue. Even Louisa had dressed in subtle colors, a mauve that bordered on gray. Tristan turned his gaze to the other side of the room. The women from Swan's Nest didn't own ball gowns. They were wearing what they'd brought, dresses that would have fit well in church. If Caroline wore the pink gown, she'd stand out like a tropical bird. He liked the idea, but he doubted she'd feel the same way.

The fiddler, an Irishman by birth, warmed up his bow with a scale, then played a melody that struck Tristan as ponderous. He supposed it fit the seriousness of the occasion, but he would have preferred something more triumphant for Caroline's entry. As the notes increased, he stared at the doorway.

He saw the hem of the gown first, then the rosettes and the pink draping and finally the bodice that fit her curves. In the gold light of the candles, the pink silk reminded him of the flamingos he'd seen in Africa. It shimmered between vibrant hues and pale ones, a mix of strength and fragility that also characterized his wife. In her hands he saw a posy made of ribbons and sprigs of pine. The evergreen made the dress even brighter.

Surrounded by women in muted colors, she stood out like a rose in the rain. He watched as her eyes scanned the room, taking in the drab dresses worn by the other women. Her chin stayed steady, but he saw panic in her eyes. He nodded his approval to encourage her, but she didn't smile back.

With every step she took, the dress reflected another candle and shimmered more brightly. Tristan scanned the faces on the Whitmore side of the room. When Caroline turned, she'd see the dowager's arched brow. The nieces both had a superior air. Pierce and Blackstone seemed bored, a reaction Caroline would interpret as disdain. Neither critical nor supportive, Louisa and Whitmore had the look of statues.

Caroline reached the end of the aisle, greeted Josh with a smile and turned. As she watched the audience, Tristan watched *her*. The instant she saw the critical stares, she flushed as pink as the dress. He willed her to stare back. Instead she focused on the doorway. The music switched to a more joyful tune and Bessie walked into the room. Caroline focused solely on her sister, smiling through a sheen of tears. Whether the tears came from happiness

for Bessie or the loss of her own, Tristan didn't know. He
knew only one thing... He wanted Caroline to triumph,
and he wanted their marriage to be everything except inadequate. He loved her. He was proud of her and the night
wouldn't end until he proved it.

The ceremony uniting Bessie and Jon couldn't have
been more different from the vows Caroline had exchanged with Tristan. Josh spoke eloquently of commitment, the joy of sharing ordinary days and the blessings of
faith, hope and love. She didn't dare look at Tristan. The
instant she saw the Whitmores, she realized the bright
dress had been a mistake.

She stayed brave through the ceremony.

She tolerated sly looks during dinner.

When the crowd moved into the great room, Adie, Mary
and Pearl surrounded her. She tried to hide behind them,
but Mary tugged her aside. "That dress is stunning," she
said in a near hiss. "Stand tall and show it off."

"I can't," Caroline murmured.

"Yes, you can." Mary had no patience with shyness. A
former actress, she enjoyed being the center of attention.
Caroline preferred to bake pies in a cozy kitchen. Tristan
had been wrong to ask her to wear the colorful dress.
Judging by the dowager's scowl and the giggling from
the nieces, she'd committed a faux pas as memorable as
the riding accident. She wished she'd worn gray or blue
or brown, anything but pink.

The fiddler played the first notes of a waltz. The banjo
player and guitarist joined in. As Jon and Bessie enjoyed
their first dance as man and wife, Caroline faked a smile.
She couldn't think of anything more awful than dancing
with Tristan, her pink dress swirling in a testament to her

failure and her heart thudding with the knowledge she couldn't be his duchess.

When the waltz ended, Jon kissed Bessie for the joy of it. Matt and Pearl stayed seated, but the other couples from Swan's Nest paired up for dancing. The Whitmores resisted the entertainment. The dowager looked especially disgruntled, a sign Caroline had sunk into even deeper disgrace.

"May I have this dance?"

She turned and saw Tristan offering his hand. His eyes sparkled blue and his face radiated good health. Even if the fevers returned, he'd live. The realization filled her with bittersweet joy. His future was bright, but she couldn't share it. She looked down at his palm, his fingers long and inviting. She didn't want to be a spectacle, but neither would she give up the one time she would dance with her husband.

She accepted his hand. "I'd love to dance."

He guided her to the middle of the floor where they spun and whirled with the couples from Swan's Nest. Her heart felt light and so did her feet. Tristan guided her expertly, matching his stride to hers and turning her with ease. She felt giddy and almost brave. He tightened his grip on her waist, drawing her close and speaking into her ear. "You're beautiful, Caroline. You make me proud."

A lump rose in her throat. "You're being kind—"

"I'm telling the truth." His eyes burned into hers. "I love you. Come to England as my wife."

"I—I—can't."

"I don't care what people say." His hand tightened on her waist. They were spinning faster and faster. Suddenly the music sounded shrill and her feet turned to lead. The other couples had stopped dancing and were watching them. She missed a step and they faltered. Tristan held her up, giving her the balance she'd lost but not the confidence. When the fiddler ended the song with a flourish, they were left face-to-face in a circle of onlookers. Behind Tristan, she saw the Whitmores.

The dowager arched a brow.

The nieces giggled.

Mr. Blackstone sniffed and Mr. Pierce sipped his punch.

Whitmore whispered something in Louisa's ear. She whispered back, then gave Caroline a tentative smile.

Tristan turned his head and saw the same critical expressions. She murmured into his ear. "Now you know, I'll never be accepted."

Abruptly he faced her. Instead of glaring at the Whitmores, he glared at her. "We're going to dance again." He raised his arm to signal the fiddler, but Caroline stepped back. "I can't." When Tristan gave her a stern look, she fled from the room.

"Caroline!"

She reached the hall and headed for the stairs. She hadn't intended to make a scene. She just needed a minute to compose herself, but Tristan's call to her had drawn even more attention. She was halfway up the stairs when he strode into the hall and looked up.

"Caroline…"

She stopped in midstep and faced him. "Yes, your grace?"

"Do *not* call me that!"

"I won't," she said. "Not ever again. I want an annulment." She saw no reason to explain. He'd witnessed the stares and snide remarks. He'd come to her rescue, yet another sign of her weakness, but they both knew her humiliation wouldn't stop. Looking at him now, she felt more deficient than ever. She had nothing left—no pride, no hope. She had her faith for comfort, but she lacked the courage to live beyond her own abilities. The admission shamed her yet again.

Tristan broke the silence. "I'm leaving tomorrow. You'll need to say goodbye to Dora."

Tears welled in her eyes. "Of course."

He pivoted and went back to their guests, leaving her to decide for herself whether to return to the celebration or to go upstairs and begin packing for Denver. She chose to pack for Denver.

Tristan returned to the great room and made excuses for Caroline. He claimed she'd been taken ill. In truth she lacked the fortitude to stand up to a cantankerous old woman and two bratty girls. He had the wherewithal to put the dowager in her place, but he also had the grace to excuse her. He did both with a few words. If Caroline hadn't left, she might have impressed the woman. Instead she'd left in shame.

Tristan stayed until Jon and Bessie left. As he said goodnight to his guests, he told them he'd be leaving for England in the morning. He accepted both condolences and well wishes, then wandered to the veranda where he inhaled cold air. The sky dimmed as clouds covered the moon, then brightened again when they passed. In the distance he saw the garden and the cottonwoods, a reminder of his own family tree, the roots and the branches named Freddie and Dora. He wanted to be a good father. He wanted his children to have a mother, and he wanted that woman to be Caroline.

Tristan, too, was a branch, and tonight he saw himself as a child much like Freddie. Confused and grieving, the boy didn't understand what had happened or why. He only knew how he felt. Tristan had greater knowledge and had tried to comfort him, but Freddie rejected him. Tonight

Tristan saw himself as Freddie and God as the father who wanted to provide comfort, hope and love to a child who didn't understand.

Humbled, he bowed his head and prayed aloud. "Father God, You love my family even more than I do. You understand Freddie and Dora, and You know what Caroline needs. Increase her faith. Remind her she's loved for exactly who she is. In Jesus' name, Amen."

He wanted to go to her and convince her of her worth, but she wouldn't listen to him. There was a time to coax and a time to exhort, a time to fight and a time to surrender. The time had come to accept Caroline's decision. His trunks were packed and ready to go. Evaline had seen to the children's things, and he'd arranged with Jon to oversee the ranch and tend to Cairo in his absence. Someday he'd return to this beautiful land, though he didn't know when.

Tomorrow he'd bid farewell to Noah and Evaline. Perhaps in the spring he'd send for them along with his horse. Looking at the sky, he considered his travel plans. The stagecoach left from Wheeler Springs, but another road ran direct from The Barracks to the bridge over the Frazier River. If Noah would drive them to Cheyenne, Tristan would save a day in travel. The annulment could be arranged in Cheyenne as easily as in Wheeler Springs. He'd also had to visit his banker. He'd never discussed an allowance with Caroline, but he intended to provide for her.

He didn't want to leave her, but with the decision made he grew restless. If he and the children left tonight, Dora might not cry, and Caroline wouldn't have to endure Freddie's hostile silence. As for himself, he had nothing else to say and he was sure Caroline had the same sense of finality. Leaving without a fight seemed kind, so he went back in the house in search of Noah. He found him sipping tea in the kitchen. The houseman greeted him with a nod. "Do you need me, Major?"

Tristan appreciated the old title. "I do. I want to leave tonight for Cheyenne." He told Noah about his plans and asked him to drive the carriage and return it to The Barracks.

Noah arched a brow. "I'll take you, sir. But it's late. Are you sure you want to leave tonight?"

"Yes."

Noah paused. "Is Mrs. Caroline accompanying you?"

"No, she isn't."

"I see." His brown eyes clouded. "I'm sorry, sir."

"As am I," Tristan said quietly. "It's a long trip. I appreciate your company."

"Yes, sir." Noah excused himself and left to tell Evaline of the plan.

Tristan went upstairs to write a note to Caroline. Maybe someday he'd come back to America. He'd find her and he'd persuade her to believe in herself. It had taken buckets of peppermint to win Cairo's trust. He didn't know what it would take to convince Caroline to turn their marriage into all it could be. He only knew that he'd failed.

Chapter Twenty-Two

Caroline stood in front of the mirror in her room looking at herself in the pink dress and wishing she'd followed her instincts and worn black. Defeated, she removed the pink diamond from her finger and set it by the lamp. Tomorrow she'd return it to Tristan. She changed from the ball gown into a calico, let down her hair and plaited it into a braid. Next she opened the trunk and filled it with her clothing, everything except the pink dress. She'd never wear it again.

When she finished packing, she put on her nightgown and slid into bed. She lay on her back for an hour with her eyes open and stinging with tears. Miserable, she gave up trying to sleep and went to the window. Staring into the dark, she took in the fallow garden, the cottonwoods and the hills where she'd raced Grandma. Tomorrow she'd say goodbye to Dora and Freddie. She didn't know which would hurt more—saying goodbye to the child who loved her or enduring the scorn of the one who didn't. She couldn't imagine Dora thinking she didn't love her, nor did she want Freddie to think she was leaving because of him. She'd made the decision on her own. As for what she'd say to Tristan, she prayed the words would come.

She didn't know how long she'd been at the window when someone knocked on the hall door. It was late. She didn't want to speak to anyone, not to Tristan and not to her friends. She opened the door with the intention of telling her visitor to leave. She expected Adie, Pearl and Mary, and that's who she saw, along with Louisa who had an odd smile. The four women were in their nightgowns and wrappers.

Adie grasped her arm and pulled her into the hallway. "You're coming with us."

"I'm tired," she said holding back.

"You can be tired later." Mary had a twinkle in her eye. "You have to see what's happening in the kitchen."

"Absolutely!" Louisa declared.

Pearl was in the back, smiling shyly.

Caroline didn't want to see anyone, but curiosity got the better of her. She followed her friends down the stairs to the brightly lit kitchen. When she stepped inside, her mouth gaped at the sight of the dowager duchess. The woman was wearing a purple satin wrapper, a mob cap and the meanest frown Caroline had ever seen. She was also wearing an apron and rolling pie dough. Armed with the rolling pin and a scowl, she'd have been intimidating except for one small problem. She had a streak of flour under her nose. It looked very much like a mustache.

Caroline suppressed a giggle. "Good evening, Dowager Somerville."

"Evening? It's not evening! It's the middle of the night and *you* should be in bed. What kind of home do you run, *Duchess* Willoughby!"

"I run a fine home, Dowager."

The woman snorted. "That's not what I see!"

"Why, I never—" Caroline bit her tongue, but she'd *had it* with the dowager's snobbery, the giggling nieces and the humiliation—and she had nothing left to lose. Furious, she put her hands on her hips. "For your information, Dowager Somerville, I run the kind of *home* where a cantankerous old woman can bake a pie in the middle of the night! I run the kind of *home* where children live their dreams and everyone is welcome regardless of titles or manners. I run the kind of *home* where love covers a person's mistakes. That includes you!"

The old woman raised the rolling pin like a scepter. "That's the way to talk, my girl! Give it to me! Give me all you've got!"

Caroline didn't think about what the woman had said. She only knew it felt good to be mad instead of defeated. She lifted a silver tray off the counter and shoved it in the woman's face. "*You* have a mustache!"

The dowager pointed the rolling pin at Caroline's chest. "And *you* have courage!"

"You bet I do!" Caroline wielded the silver plate like a shield.

Looking positively gleeful, the dowager brandished the rolling pin like a sword. "En garde, Duchess! Choose your weapon!"

Slowly, like the sun rising on a cloudy day, the absurdity sunk into Caroline's mind. Adie started to laugh, and Mary let out a hoot. Pearl was laughing so hard she had to hold her stomach, and Louisa let out a very unladylike guffaw. All four of them had tears of laughter streaming down their faces. Caroline turned back to the dowager.

Lowering the rolling pin, she smiled like a grandmother. "I knew you had it in you, Duchess. I just *knew* it! My maternal grandmother was an American. She gave my grandfather all his gray hair, but he loved her for it."

"You did this on purpose?" Caroline asked.

The old woman nodded. "Someone had to make you

see your abilities. Your husband tried, but we don't always trust the judgment of those who love us. They see us with blinders on, which is rather convenient. Sometimes it takes a stranger to test one's grit. And you, Duchess Willoughby, have grit!"

Caroline's eyes widened. "I believe I do."

"I'm sure of it," Adie said.

"Me, too," added Pearl.

"I quite agree," Louisa answered.

Mary grinned. "We did a good job, didn't we? I thought of the mustache."

The dowager's eyes twinkled. "I've wanted to make a flour mustache since I was a little girl." Looking positively impish, she dragged her finger through the flour and ran it under Caroline's nose. Laughing, Caroline gave a mustache to Adie, who shared the fun with Mary and Pearl. Pearl did the honors for Louisa, who still looked dignified with flour on her nose. The women laughed and hugged, wearing flour mustaches and feeling like the best friends they were.

The dowager drew back first. "I do hope to see you in England, my dear. We're a stuffy lot, but I'm sure you can cope."

Louisa hugged her. "She means it, Caroline. No matter what happens, I'll be your friend."

Tears of happiness pushed into her eyes, but then she thought of her quarrel with Tristan. "I'm afraid I owe my husband an apology."

"So make it," the dowager said.

"I will."

"Good," Adie replied. "I know you and Tristan took vows, but perhaps you'd like to renew them? I feel cheated not being at your wedding!"

"Me, too," echoed Mary and Pearl.

Caroline's eyes brimmed with happiness. "That would be wonderful, but first Tristan has to forgive me."

The dowager harrumphed. "He's already forgiven you. I saw how he looked at you in that *scandalous* pink dress. He was positively smitten."

Caroline hadn't even noticed. She'd been so concerned with the opinion of others that she'd missed her husband's admiration. Turning to the dowager, she hugged her again. "Thank you for everything."

"My pleasure," the dowager said sincerely.

The women blew out the lamps and retreated upstairs. Caroline hugged her friends goodnight, went to her room and slipped quietly through the closet to Tristan's suite. His room was dark and cold, a sign he hadn't bothered with a fire. She imagined him sleeping alone, chilled between the sheets. In the dark she inched forward, softly calling his name. "I'm so sorry, Tristan. Will you forgive me?"

Silence answered. Not a breath, not a stirring of the bedding. She inched forward, blind and lost in the dark, her hands reaching for the man she loved. "Tristan? Can you hear me? Please say you forgive me—"

She touched the corner of the mattress, then a blanket that had no wrinkles. With her heart pounding, she found a match and lit the lamp. The golden flare revealed the empty bed and a letter on the pillow. It was addressed to her.

My dearest Caroline,

It seemed wise to avoid more painful goodbyes, so I left with the children for Cheyenne. Rather than travel by stagecoach, Noah is taking us directly. He'll return in a week or so with the documents for the annulment. When we took vows, I promised to

*provide for you. Please accept the gift of an annual
allowance for the rest of your life.*

*If I could, I'd give you riches far greater than
money.*
With love,
Tristan

Caroline didn't want an allowance! She wanted her husband. It was dark, but the sun would rise in an hour or so. If she rode hard, she could catch up with Tristan and the children. She had the courage to make the trip, but she wasn't foolish enough to do it alone. She hurried to her room, put on her riding habit and raced up the stairs to the third floor. Any of the men could help her, so she pounded on the first door she reached.

Jonah opened it with his typical caution. If he'd been sleeping, it didn't show. Mary came up next to him. She still had a spot of flour on her lip. "What's the matter?" she asked.

"Tristan left with the children—"

"When?" Jonah asked.

"A few hours ago." She told them about the note and the direct road to Cheyenne. "I'm going after them."

"You're not going alone." Jonah had his boots on before she could blink, and Mary was handing him a canvas duster.

"Let's go," he said as he punched into the sleeves.

Behind her another door opened. Matt came into the hall. Josh came out of the third door. He'd been sound asleep and it showed. Mary, Pearl and Adie crowded into the hall with their husbands, murmuring and looking worried.

Jonah took charge. "Get dressed, gentlemen. Tristan left with the kids. We're taking Caroline to find him."

"Where'd he go?" Josh asked, yawning.

"Cheyenne," she answered. "And then to England. We have to hurry."

The men put on boots and jackets, kissed their wives and left the house with Caroline in the lead. Behind her they formed a shield of sorts, guarding her back as they paced to the barn in silence. She'd have ridden after Tristan alone if she'd had no other choice, but God had provided these good men to help her.

When they reached the horse barn, Matt and Jonah surveyed the stalls. In addition to Cairo and Grandma, the two Arabians were ready to ride. The other horses were out to pasture. They saddled the Arabians and led them to the yard. Figuring she'd ride Grandma, Josh approached Cairo. "Hi, fella."

The stallion snorted at him.

"He's not fond of me," Josh said drily. "I guess I'm staying."

Matt came up behind him. With a twinkle in his eyes, he jerked a thumb at the stall holding Biscuit. "You could ride that one, preacher."

Josh laughed and so did Caroline. It eased the tension, but only a bit. It didn't seem right for Josh to stay behind. Looking at the stallion, she thought of the peppermints she'd given him. He was the fastest horse in the barn. With Matt and Jonah on the Arabians, Grandma would be the slowest. She welcomed the men's protection, but she intended to reach Tristan first. She went to the tack room, fetched a handful of peppermint sticks and approached the stallion. "Let's see if Cairo will let me ride him."

"But why?" Josh asked.

"He's the fastest." A month ago his speed would have terrified her. Today she needed it. Murmuring to Cairo the way Tristan did, she fed him the treats. He knew her from the riding lessons and calmed immediately.

"You have the touch." Josh gave her a questioning look. "If you can handle Cairo, I'll ride Grandma."

"She beats the pony," Matt joked.

Caroline soothed Cairo while Josh saddled him. When he finished, she led the stallion to the mounting block and climbed on. To her relief, the horse gave her the respect he usually reserved for Tristan.

Matt and Jonah mounted the Arabians. Josh led Grandma out of the barn and swung into the saddle. With Caroline in the lead, the four of them headed for Cheyenne. Tristan had described Grandma as a rocking chair with legs. Cairo moved like a locomotive on a flat plain. Steady and powerful, he set a fast but sustainable pace. Caroline gripped the horse with her legs and moved with him. In the cold light of dawn, the woman and the horse went after the man they both loved.

Tristan, Noah and the children had been on the trail for two hours when the sun rose in the eastern sky, turning it the same shade of pink as Caroline's dress. Another hour passed, and then another.

Noah was perched on the driver's seat, humming quietly as he steered the carriage along the road that led to the Frazier River. Tristan was in the passenger compartment with Dora asleep in his lap and Freddie next to him. The boy had scooted to the side and hadn't budged. With hours of travel ahead of them, Tristan considered Freddie's silence and how best to break it. He knew all about leading horses to water and getting blood out of stones. He'd been as reluctant to speak to God as Freddie was to speak to him now. In the end, it was love that had broken through to him. If Tristan had learned nothing else, he'd learned that a father's love had no conditions. With Freddie in a pout, Tristan could show that kindness to his son.

"I think you'll like Willoughby," he said amiably. "It's different from Wyoming, and it's certainly different from the West Indies."

The boy kept staring out the window. "Grandfather said England is foggy."

"It is."

Tristan had kept his voice low, but Dora yawned and stretched awake. Last night, he'd asked Evaline to dress the child for travel. She'd roused, but only barely. Tristan had lifted her into his arms and carried her, feeling the weight as she slouched against his shoulder. She'd been asleep when they'd entered the carriage. Now, startled by her surroundings, she came fully alert. "Where are we?"

Tristan made his voice jovial, though he felt no pleasure. "We're going on a trip, my dear."

"A trip?"

He couldn't bear to tell her they were going to England without Caroline. He thought of the woman he loved, the dream game and Dora's desire to be a princess. He'd use whatever he could to lessen the emotional blow he had to deliver to his little girl. "We're going to England, Dora. You're going to live in a castle like a real princess."

"Where's Mama?"

He'd heard Dora use the endearment with Caroline, and it had charmed him. Now the words were a knife to his heart. "She's staying in America."

"But why?" Dora's voice rose to a shriek. Dissatisfied with Tristan's answers, she turned to Freddie. "I want to go home! I want Mama!"

Freddie's eyes widened with confusion, then dimmed with emotions Tristan couldn't discern. When the boy turned abruptly to the carriage window, Tristan dared to hope his son was feeling the sting of regret for how he'd treated Caroline, and how he'd indirectly hurt Dora by pushing Caroline away. The girl was weeping copious tears, muttering that she wanted to go home. Tristan soothed her as best he could, but Dora kept crying. Caroline would have known what to say. She had a mother's heart. If only she'd had the courage to come with them...

Dora cried herself into exhaustion. With his own heart in tatters, Tristan stared out the window.

"Father?"

Turning, he faced his son. Freddie's eyes had the sharp gleam of shattered crystal. He'd worn that expression for days after Molly died. Tristan put his own grief aside and spoke kindly. "What is it, son?"

"I've been thinking about something Grandfather said."

Tristan braced for trouble. "What was it?"

The boy looked at his sister, sleeping now, then he murmured. "He said I was more important than Dora."

Favoritism. It was the most diseased root of the Smythe family tree. What made one child valuable and another worthless? He thought of the saying about beauty being in the eye of the beholder. Perhaps that was true of paintings and possessions, but children were beautiful just as God created them. Freddie needed to understand that bloodlines didn't give a man worth. The boy was no better than anyone else. Ironically, Caroline needed to know she was no less worthy than the duke, the dowager or anyone else.

Tristan kept his voice matter-of-fact. "You and Dora are equals. There are no favorites in this family." Certainly not in Tristan's heart, or in God's heart.

Freddie looked troubled. "That's not what Grandfather said."

"What did he say?"

"He said I was his favorite because I'm like him."

Tristan held back his disgust, but just barely. He'd forgiven his father before, and he'd do it again. He'd do it until the poison had been purged from his family tree. "You resemble him, but you have your own mind and your own dreams—"

"I want to be a scientist."

"And you can be," Tristan agreed. "Someday you'll be the Duke of Willoughby. You'll have a title and responsibilities, but you'll still be a man just like Noah and Jon and your grandfather."

"A man like you?" Freddie said with admiration.

Tristan's chest swelled with pride. He couldn't hug Freddie without embarrassing him, so he patted Dora's back. He'd lost Caroline, but she'd given him back his children. He smiled at his son, a boy who had his eyes, Molly's nose, Caroline's wisdom and a mind of his own. "You'll be a better man than I am, son. I'm sure of it."

Freddie still looked troubled. "Grandfather said something else. He said Miss Caroline was common."

"Far from it," he replied. "She's one of the finest women I know."

Freddie was chewing on his lip, a sign of the burden he carried. Finally, he looked into Tristan's eyes. "He said she'd ruin our family tree with her American blood, but I like her. Even when I was mean, she was nice."

"Yes, she was."

"I was wrong about her causing Grandfather to fall. He was riding too fast." Freddie turned back to the window. "I'm sorry. I wish I could tell her."

So did Tristan. He considered turning the carriage around, but Caroline had made her decision independent of Freddie's resentment. "Perhaps you could write to her from Cheyenne."

"I'll do it," he said in a solemn tone. "Do you think she'll forgive me?"

"I'm sure of it." He gave Freddie a crisp nod, an acknowledgment of the boy's new maturity. "She loves you, son. So do I. Love and forgiveness go hand in hand."

"Maybe Aunt Caroline will change her mind," the boy said hopefully. "She could still come to England, couldn't she?"

"Yes, she could." Tristan would welcome her with open arms, but he doubted Caroline would reverse her decision.

They were nearing the Frazier River. The bridge had been repaired, so the crossing would be nothing like what Tristan had experienced with Caroline. Instead of feeling the water on his boots, he'd hear the wheels on the fresh planks. Now, though, he was hearing something different... He heard hoofbeats, several of them, and they were approaching fast. The Carver gang hadn't been apprehended, so he prepared for the worst.

"Get down!" he commanded Freddie.

The boy dropped to the floor of the carriage. Tristan set Dora next to him. She roused, but Freddie consoled her. Noah slowed the rig, turning it slightly for reasons Tristan didn't understand. As the wheels ground to a halt, he slid a pistol from under the seat and aimed at the closest rider...a rider on a black Arabian stallion...a rider wearing a split skirt...a rider with long brunette hair.

"Tristan!" Caroline shouted. "Wait!

Just as she'd once aimed a gun at him and lowered it, Tristan uncocked the pistol and removed it from the window. "Children, you can get up, but stay here."

He climbed out of the carriage, handed Noah the revolver and strode to the woman and the horse. In the distance he recognized Matt, Josh and Jonah. Seeing Caroline's safe arrival, they had stopped at a distance. She slid off Cairo and tumbled into his arms. "Don't leave. Please, don't go. I love you."

He loved her, too. But he had responsibilities. Was she asking him to stay, or did she want to go with him? He didn't know, and he couldn't hold her close until he understood. "What are you saying?"

She told him a crazy story about the dowager, a rolling pin and flour mustaches. When she finished, he was more confused than ever. He needed to sort through the facts. "So you're friendly with Dowager Somerville?"

"I am."

He hesitated, then asked the question that would set the course for the future. "Exactly where do you intend to continue that friendship, here or in England?"

"Oh!" Her eyes twinkled. "I didn't make that clear, did I, your grace?"

The title usually irked him, but she said it with a smile. He didn't dare smile in return. "No, you didn't."

"Then let me be direct." Stepping back, she held her head high and squared her shoulders. "If the Duke of Willoughby will accept my apology, I intend to accompany him to England. Not only will I be a mother to his children, I'll assume my duties as Caroline Bradley Smith, Duchess of Willoughby."

"I see." Tristan's dreams were coming true, but he was still a man and he wanted to be in charge. With a glint in his eyes, he arched his brows. "You *do* realize what such a position entails."

"I do, your grace."

"I expect you to follow orders."

Her hazel eyes sparkled with mischief. "And I expect the same of you. Is that agreeable?"

"It depends on the order." He cupped her chin.

"Kiss me," she murmured.

As far as orders went, he couldn't think of a better one. Her eyes drifted shut and so did his, then the carriage door slammed and startled them both. Looking up, he saw Dora running to them, her arms outstretched and her eyes on Caroline.

"Mama!" she cried.

Caroline scooped the girl onto her hip. Freddie trailed after his sister but with a firm stride. He traded a look with Tristan, then approached Caroline.

"I'm sorry, Aunt Caroline." He swallowed hard. "I was mean about Grandfather's accident. It wasn't your fault."

Her eyes misted. "Thank you, Freddie. That means a lot to me."

The boy looked at her with a new eagerness. "Are you coming with us to England?"

"That's up to your father, but I'd like it very much."

Tristan cleared his throat. "We were just discussing the possibility. Freddie, take your sister and wait with Noah."

"Yes, sir."

Caroline kissed Dora's forehead and set her on her feet. Freddie led the girl to the carriage, bending to the side to whisper something that made her giggle.

Tristan faced his wife. "Where were we?"

Her cheeks turned as pink as the fancy gown. "We were discussing orders," she said shyly.

"Ah, yes." He wasn't ready to end this moment. In essence, it was all the courtship they'd have. He wanted to enjoy watching her blush, so he gave her a private look she'd soon know well. "I believe it's my turn to issue an order."

"Yes, your grace." She put her hand on his chest, palm flat in a pledge of sorts.

The desire to tease her evaporated like a mist. He could only think about the love they'd almost lost and the future that awaited them. He put his hand over hers and pressed. "Promise that you'll never leave me."

"I promise." Her eyes misted. "I love you, Tristan. I can't imagine life without you."

He looked at her hand and saw that she'd removed the wedding ring he'd given her. Whether she'd taken it off in a fit of despair or removed it only for the ride, he didn't know and it didn't matter. They were starting anew and he wanted matching gold bands. "Marry me again," he said. "Let's say the words before God and mean them."

"Yes," she cried. *"Yes!"*

He pulled her into his arms, drawing her close as he matched his lips to hers. She was his wife, his duchess, the mother of his children and of the children to come. When he kissed her, it was far more than adequate. It was spectacular.

* * * * *

Dear Reader,

Writers are always looking for fresh ideas. Maybe that's why I matched Caroline Bradley, the last of the Swan's Nest heroines, with a retired British Army officer. To make the romance more challenging, I gave him malaria. Somewhere along the line, my hero surprised me yet again by announcing he was the third son of a duke and that he'd become heir apparent.

Tristan's disclosure led to more questions than I ever imagined. How are titles passed on? What are the proper forms of address? What's the difference between a duke, a marquis, a marquess and an earl? Then there are the titles for women and how they're used... And that's just the beginning.

The rites of inheritance were crucial to this book, and I started off with the mistaken notion that a man could refuse an inherited title. I owe a debt of gratitude to the online community of romance writers who graciously offered help with the facts and led me to websites with oodles of information.

This Western writer did her best, but a Stetson fits me better than a tiara. Any mistakes are mine.

With Caroline happily married, the WOMEN OF SWAN'S NEST series has come to an end. I've enjoyed telling these stories and hope you've laughed and cried along with the characters. In my imagination I see them all in twenty years. The women will still be friends, and they'll be cheering for each other. The men will be working to support their families, and they'll be loving their wives, children and grandchildren for years to come. After all, a good love story never really ends.

All the best,

Victoria Bylin

Questions for Discussion

1. Why does Caroline accept a position as a governess? What is your opinion of her decision? Is she compromising or being realistic?

2. Tristan is ill with malaria. What does he most fear? How does he handle his anxiety, especially in relation to his children?

3. Caroline is afraid of horses. What caused her fear? When is fear justified and when must it be overcome?

4. Tristan has a negative relationship with his father. How does his childhood affect his perception of God? What events in the story change Tristan's perceptions and beliefs?

5. Caroline and Tristan marry to protect his children from his father. What obstacles do they each face? What compromises do they each make?

6. The "dream game" is Caroline's way of telling the children about the unexpected marriage. Tristan wanted to tell them in blunt, unemotional terms. What might have happened if they'd told the children about their marriage using Tristan's method? How do you think Freddie would have reacted?

7. Louisa's arrival is a surprise. If Tristan wasn't married to Caroline, what might his reaction have been to her? In what way was Caroline a better match for him than Louisa?

8. Tristan takes unique steps to prepare Caroline for her first riding lesson. What does his careful approach say about his personality? Where do you think he learned to be compassionate?

9. Caroline doesn't want her friends from Swan's Nest to attend the house party, but she's very pleased when they arrive. What words of wisdom do the women share? In what ways do they support Caroline?

10. The outcome of the horse race is devastating for Caroline. Do you think she's at all responsible for the duke's accident? What are some of the ways she could have reacted to the criticism and gossip?

11. Caroline lacks the confidence to be a duchess, but she tries hard to learn how to behave properly. What are her biggest obstacles? Who helps her the most?

12. Tristan's illness humbles him. What experiences have you had in your life that have caused you to rely on others? How did the experience shape your character or change your values?

13. The Duke of Willoughby is the kind of father who "plays favorites." How does this trait affect his relationship with Tristan? What social factors contribute to the duke's favoritism? Is his favoritism at all justified? What damage does it do?

14. If Tristan had died and Freddie returned to England with his grandfather, what kind of man would he have become? What might have happened to Dora?

15. Describe what life will be like for Caroline and Tristan in twenty years. Do you think she'll acclimate to England? What will be the benefits? What challenges will she face? How is she equipped to face them?

INSPIRATIONAL

Inspirational romances to warm your heart & soul.

Love Inspired.
HISTORICAL

TITLES AVAILABLE NEXT MONTH

Available November 8, 2011

REQUEST YOUR FREE BOOKS!

2 FREE INSPIRATIONAL NOVELS
PLUS 2
FREE
MYSTERY GIFTS

Love Inspired
HISTORICAL
INSPIRATIONAL HISTORICAL ROMANCE

YES! Please send me 2 FREE Love Inspired® Historical novels and my 2 FREE mystery gifts (gifts are worth about $10). After receiving them, if I don't wish to receive any more books, I can return the shipping statement marked "cancel". If I don't cancel, I will receive 4 brand-new novels every month and be billed just $4.49 per book in the U.S. or $4.99 per book in Canada. That's a saving of at least 22% off the cover price. It's quite a bargain! Shipping and handling is just 50¢ per book in the U.S. and 75¢ per book in Canada.* I understand that accepting the 2 free books and gifts places me under no obligation to buy anything. I can always return a shipment and cancel at any time. Even if I never buy another book, the two free books and gifts are mine to keep forever.

102/302 IDN FEHF

Name	(PLEASE PRINT)

Address		Apt. #

City	State/Prov.	Zip/Postal Code

Signature (if under 18, a parent or guardian must sign)

Mail to the **Reader Service:**
IN U.S.A.: P.O. Box 1867, Buffalo, NY 14240-1867
IN CANADA: P.O. Box 609, Fort Erie, Ontario L2A 5X3

Not valid for current subscribers to Love Inspired Historical books.

Want to try two free books from another series?
Call 1-800-873-8635 or visit www.ReaderService.com.

* Terms and prices subject to change without notice. Prices do not include applicable taxes. Sales tax applicable in N.Y. Canadian residents will be charged applicable taxes. Offer not valid in Quebec. This offer is limited to one order per household. All orders subject to credit approval. Credit or debit balances in a customer's account(s) may be offset by any other outstanding balance owed by or to the customer. Please allow 4 to 6 weeks for delivery. Offer available while quantities last.

Your Privacy—The Reader Service is committed to protecting your privacy. Our Privacy Policy is available online at www.ReaderService.com or upon request from the Reader Service.

We make a portion of our mailing list available to reputable third parties that offer products we believe may interest you. If you prefer that we not exchange your name with third parties, or if you wish to clarify or modify your communication preferences, please visit us at www.ReaderService.com/consumerschoice or write to us at Reader Service Preference Service, P.O. Box 9062, Buffalo, NY 14269. Include your complete name and address.

LIH11B

Adopted as a baby, Mei Clayton never felt like she belonged in her family, or in Clayton, Colorado. When she moves back to fulfill the terms of a will, she's reunited with handsome Jack McCord, the man she secretly loved. Their families have feuded for years…can faith and love open their hearts?

The Loner's Thanksgiving Wish
by Roxanne Rustand

◄ ROCKY MOUNTAIN HEIRS ►

Available November 2011 wherever books are sold.

www.LoveInspiredBooks.com

LI87704

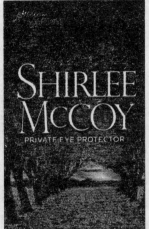